AFTER LIFE

ANDREW NEIDERMAN

BERKLEY BOOKS, NEW YORK

AFTER LIFE

A Berkley Book / published by arrangement with
the author

PRINTING HISTORY
Berkley edition / November 1993

ISBN: 0-425-13974-3

BERKLEY ®
Berkley Books are published by The Berkley Publishing Group,
200 Madison Avenue, New York, New York 10016.
BERKLEY and the "B" design
are trademarks belonging to Berkley Publishing Corporation.

PRINTED IN THE UNITED STATES OF AMERICA

10   9   8   7   6   5   4   3   2   1

FOR UNCLE FRANK,
WHO WILL ALWAYS BE
MY GODFATHER

AFTER LIFE

PROLOGUE

Kurt Andersen stabbed the trunk lock with his key and heaved his duffel bag in as soon as the trunk snapped open. Then he brought the door down quickly with a slam that shook the very frame of his '89 Ford Taurus. It was as if his duffel bag was an animal he wanted to keep incarcerated, something he had trapped or wanted to punish. He clutched his car keys in his fist and turned slowly to look back at the Gardner Town High School.

The shadowy hand of twilight now spread over the pale red-brick building. In the dim light the bricks looked more ruby, more like the color of dried blood; but whenever Kurt first set eyes on it in the morning these days, the building looked ablaze.

He scanned the windows, now no more than frames surrounding mirrors that reflected the brooding fall sky. Bruised clouds had begun to roll over the dark blue, dragging in a curtain of thunder and rain from the east. His gaze settled for a moment on the set of windows at the corner of the building on the second floor, windows he knew belonged to the principal's office. Immediately the shadows in the glass took the form of two giant eyes.

1

Kurt blinked and shook his head to deny what he saw.
When he looked back, the eyes were gone.

Still, it made him feel as if he were standing barefoot
in a pool of ice water. He shuddered and hurried around
to unlock his car and get behind the wheel. It wasn't until
he backed out of his space and drove out of the lot and
onto the highway that he felt any sense of relief. The
school grounds dwindled in his rearview mirror and he
fixed his eyes on the lush scenery before him.

Summer had held on tenaciously. Warm rains and
warm nights had kept the forests luxuriant and green.
Home owners in this relatively small, upstate New
York residential community were cutting their lawns
and pruning their hedges as often as they were in July.

"The grass will grow into February this year," George
Freeman, the ageless science teacher predicted in the
faculty room yesterday. Ordinarily everyone would have
laughed or smiled at his earthy humor, but these weren't
ordinary times. The subtle yet dramatic changes that
had come over the school community created an aura
of fantasy. The community was changing: the students
were different; even some of the old-timers like himself
were cutting corners and saying things he had never
imagined they would do and say. This was especially
true of Henry Young, who had been the principal almost
as long as Kurt had been a teacher.

"Blame it on his pneumonia and his rendezvous with
death," George said when Kurt complained to him about
some of the things Henry was doing, or more accurately,
not doing. The school was coming apart at the seams.
Why didn't more people see it?

Sometimes Kurt would look down the corridors during the changing of classes and think the world had
fallen into slow motion and all sound had dropped ten

decibels. But that was one of his far less horrifying visions. In others the corridor walls became pulsating flesh; the students were swallowed and sucked down into the bowels of the school, where they were churned into a syrupy liquid that poured out the rear of the building and seeped down into the earth. He even saw himself running over the muck, his feet sinking. When he pulled them up, strings of hair and teeth, bones and skin clung to the soles of his sneakers.

Whenever these visions attacked him, he retreated to his physical-education office and fortified himself with his administrative duties. As department head, he was responsible for all purchasing. He taught only two classes, but he coached soccer and varsity basketball, as well as varsity baseball in the spring. He had been teaching at Gardner Town a little less than five years when the department-head position had been offered him. Now, nearly twenty years later, at forty-eight years of age, he was considered an institution at this high school. His teams had won more than their share of trophies. For years now he was known simply as the Coach. Even people in the community didn't call him by his name anymore.

Perhaps being a bachelor had made all the difference. Married only to his profession and his love of sports, he was at it day and night with a seemingly monomaniacal passion. He lived and breathed his work. His boys were his family. People were so accustomed to him being dressed in his sweat suits and sneakers that he looked out of place in a jacket and tie. It brought smiles instantly to the faces of those who saw him. He was a solid jock, standing six feet two, muscular, his light brown hair in a permanent crew cut.

Although he had had two slight romances, he had never been able to make the compromises necessary to take someone else significantly into his life. His friends kidded him: he would have to find a woman with a good jump shot or one who favored the scent of perspiration over the scent of perfume and cologne. There were women like that, but they demanded too much of his space; they were too competitive.

Bachelorhood was comfortable and he had his extended family without the obligations that accompanied it. Usually, once he left the school, he left the problems behind. Sometimes one of his players had personal problems and sought him out for advice; but the point was they left afterward and he could sit back in his oversized, cushion chair and turn on ESPN. What could be better? Why disturb it?

He looked into his rearview mirror again as he made the turn that would take him onto County Road 17 and to his small, but cozy ranch-style home between the hamlets of Gardner and Sandburg. It had been his home ever since he had begun teaching here, first renting it and then buying it.

The road behind him was empty and dark now, the darkness so deep that night seemed to be swallowing him. The moment his car headlights washed through a section of road, the darkness poured behind him like ink. It made him speed up. His tires squealed as he turned and accelerated.

These periodic jitters were beginning to annoy him. He hated when it came over him at school, and now it was happening outside the school. When he saw his house ahead of him with the solar sensitive porch light triggered by the curtain of darkness, he felt his muscles relax and the tightness go out of his stomach. It wasn't

ever like this, he thought with regret. There were times
the custodians practically had to chase him out of the
building so they could clean his office and the gym.

He turned into his driveway and waited as the door to
his small, unattached garage lifted on command, turning
on the garage light. Then he drove in and shut off the car
headlights and engine. He went around to the trunk and
took out his duffel bag. It seemed heavier, remarkably
heavier. The sensation brought a smile of confusion to
his face.

How could his sweat suits, shorts, sweat socks, and
jocks suddenly weigh so much? What, was he getting
weaker by the second? He started to laugh at this illusion when the bag turned so heavy it made him lean to
the side.

"Huh?"

He dropped it to the concrete floor and stood up, his
heart pounding.

"What the hell . . ."

He bent over and grasped the handles again, but this
time he couldn't lift it off the floor. He nearly wrenched
his back in the attempt. For a long moment he stared
down at it. Then, with his fingers trembling as he did so,
he leaned over and pulled the zipper open. He separated
the sides and gazed in.

Somewhere at the pit of his stomach, a primeval scream
began and reverberated its way up his body, through his
chest, and to the base of his throat, nearly gagging him
on the effort to get it out. He exploded in a high-pitched
screech so unfamiliar and so unlike him, he thought it
came from another being living within his body. It drove
him back. He felt his eyes widen so fast and so hard,
his forehead ached and burned with the resulting folds
of skin.

He clutched at his chest. His heart thumped with deadly force; he could actually feel the cardiovascular strain, hear the ripping of precious tissue and the gurgle of blood, blood that had rushed into his face with great force, lifting the skin from his bones, inflating his face like a balloon. His tongue curled up with the effort of the scream and contorted like a snake whose tail had been squashed under a jagged rock. Its struggle to tear lose drove it to self-destruct, to rip that part of its body that was free from that part that was trapped.

He shook his head to deny the sight before him, but it didn't disappear. There, stuffed into his duffel bag, a recent gift from one of his teams, were the decapitated heads of his starting five basketball players, their mouths open, their eyes in the glassy hold of death. They bobbed in a pool of their own blood, one disappearing, another appearing.

Kurt Andersen screamed again, but this time he made no sound. The scream was caught in his throat and reverberated throughout his body, growing louder and louder as it bounced from his chest to his spine to his neck and into his brain, where it lodged itself and turned into a chorus of screams. He felt the bones in his legs soften until they were no more than straw and he began his collapse to the garage floor, a slow descent that seemed to take him forever and ever, as if he were dropping down a deep well.

— 1 —

Lee Overstreet paused for a moment in his unpacking of cartons and gazed out the side window in the kitchen. Despite the size and brightness of this apartment and the reasonableness of the rent, he couldn't get used to the idea of living right next to a cemetery.

He never told Jessie about the cemetery when he described the apartment he had found for them. One thing they didn't need now was something else to depress them. The car accident would last for a lifetime. Whenever there was a chance for any happiness, all he had to do was watch her grope her way about their apartment or watch her reading in braille and that would put things back into perspective.

Of course, he had anticipated that the accident and her subsequent blindness would change her; he had expected her to become bitter if not frustrated and full of self-pity. Instead she became oddly mysterious, often uttering things that seemingly made no sense. And those voices! It gave him the jitters how she could look up suddenly and say, "Who's here, Lee? Who's in the kitchen?" or "Who's out in the hall?"

"What who? There's no one there."

"Yes, there was," she would insist. "Listen."

He heard nothing.

"Someone was whispering," she would say. They were just out of range for her to make out the words . . . or at least all the words. Sometimes she heard one or two.

"You're imagining it," he would tell her, stroking her long, light brown hair and kissing her softly on the forehead.

Life had taken another downturn for them when he had had his job cut at Hicksville High School on Long Island. He had been unable to find another teaching position in physical education nearby and had had to work for a taxi service, doing the late shift. He was desperate, so they could give him whatever they wanted. Then, seemingly out of nowhere, came this advertisement in the mail for an immediate opening at the Gardner Town High School in the Catskill Mountains of New York. He applied and forgot about it until he received a telephone call inviting him to come for an interview.

He had met with Henry Young, the principal, who explained why the school responded so quickly to his letter of application and why there was such urgency to fill the position.

"Kurt Andersen was more than just one of our better teachers here," Henry Young had said. "He was, in every sense of the word, Mr. Gardner Town High. And," he added, "a friend." The tall, lean man with the kind of tired, drawn, and melancholy face that reminded Lee of Abraham Lincoln swallowed back his sorrow. It was understandable. Andersen's death was so recent.

"Massive coronary," Henry Young explained, and shook his head. "No one expected it. The man was as strong as a horse, but as old Doc Beezly says, 'tension wears on you in places you can't see, can't even feel,' " Young added, raising his eyebrows. "Good thing to keep in mind."

Tension, Lee thought, how do you hold it at bay?

"Daydreaming?" Jessie asked.

She felt her way through the kitchen door and stopped by the kitchenette set, her hands on the back of a chair. She sensed where he was standing and turned in his direction. With her ebony hair tied up with a bandanna and with her dark complexion, silvery gray eyes, and gold teardrop earrings, she looked like a fortune-teller.

Jessie stood only two inches shorter than Lee, who was six feet tall. She had long, graceful legs and a slim figure with perky breasts that often drove him into a lustful frenzy whenever they began to make love. He loved to trace his forefinger down the slope of her soft shoulders, over her collarbone, and through the valley of her bosom. His roadway to ecstasy, he called it, and three years of marriage hadn't dimmed the passion or slowed the beat of his heart whenever she brought her lips close to his.

"How did you know I was daydreaming?" he asked. Her new sensitivity to things around her constantly astounded him. The doctors had told him her sense of smell and hearing, even her sense of touch, would improve, grow sharper to compensate for her loss of sight, but sometimes she seemed to possess radar.

"I heard you stop unpacking. Want me to help? I could hand things to you, couldn't I?"

"No, everything's just about out of the cartons, Jess. I was just . . ."

"Admiring the scenery? Describe it to me," she said, working her way to him. "Is it pretty? Do you see mountains? There's not much traffic here. I don't hear many cars go by."

"It's off the main drag, just like I told you."

He looked out the window again. You could see the mountains in the distance, and beyond the cemetery there was a lush forest filled with pine and birch, maple and some hickory. He skipped over the graveyard and described the rest.

"Sounds beautiful. We'll be happy here, Lee. I know it. Well," she said, her right hand on his left upper arm, "if you have put everything in its place, it's time for you to show me. I want to be just as independent in this apartment as I was in Hicksville, even though this one is a lot larger."

"Okay," he said, shaking his head and smiling. He had searched for a ground-floor apartment and had found this one in this turn-of-the-century, two-story Victorian. He suspected it was inexpensive because of the proximity of the graveyard, but it fit the bill. It would be easy for Jessie to work her way around it, and that was what was most important.

Jessie smiled, that dimple in her right cheek flashing. There was always so much animation in her face—the way she raised her eyebrows, twitched her small upturned nose, quivered the corners of her mouth. He doted on her features.

"You're laughing at me, aren't you?" she said.

"How did you know?"

"I can feel it," she said, and he believed her.

"All right." He took her hand. "Let me show you around your kitchen. I put everything left to right just the way you had it in Hicksville, beginning with the toaster, the coffeepot, and the Mixmaster.

"First cabinet," he continued, and took her through the kitchen, dish by dish, pot by pot. When he was finished, she began on the left by herself and reviewed it, not making a single error, and ending up sitting at the kitchenette table. He shook his head. She was truly amazing.

"Our bed is made," she said, "and I put away all my things and most of yours."

"Great." He put away the remaining articles and folded the last carton. "I've got to cut up all these cartons and make them flat. Then I have to tie the bundle up," he said. "Those are the rules from the sanitation company here. I'm surprised they didn't ask us to tie pink ribbons around everything. Talk about your prim-and-proper little communities."

Jessie laughed.

"Tell me about the school, Lee. You've hardly spoken about it. You're not ashamed of it, are you?" she asked perceptively.

"Well . . ."

"You are, aren't you?"

"It's nothing like what I had in Hicksville. They've got a gym, of course, but no separate exercise room and very little gymnastic equipment."

"No football then?"

"Too small a school. K to twelve is just under a thousand."

"That must be nice, though. You'll get to know everyone quickly." She smiled and then reached out for him. "Come here. I hate when you're so far away from me when I speak to you. I can't see your face with my fingers, and I don't know how you're reacting to what I say."

"Really? I thought you could sense things a mile away," he said, and sat beside her. She pressed the tips of her right hand over his lips and eyes.

"What is it, Lee? What's wrong?"

"Jesus."

"There's something wrong," she insisted. "Tell me. Is there something the matter with the apartment?"

"No."

"What then? Come on," she coaxed.

"I don't like my good luck being based on someone's bad," he confessed.

"Mr. Andersen," she said, nodding. "I suspected as much. Was he married?"

"To his job, from what I hear. He taught here for over twenty years."

She nodded again, her face full of concern. Then her expression changed.

"Someone's at the door," she declared.

"Huh?"

The door buzzer sounded.

"How the hell . . ."

"I heard footsteps on the porch steps," she explained.

The buzzer sounded again. Lee got up slowly, still shaking his head, and went to the door to greet Bob Baker, an English teacher he had met briefly when he had first come for an interview. Baker was just over six feet tall, in his late forties, with that distinguished gray tint in his temples. He had an impish twinkle in his cerulean-blue eyes. He wore a tweed sports jacket, matching brown slacks, and a white shirt opened at the collar. Lee thought he either had the remnants of a late summer tan or he was a naturally dark-skinned man. Baker carried a bag that obviously contained a bottle of some alcoholic beverage.

But Lee's gaze was quickly drawn to Baker's wife, who though not quite as tall, somehow evinced a taller appearance with her statuesque figure. Her face was an artist's dream, sculptured features, high cheekbones, deep-set green eyes, and a straight, sensual mouth. She wore her light brown hair brushed back and down over her shoulders. It lay softly and had a healthy, silky sheen.

"Lee Overstreet?" Baker said.

Lee smiled.

"Yes?"

"As faculty president, I make it my business to formally greet newcomers and see to it that they are properly christened." He handed Lee the bag, which Lee saw contained a bottle of champagne. And not a cheap one at that.

"Well, now, thank you. Come in, please."

"Actually it's only an excuse for Bob to drink," his wife said, extending her hand. "I'm Tracy Baker. I hope this is not a bad time, although I can't imagine when it could be a good time for you, having to move in practically overnight."

"No, no. It's—"

"Nervy of us," Bob said, stepping past him. Jessie had made her way back and was standing in the hallway, smiling. "Hi," Bob said.

"Hello." Jessie extended her hand and Baker moved forward quickly to shake it.

"Bob Baker. And this is my wife, Tracy," he said, turning.

But before she greeted Tracy, Jessie pulled her hand from Baker's abruptly because it felt loathsome, felt as if she had joined hands with a rotting corpse. She pressed her palm against her bosom and covered it with her other hand protectively.

"Jess?" Lee said.

She shook off the grotesque image quickly. These images, voices, when would they stop haunting her?

"I'm all right," she said quickly, and forced a smile.

"It's terrible of us to barge in on you like this," Tracy said, "but Bob insisted."

"No, no, it's all right," Jessie said. "Really."

"It's one of the few duties I have that I thoroughly enjoy," Baker quipped. He gazed around. "You haven't done too badly. I think it took us . . . what . . . ten days to unpack, Trace."

"More like ten months."

"How long have you lived in Gardner Town?" Jessie asked.

"A little over ten years. Teaching was going to be my temporary job," Baker said. "I had high hopes of becoming another Brando."

"Oh, I'm sorry," Jessie said. "I can appreciate what it means to be frustrated."

"Ah, I've adjusted," Baker said. "Besides, teaching is really a performance. Look at what we're competing with for the students' attention these days: MTV, the Laugh Channel, and home videos." He slapped his hands together and looked at Lee. "We can just open the bottle and pass it around, if you don't have your glasses unpacked yet."

"Lee!" Tracy exclaimed. "He's incorrigible and I think he tipped a few at O'Heanie's before he came home from school today."

"Absolute poppycock," Baker said.

"I'll get the glasses," Jessie said. "Take them into the living room, Lee. Do we need a corkscrew?"

"Naw, it's a twist-off," Baker said. "Old wine in a modern container."

Jessie smiled and then began her slow journey back to the kitchen, feeling her way down the corridor. The Bakers stared and then turned slowly toward Lee, who nodded.

"Yes," he said softly, "she's blind. A car accident a little over a year ago."

"Oh, I'm sorry," Tracy said quickly. "Bob, I told you it wasn't right to intrude."

"No, it's fine," Lee said. "She doesn't let it prevent her from doing much. She's already memorized her kitchen. Come on in and sit down. I appreciate the break and chance to relax."

"This is a roomy apartment," Tracy said, gazing around. "I didn't know it was available. Old man Carter, the cemetery caretaker, still lives upstairs, doesn't he?"

"Yes," Lee said, and then indicated they should sit on the sofa. He sat across from them in the high-backed, thick-cushioned easy chair.

"I heard he's in his nineties," Tracy said, "but I guess he still does his work satisfactorily."

"How do you know? Just because none of his residents have voiced any complaints?" Baker said, and laughed at his own joke.

"Bob, that isn't nice."

"One thing," Lee said, quickly gazing toward the doorway. "Jessie doesn't know we're practically on top of a cemetery. I left out that detail when I described the surroundings. I'll break it to her slowly," he added.

"Understandable," Baker said. He slapped his hands together and leaned forward. "Well, you've come from a rather big school system. It's going to be a lot different here, but I think you will like it. We have a fairly intelligent faculty and the board of education isn't bad if you look at them relatively. It's nothing like some of the outlying communities with schools governed by crew-cut conservatives who think the blackboard is a frill."

"And," Tracy added, "you'll find the community very sports-minded, especially when it comes to the basketball team."

"Yeah, I know. I've already been told about two hundred times how well liked Mr. Andersen was and how important it is to the school to have a good basketball team. I think the reason I was hired was because of my record as a basketball coach and my own achievements as an undergraduate."

"Very astute of you," Baker said. "You're in your element, buddy."

"Now, Bob, don't say anything to discourage him," Tracy warned. "He can be a terrible iconoclast when he gets started."

"Oh?"

"What is that, Bob?" Jessie asked from the doorway. "Don't tell me teaching has made you cynical." She placed the glasses on the coffee table carefully. The Bakers were mesmerized by her every move. She sensed it in the silence. "I'm fine," she said, smiling. "Bob, you sound like a very nice and very interesting man. Are you cynical?"

"Oh, I don't know. I suppose I get a little envious sometimes. I mean Lee here will get my students absolutely riled up into an hysteria with his basketball team, but I will struggle to get them to stay awake and try to understand why poetry has any purpose. But let's not get too philosophical here," he added quickly, and leaned over to open the bottle. "Let's get right to a toast."

He poured the champagne and Lee gave Jessie hers. They raised their glasses.

"To Lee and Jessie Overstreet. May their lives flourish and be productive and happy here in Gardner Town. Good luck and welcome from the faculty of Gardner Town High. Here, here," Bob said, and tilted his glass. They all drank.

"Did you teach anyplace else before Gardner Town, Bob?" Jessie asked. She turned her head so that she faced him directly. Although the wires had been tragically shut down behind those silvery gray eyes, they still held a glint of exuberance, a sparkle of life. It was as if she had the aim of someone in meditation, focusing her entire being on whomever or whatever she attended to.

"Like Lee, I taught for a few years in a bigger system. I was in Yonkers. I wanted to be very close to New York City in those days, and the theater," Baker explained.

"Don't you miss the livelier urban area, the richer school system?" Jessie pursued.

"Well . . ."

"We did in the beginning," Tracy replied quickly.

"What changed for you?" Jessie asked. Her hand searched for Lee's. He closed his fingers around hers and smiled at the Bakers.

"Jessie's a writer; she likes to know what makes people tick," he explained, gazing at her with some pride.

"A writer!" Baker leaned forward. "Really? Have you published anything?"

"Short stories in small magazines, some poetry. Nothing major yet. So," she said, the smile around her lips rippling through her cheeks and around her eyes, "you do like living in a small-town world?"

"Yes. It sort of wears on you after a while. It's nice not to have to fight for a place to park when you go shopping."

"Certainly you don't have the same sort of problems big schools have," Jessie said. "I'm sure kids here aren't as into drugs and alcohol, are they?"

"I guess we have our share of delinquents, but you're right—it's not as bad as the inner city. And as far as the school goes, Henry Young has a handle on things," Baker said.

"Yes," Lee said. "I got that impression. I never heard so many superlatives when it came to an administrator. Is he really that good?"

"Who told you all these good things about him?" Tracy inquired.

"His secretary, naturally, but some of the teachers I met, too. Why?" he asked when he saw her pensive look. "Isn't it true?"

"Of course it's true," Bob insisted. "There's no one I'd rather work under." He lifted his glass. "To Henry Young." He emptied his glass in a gulp.

"In my house it's practically as blasphemous to say anything that could in any way be construed as negative about Henry Young as it is to say anything negative about Jesus Himself," Tracy quipped.

"Tracy!"

"Take it easy, Bob. These walls aren't bugged, and the Overstreets aren't going to run right out and say I criticized your precious leader." She looked up at Lee quickly. "Are you?"

Lee started to laugh, but saw that Jessie's soft smile had evolved into a look of deep concern.

"Hey," he said in an attempt to lighten things up. Instinctively he put his arm around her. "I thought I was coming to work in a nice little old country schoolhouse with none of the tensions and politics of the bigger systems."

Baker looked up sharply.

"You are," he said. "Believe me, you are," he added, and shot a reproachful glance at Tracy.

Tracy managed to change the subject and get them talking about the things new residents would appreciate: the best dentist, places to shop, and the best doctor.

"Actually," she said, laughing, "we have only one in this community, and he's so old-fashioned, he still makes house calls."

"Really?" Lee smiled.

"Old Doc Beezly," Baker said. "I'd sooner have him treat me than any of these computerized wonder boys coming out of medical schools these days. He saved my life."

"Oh, what happened to you?" Jessie asked.

"I had a heart seizure. The old ticker actually had stopped, but Dr. Beezly used CPR and brought me back."

"What a fright," Jessie said.

"I've been all right since. No problems. I go to him for regular checkups. Wouldn't go to anyone else," he reiterated.

They chatted some more and then a little over a half hour later the Bakers left, Tracy promising to come by in a day or two to show Jessie around the town.

"They seemed like a nice couple," Jessie said after Lee closed the door behind them. "I like her."

"He's a bird," Lee commented. He stared at her a moment. "What made you jump when he shook your hand? Static electricity or something?"

"Yes," she lied, and flashed a false smile. But Lee didn't pursue it; he sensed it had something to do with those damn nightmares and voices.

"Well," he said, rubbing his hands together, "shall we attempt our first meal in our new home?"

After the accident Lee had taken on more domestic duties, but as Jessie gained confidence and became more adept at overcoming her handicap, he drifted back into the role of a mere assistant. They fixed their first meal in their new apartment, ate, and enjoyed coffee and conversation. As soon as they had cleaned up, Jessie went to what would be her writing office, one of the extra bedrooms, to see about setting things up, while Lee watched some late news on television.

Just before he turned off the set to get ready for bed, Jessie came in, moving so slowly and with such purpose, she looked like she was gliding along an invisible wire.

"Hi," he said. "I was just . . ."

She didn't reply. She went to a side window and pressed her forehead to the glass as if she could actually look into the darkness.

Because they were on a side road and away from the center of town, there were no streetlights. The only illumination on the road and surroundings came from the half-moon that peered around the shoulder of a large, dark cloud. The resulting yellow glow looked like a pool of amber water flooding the graveyard. Lee came up beside Jessie and put his arm around her.

"What is it, honey? What's wrong?"

"All those voices," she said softly, and raised her head from the window to turn to him. "Don't you hear them?"

"Hear them?" He listened. "No, honey, I don't hear any voices. It's as quiet out there as it must be on the surface of the moon."

"No," she said. "It's as noisy as a congregation full of Sunday worshipers, everyone talking at once," she said, putting her hands over her ears.

"Jessie, baby . . ." He took her hands into his, but she continued to grimace in pain. "You've got to see a doctor about this. There's no one out there, honey. Honest, we're—"

"Right beside a cemetery," she said, her eyes wide. The way she said it drove a sword of ice through his heart. She turned back to the window.

"A cemetery," she whispered. "And something's very wrong, very wrong."

— 2 —

Lee studied the twelve boys standing before him for a moment. Barry Gilmore held the basketball against his side as if he owned it and he was only letting the rest of them play with it. He looked impatient and openly telegraphed so with his distinct smirk. The caramel-skinned boy was six feet five and, from what Lee had been told, was supposed to have an excellent opportunity to achieve high scorer's honors in the Southeastern Zone this year.

Donald Hodes, a six-foot-two-inch pasty-white boy, looked awkward and gangly standing beside Gilmore. Gilmore's body was lean and well proportioned for a basketball player. The power in his legs and his shoulders was evident. Hodes had trouble standing straight when he stood still. His prominent collarbone protruded and the bones in his shoulders stuck up so sharply it looked as if his body were on a metal hanger. Like Gilmore, Hodes appeared bored with Lee's opening remarks, and Lee wasn't very impressed with him. Yet Larry Thompson, the temporary substitute, had told Lee that Donald was strong under the boards.

"He's all elbows and hips, bumping and poking," Thompson had said. "Swear, he could stab someone with that sharp, right elbow. He doesn't hesitate to get away with it," Thompson had added, and winked. Lee didn't like the implication.

"Now, I know it's hard for any team to pick up a new coach halfway into the season," Lee began when he faced the boys after school for their first practice with him, "but maybe we can turn this into an advantage. The way I see it, all you guys are going to have to prove yourselves again. I look at you with fresh eyes."

"Does that mean there's no such thing as a second team, Coach?" Paul Benson asked. He was a five-foot-ten-inch muscular white boy with very dark black hair and heavy sideburns. His remark was greeted with much laughter.

"There's a second team, Paul. We just gotta see who's on it." Lee sat down on the bench, clipboard in hand. "All right," he said, "we'll begin the scrimmage. You guys on the benches watch the clock and substitute yourselves every ten minutes."

"Who's gonna be the ref, Coach?" Billy Simins asked. The wiry six-footer had a way of tilting his head to the side when he spoke. It made him look sly.

"Ref yourselves. I want to be able to sit back and observe everyone out there to see who stays back and lets the other guy do it. I'm looking for hustle."

Shortly after the boys had begun playing, however, the scrimmage came to a halt when they saw Henry Young enter the gym. They stopped in their tracks and stood at attention. At first Lee didn't know what was happening. Then he turned and saw the principal coming toward him.

"Carry on, boys," Mr. Young said.

Gilmore passed the ball sharply to an unprepared Paul Benson, almost knocking him over. Lee caught the anger in the guard's eyes when he received the ball, but his concentration on the boys was broken as Young drew closer.

"Didn't mean to interrupt," the principal said, and sat down beside him.

"No problem."

"First few days are always the hardest, getting the boys to accept you, learning the ropes, finding the squeaks, eh?" He gazed out at the players, his eyes growing small, intent. "These kids are tough, real competitors. Kurt was proud of them, proud of all his teams, but especially proud of this one."

"Oh?" Lee wondered why. He saw nothing outstanding in this group of boys, especially in light of the championship banners that hung on the walls and trophies that were displayed in the glass case in the lobby of the gym. Andersen's previous teams had to have been head and shoulders above this present one.

"Gilmore's got some jump shot from the corner, doesn't he?" Young asked.

"Much more effective when he doesn't waste time on the first bounce."

"Of course, but you see it with more expert eyes. My secretary, Mrs. Schwartz, explained our referral system to you, I take it," Henry Young said.

"Yes, she did. Seems rather organized."

"Most important," the principal said sharply. "Discipline breaks down when it's conducted in a slipshod fashion. I like to know what's happening in my building. I don't like surprises," he added with an ominous note in his voice.

Young paused to look at a heavyset black boy who came into the game as a substitute. Lee saw the way the principal smiled and thought they were thinking the same thing.

"Billy Dyes doesn't look in shape for basketball, does he?" Lee said. "Wonder why Andersen kept him on the squad. He's out of breath just running onto the court."

"He's a bull out there," Young replied, his smile now coy, "when you need a bull."

"Bulls are for football," Lee said dryly. "Basketball's a game of grace, skill, and stamina, as well as strategy."

"Of course, but you'll find this isn't exactly a league of gentlemen. These little towns take their sports seriously; winning is a matter of pride because all these upstate communities have such a definite sense of identity." He laughed. "One thinks it's better than the other. It takes some getting used to, I guess. But," he said, slapping his knee and standing, "you'll get into it before you know it.

"Anyway, I just wanted to stop by and wish you the best of luck with the team and see if there was anything I could do for you. Don't hesitate to ask."

"Thank you," Lee said. He rose and shook the principal's long, firm hand. It felt so warm, he thought the man was feverish.

"Pick it up there, Dyes," Henry Young coached. "This isn't a Sunday-school picnic." He laughed and started away. Lee turned back to game.

Dyes took the ball and began dribbling awkwardly down the court. The boy guarding him charged forward, stabbing at the ball. Dyes turned his back and tried to dribble in another direction, but the boy shot to his right quickly to block him. The other members of Dyes's team were shouting at him to pass. He stopped dribbling and searched frantically for an open member of the squad. The boy guarding him was all over him, waving his arms frantically. Lee thought he was doing a very good job and started to make note of him on his tablet when suddenly Dyes snapped the ball directly at the boy's face. It struck him smack at the bridge of his nose and sent him backward, sitting him down sharply on his ass. Blood spurted from his nostrils. Instantly a number of his fellow teammates began to laugh.

"What the hell . . ."

Lee ran out to the middle of the court. As he did so he could see Henry Young standing in the gym doorway, smiling.

"What the hell did you do that for, Dyes?" Lee cried.

"I was just tryin' to pass, Coach, and he got in the way," Dyes said, making a weak attempt at denial.

"Like hell he did," Lee said, kneeling beside the stunned boy. He examined his nose bone quickly. "It's not broken. Go into the locker room and get some tissues. Hold them tight with your head back."

"Gilmore," Lee ordered, "go with him and help."

"Aw, Coach, let him go to the school nurse."

Lee looked toward the doorway and saw that the principal had left without even checking to see if the boy was seriously injured.

"The nurse is gone for the day," Lee said.

"So?" Gilmore said sullenly. "It's just a damn bloody nose."

"He's a member of your team," Lee said, helping the boy to his feet, "and you're supposed to be the captain. Know what that means?"

"Means shit," Gilmore mumbled.

"What was that?"

"Nothin'," the boy said sullenly. "C'mon, asshole. Next time learn to duck."

Lee watched them go off. Then he turned to Dyes.

"This sort of stuff doesn't go with me, Dyes. It's a cheap shot. Take ten laps."

"Huh?"

"You heard me, run around the gym ten times," he ordered.

"He does that, Coach," Benson said, "and he'll drop dead." Everyone smiled; Hodes laughed.

"If he can't do that, he can't be on my team," Lee said. "That goes for everyone here," he added, spinning on them sharply. Some still held their smiles. "Physical conditioning is essential. I don't even want to hear about any of you smoking, understand. Starting tomorrow, we begin each practice with twenty laps and we finish with twenty."

There was a chorus of groans.

"Dyes?"

The overweight boy looked ready to lunge at him. He turned toward Hodes and Lee thought he saw a slight nod. Then Dyes lowered his head and started to run, mumbling obscenities under his breath.

"All right," Lee said, releasing his breath. "Back to the scrimmage. So far I haven't seen anything to lead me to believe you guys have a chance to beat the girls' team in my last school. Hodes, take it out."

Lee returned to his bench and watched. Dyes ran with his arms against his sides as if he had to hold in his stomach, but Lee noticed he had his middle finger on both hands extended in silent, profane defiance. The other boys noticed, too, and some smiled.

Gilmore returned and took his position, the injured boy behind him walking with tissues in his nose.

"You okay?" Lee asked him. The boy nodded. When Dyes ran by, he glared at him hatefully and the boy cowered and retreated to another, more out-of-the-way place on the bench. The scrimmage continued until Lee saw Hodes jab his elbow into another boy's face, causing him to bleed at the mouth. Lee blew his whistle and called them to gather in a circle before him.

"I wonder," he said slowly, "if you guys ever heard about something called personal fouls."

"Ain't that something that happens when you get caught," Benson quipped.

There was a short burst of tittering.

"From now on," Lee said, ignoring it, "whenever we scrimmage, everyone has the same limit we have in a game. Then you're out."

"Shit, we all be out then," Gilmore said, and the boys laughed again.

"Then you'll all be out," Lee said as nonchalantly as he could. He perused the squad. To a man they were glaring back at him, and for the first time since he had begun his initial practice with his squad, he understood what was giving him this sense of foreboding.

The team, his team, looked more like a pack of rabid dogs panting as they stood there staring back hatefully at him than they did a group of teenage boys training to compete in a civilized sport.

Jessie paused in her preparations of the meat loaf she and Lee were to have for dinner. She held her breath and listened again. It was the oddest sound and it came from above, from old man Carter's apartment. It sounded like some sort of steel-toothed creature gnawing away at the floor. The crunch, crunch sound was followed by a soft gasp. It gave her the chills. She embraced herself and waited. After another series of crunching and another gasp, it ended. She heard footsteps. Then she heard the door of the upstairs apartment open and close. She moved toward the front of their apartment to hear even better.

Someone, obviously much younger than the aged tenant above, was coming down the stairs quickly. His steps pounded with a firmness and an authority old man Carter's lacked. The heavy oak outside door opened and closed and the footsteps continued over the loose slats of the porch floor and down the stone stairway. Jessie went to a slightly opened front window and continued to listen. The sounds trickled away as whoever it was continued rapidly over the fieldstone walk.

Lee had done a good job describing the structure and the grounds, so she could easily imagine someone moving about out there. But whoever it was didn't get into an automobile and drive off as she was anticipating. Instead he turned to the right and walked toward the cemetery, the footsteps becoming different. Jessie listened until the sound ceased.

How odd, she thought. She knew that by this time of day, the late-fall twilight had set in and it must be rather dark outside. Lee had described the street, so she knew there were no streetlights to push away the heavy, black curtain of night. Who was this person? Where was he going in the dark?

For a moment she didn't move. She waited to hear old man Carter above, but there was only a deep, ominous silence. Just as she turned to go back to the kitchen, she caught a whiff of some putrid odor slipping under the front door of their apartment. It was so rancid and foul, she imagined some field animal had come into the house and died in the entryway. Perhaps it was a poisoned rat.

The stench made her gag. She retreated quickly to the
kitchen and got herself a cold glass of water. The cool
liquid bubbled when it hit her stomach, but it seemed to
clear away the stench that had lingered in her nostrils and
throat.

Poor Lee, she thought. He's going to walk right into
that, whatever it was. She felt for the clock with the
raised numbers and confirmed that he wouldn't be home
for at least another hour or so. Then she returned to her
dinner preparations, but kept a keen ear out for sounds of
Lee's return. She was surprised when she heard him pull
his car into the shale-stone driveway beside the house
only fifteen minutes later.

That was one thing they would definitely miss, she
thought, a garage. This old house didn't even have a
carport. Then she remembered that Lee had told her
that old man Carter, although easily a man in his late
eighties, still drove his '72 Chevy.

"He claims he's had that car for nearly twenty years,"
Lee had said, "and never parked it in a garage. Of course,
all he has on it is thirteen thousand miles. He only uses
it to go to get what he needs. Can you imagine? The
inside's immaculate, but the outside's quite rusted and
faded. No dents or bumps to speak of, however. And
the engine sounds like it will go on for another twenty
years. Just like him," Lee had added, and Jessie had
thought, Yes.

Her initial meeting with the old man had left her confused. Lee had introduced her to him the morning after
she had sensed they were living adjacent to a cemetery.
The cemetery caretaker's voice cracked with age, and the
skin around his hand felt wrinkled and dry, but he had
a youthful firmness in his grip and she heard something
underneath the cracking, something buried just under

the croaking, rasping voice that to her suggested youth. It was only one of those incomprehensible, intuitive things that Lee thought were symptoms of some mental disturbance lingering from the accident. Maybe he was right. She certainly couldn't put her feelings about old man Carter into words.

Jessie had the table in the dining room set and everything warmed and waiting in the kitchen when Lee entered the house. She turned toward the front door as soon as she heard him insert his key in their apartment door.

"Hi," he called out. She moved quickly to greet him. She had remained at the rear of the house ever since she had heard the footsteps and smelled that horrible stench, but as she made her way toward Lee she didn't smell it anymore.

Lee embraced and kissed her.

"Something smells great," he said.

"You didn't smell anything horrible on the way in, then?" she asked.

"Horrible? No. Why?"

She told him, the two of them still holding on to each other.

"No," he said again. "Nothing like that. Maybe the old man had an exterminator in and they caught whatever it was and that was what you caught a whiff of. This house is probably old enough for that kind of problem. Don't forget, we're out in the country."

"I know. You told me the nearest neighbor was at least a good half mile away in either direction. But why would an exterminator park his vehicle so far from the house?"

"I don't know, honey. Maybe you just didn't hear him get into the truck," Lee said, and released a heavy breath of stored tension from his lungs. She sensed it in the tightness of his muscles and even heard it in his voice.

"You don't sound as if you had a good day, Lee," she said when he released her and started toward their bedroom to change for dinner.

"I'll tell you all about it after I get out of these clothes."

"Why didn't you shower and change at school like you used to?" she asked.

"I don't know. I just felt like getting out of there quickly today. I'll just be a few minutes," he added quickly, and continued on to the bedroom. She listened after him.

Strange how she had come to be able to sense his mood even in the way he walked. But then again, she could tell a great deal about someone from the way they walked. Heavy ponderous steps conjured up the image of a big person or someone with a lot on his mind. Light tread was carefree, young. She could sense age, temperament, confusion, firmness, and determination just from the sounds of footsteps.

That's what made those footsteps she had heard before so confusing, she thought, now that she recalled them more thoughtfully. They were fast, energetic, but there was an intermittent shuffle, especially after whoever it was went out of the house.

Yes, she thought, almost crying out, the dying away of sounds . . . it didn't come because of distance; it came because the footsteps changed until it sounded more like the individual was dragging himself or herself over the walk. How odd, she thought, but she put her confusion aside for the moment and went into the kitchen to get the dinner on the table.

Lee's mood was dramatically changed when he returned from his quick shower. It was as if the water had washed away the turmoil that had somehow formed a crust of depression over him.

"I am hungry," he announced, slapping his hands together, "and this does look great. I don't know how you do it."

"From memory mostly," she said. "Don't forget, I did a lot of cooking for my mother before I met you."

"Well, remind me to thank her for being so lazy," Lee quipped, and laughed.

"You want to talk about your day now or wait until after we eat?" Jessie asked.

"Naw, it's all right. The regular day went great . . . small classes, manageable, most of the kids quite nice. I met a few more faculty members, mostly old-timers, a few newcomers, which in this school means being here less than ten years. These places don't have the same kind of turnover we saw around the city."

"So," Jessie said, her smile quickly evaporating, "what was it that turned the day around for you?"

"The team, I'm afraid. They're so undisciplined, wild, and so many of them are quite self-centered. Frankly I'm very surprised. Everything I've heard about Kurt Andersen would have led me to believe his players were different. A number of people told me he was an old-fashioned coach who demanded respect and was admired by his boys. I can't envision these boys admiring anyone who demanded they treat each other with respect, much less him."

"Aren't you being a little hard on them, Lee? It is traumatic for them, too, to have their coach die unexpectedly and have to adjust to a new man."

"Ah, it's not just dealing with me," he said, "or Andersen's death. Matter of fact, no one so much as brought up his name, and when I mentioned him, I didn't see any sorrow. Some of them were even smirking, especially the team's so-called stars—Gilmore, Hodes, Benson." He paused.

"There's more?" she asked perceptively.

"Yeah. A very strange thing happened at practice. One of the boys deliberately hurt another, hit him directly in the face with the ball."

"My God."

"That wasn't what was strange, however. I've seen malicious kids in action before. What was strange was Henry Young was there at the time. He saw the whole thing."

"The principal? What did he do?"

"That's it. He did nothing, Jess. In fact, I thought I saw him laugh."

"Oh, come on, Lee. You must be mistaken."

"I don't know, honey. But even if I am mistaken about that, he never even checked to see how the boy was."

"Is the boy all right?"

"Yeah, just a bloody nose. I've got a lot of work to do," Lee said, sighing. "A lot more than I ever anticipated. Basketball skill might be the least of it," he added. He reached for another scoop of mashed potatoes, but stopped when he saw the expression on Jessie's face. "I'm sorry," he said. "I should have waited until afterward. Didn't want to disturb you at dinner."

"No, Lee. That's all right. In fact," she said, tilting her head back so that she looked as if she were gazing through the ceiling, "I somehow anticipated you would have problems."

"Aw now, Jess, you're not going to start that talk about dreams and premonitions, are you?"

She pressed her lips together as if to keep herself from speaking and shook her head.

After they had eaten and cleaned up, they retired to the living room and Lee described some of the other people he had met.

"Oh, before I forget," Jessie told him, "Tracy Baker called today. She wants to come by tomorrow to pick me up and show me around. And the Bakers want to have a dinner and introduce us to some of their friends, one of whom is Dr. Beezly, the doctor they spoke of so highly when they were here. I said I would check with you as to the date."

"Any night's as good as another right now, Jessie," Lee said. "My social calendar isn't quite set yet."

"I know. I as much as told her that."

"Great," Lee said, stretching. "Gosh, I can't believe how tired I am already."

"Tension does it to you, honey. After you're settled in and you start getting things to go more the way you want them to, you'll relax."

Lee got up and sat beside her on the couch. He took her hands into his.

"What makes you so wise. And so patient?" he asked.

"Oh, I'm not so wise."

"Don't tell me. I know wisdom when I see and hear it," he insisted. She grew serious, the lines around her mouth tightening.

"I think it's because of the darkness. I have to turn into myself to see things now, and there are many things to discover about yourself when you do that, things you've inherited, things below the surface, things we can't see because we are usually distracted. Does that make any sense?"

"No," he said. "But I know what you're doing—you're trying to make me feel better, which is just like you, Jess. No matter what you say, and no matter what

you do, I'll never forget that I was driving that day and
that—"

She put her fingers on his lips so quickly and so
accurately, it was as if she did see.

"Please, Lee, don't," she said.

He kissed her fingers and then her lips.

"Okay," he said. She felt him lighten up and knew he
was smiling.

"Are you trying to tell me you're not that tired?" she
asked. He laughed.

"How did you guess?"

He helped her to her feet and they started out of the
living room toward their bedroom, he putting the lights
out as they went.

When he looked back, it seemed as if the darkness was
closing in around them. He shuddered, thinking this was
Jessie's world now. No wonder she had so many strange
thoughts and ideas. He vowed to be more loving and to
stop bringing home his own problems.

But something instinctive told him that this might be
harder than he thought.

— 3 —

The defiant-looking shadows just out of the reach of the streetlights retreated before the dim headlights of a '72 Ford pickup whose red exterior had faded into a pale shale color. It was quite rusted, especially around the wheel wells. The truck crept down Main Street, Gardner Town, passing by the darkened windows of the closed stores, windows that reflected the emptiness and solitude of the sleeping hamlet. The only sound came from some metal signs above the garage at the west end of Main Street. They groaned and complained about the wind that lifted and dropped them with a monotonous regularity. The subsequent screech sounded like the cry of some metallic cat agonizing about its loneliness under a sky devoid of moon and stars.

The truck came to a slow stop at the blinking traffic light and then turned to the right, picking up some speed as it moved through a residential neighborhood with its quaint homes and neatly manicured lawns and hedges. Only the bright lights above front doors and gates to discourage prowlers and burglars provided any illumination on the side street. The man sitting in the cab of the truck was barely visible. Most of the time he appeared a dark phantom. He looked like a ghost who, together with his decrepit vehicle, had emerged from some car dump on a ghoulish mission, perhaps to get revenge on the vehicle and driver who had plowed him off the highway years and years before.

The truck snaked around another turn and headed out toward the cemetery. The homes began to become few and far between until the street was bordered on both sides by long fields and forests, the trees now standing like mute and belligerent sentinels guarding the secrets within their pockets of darkness. When the truck reached the Gardner Town cemetery, the driver turned off his headlights.

Becoming one with the night, the truck passed the gray stone archway of the cemetery with its high reliefs of trees and flowers. The vehicle stopped about a hundred yards from the house in which old man Carter and the Overstreets lived. For a moment the driver focused on the lighted windows upstairs. Then the truck inched forward as if on its own.

A startled owl flew off a nearby tree limb and sailed across the truck's path before disappearing into the night. The driver didn't seem to notice. Nothing took his concentration off the windows. Not more than fifty feet from the house, he stopped the truck again and just stared. Finally he lit a cigarette. Its glowing ash looked like the single eye of a terrified alley cat reflecting the stray glitter from garbage cans. The driver rolled down his window, but the escaping smoke was barely visible. After a few more moments he flipped the cigarette into the night. It landed with an explosion of sparks and remained a tiny, red-orange bead against the blackness.

A shadow crossed the first lit window.

Reaching over to the dashboard, the driver of the truck opened the glove compartment and took out a pint bottle of rye whiskey. He unscrewed the top carefully and took a long swallow. He shuddered as the whiskey burned down his throat and warmed his chest. Then he screwed on the bottle cap and put the bottle back in the glove compartment, catching a glimpse of himself in the rearview mirror.

Only he didn't see himself; he didn't see a drawn, unshaven man with sunken cheeks and a pronounced jawbone. He didn't see his own bloodshot eyes or his disheveled, thin brown hair. Instead he saw the face of a teenage boy, round and full of health, a face of smiles and optimism.

The driver paused to smile back.

"Just a little while longer now, Paulie boy," he muttered. "Just a little while longer. You're gonna know it, too, boy. I can feel it. It's gonna wake you up, bring you back to the way you was. Just a little while longer."

The dark silhouette in the house moved across a second window. The driver reached behind his seat and brought out a rifle.

"Oh yeah, Paulie boy," he muttered. "Oh yeah."

He started to open the truck door, but the handle didn't turn. He pressed down on it again and again. It didn't move. He leaned on it with all his weight, but the handle did not budge.

"What the hell . . ."

He slid across the seat impatiently and reached for the handle on the passenger-side door, but that, too, did not budge. He banged on it with his closed fist until his hand screamed with pain and then he raised his rifle and slammed the handle with the rifle butt. Nothing happened.

Except the windows rolled up.

The driver sat back in shock. They were certainly not power windows.

"Huh?" he said to an invisible passenger.

He kicked at the door, but it was like kicking at a cement wall.

The truck started. He jumped back as if the steering wheel were on fire. The engine raced.

"What the hell's going on?" He turned the ignition key, but it was already on off. The truck shook and rumbled as the engine raced harder and harder.

Panic set in. The driver slammed the windows with his rifle, but they didn't as much as crack. He felt as if he were choking, as if all air were cut off. Then he realized . . . the faulty exhaust system, the carbon monoxide . . .

He flailed about like a man going down in quicksand, but nothing helped. Nothing.

Finally, seeing no other way, he pointed the rifle at the side window and pulled the trigger. The report was ear shattering, and he thought, as crazy as it seemed, that he actually saw the bullet bounce off the window and turn around. It seemed to hesitate for a moment as if it, too, didn't believe what was happening, or didn't want what was happening to happen. But neither he nor the bullet had any say in the matter.

It continued its ricochet and crashed through his forehead, lifting him slightly off the seat and throwing him back against his door, the rifle flying out of his hands and landing on the seat.

The engine stopped. The door handle went down and the door opened. The driver fell back, but his legs got caught under the steering wheel and he dangled there, his body swaying in the wind.

• • •

Jessie woke with a start. Her body was comfortably curled in the pocket of Lee's embrace, his right arm lying lightly over her shoulder. They had fallen asleep almost immediately after making love, both enjoying that gentle and welcome fatigue that followed. Jessie recognized that through their lovemaking they both rid their bodies of the day's anxiety. Sex was an antidote for tension, for loneliness, and especially for fear. With every kiss, with each touch, they reinforced their alliance and assured each other that no matter how cold and dark the world seemed to be around them, they were in a warm, protective cocoon.

Lee would tease her about their sexual relations now. It was the only time he inserted any humor into a discussion of her blindness.

"Wait a minute," he said after they had made love one night, "if the doctors are right about you and your other senses have become sharper, you're probably getting more out of this than I am now."

"So practice keeping your eyes closed when we make love," she replied, and they laughed.

But it was true. Often, when they made love, she felt something beyond what she had felt before the accident: she reached a higher plateau. Right at the point of orgasm, she seemed to leave the confines of her body and become part of some ongoing stream, a flow of souls, a greater, higher form of life. It was an altogether different sort of ecstasy, not sensual, not pleasurable in the common sense; her body didn't tingle and feel filled with electricity. This ecstasy came from a sense of completion, as if . . . as if she had a taste of what would come in the hereafter.

Of course, she didn't mention a word about it to

Lee. He would just lay the blame on her overworked imagination again, and she instinctively sensed he might not appreciate knowing she wasn't thinking of him per se when they made great love.

They had made great love tonight, both of them driven by a need to comfort themselves as well as each other. Lee had taken his time, titillating her with what he playfully called his mystery kiss. It was their closest thing to kinky sex. She would lie nude, her arms up over her head. He would begin by kissing her feet or her stomach, and then she had to anticipate where he would put his lips next. In her perpetual darkness, his kisses felt like drops of warm rain, one falling on her breasts, another on her lips, and then another just inside her thighs.

Sometimes he lingered between kisses, making the anticipation that much greater, drawing out the exquisite torment until she cried out and reached up for him. He would laugh and come to her and they would cling to each other with a delicious desperation. It had been like that tonight. And they had drifted into a gentle repose.

Until the noise shattered her peace.

"What was that?" she cried, sitting up. Lee's arm fell away from her shoulders and he groaned. "Lee?"

"Huh?" He fought opening his eyes. It was too sweet, too comfortable. She poked him. "What?" he said, and groaned as he turned over on his back.

"Didn't you hear that bang?"

"What bang?" He wiped his eyes and reluctantly lifted his head from the pillow to listen. "I don't hear anything," he said.

"Not now." She threw her legs over the bed and found her slippers.

"Where are you going?"

"I heard something . . . something terrible," she said, and started for the doorway.

"Oh Jessie, Jesus." He wiped his cheeks vigorously and sat up himself. By the time he found his own slippers, she was down the corridor and entering the living room. He was nude, but he didn't pause to get a robe. He flipped on the hallway light and found her with her ear pressed against the front window. For a moment he almost burst out laughing. She looked like someone eavesdropping on the neighbors in the next-door apartment.

"Jessie?"

"Someone's out there," she said. "I hear an engine running."

"Oh boy," he said, and joined her at the window. It took a moment for him to see the truck silhouetted in the darkness. Without its headlights on, it had blended in with the other shadows and forms in the night. "What the . . ."

"There's someone there?"

"A truck," he said. "No lights. I can't tell if anyone's sitting in it or not."

"The engine's running," she insisted. He couldn't hear it through the closed window, so he opened it and knelt down to place his ear close to the screen.

"Yeah," he said, "it is."

"Well, what is it?"

"I don't know."

"I heard a terrible, loud sound before, Lee. It sounded . . . like a gunshot."

"Huh?" An icy finger of fear traced the length of his spine from his neck to his waist. He shook his body like a bird shaking off rain. "Shit," he said. "I'm standing here naked. And," he realized, "so are you."

"Maybe you should phone the police, Lee," she said, unconcerned with her own exposure in the window.

"And tell them what? There's a truck parked on the street with its engine running."

"It's very late. And whoever it is has the lights off. That's peculiar, Lee."

"Oh Jesus," he groaned. "I'll get some clothes on and see what the hell it is."

She grabbed his arm.

"No, Lee. Just phone the police. I'm afraid."

"They won't come up here if I just tell them there's a truck outside with its engine running, honey. There's no law against that. I'll see if there's anything wrong and then I'll phone." He patted her hand and returned to the bedroom.

Jessie turned her attention back to the window and continued to listen. There was the distinct sound of those shuffling footsteps again. The cool night air came in through the opened window, but it wasn't the chill that made her step back; it was the odor, a whiff of that horrible stench. She brought the window down sharply and stepped back, her heart pounding. A moment later she heard Lee coming down the hallway toward the front door.

"Wait," she cried.

"What?"

"There's something out there, Lee."

"What?" he asked.

"I don't know, but it's something . . . horrible."

"Oh Jessie," he groaned. "I have a flashlight with me. I'll check it out first before I go too far, okay?"

"Don't go off the porch," she advised.

"Right," he said. He opened the door and went out.

"Lee!" she cried when he closed the door behind him. She rushed to it and opened it again just in time to hear him walking down the steps. "Lee?"

"It's all right," he called back. "I'm okay. Get back inside, you exhibitionist," he said, and she finally realized she was standing naked in the doorway.

"What do you see?" she asked, covering her bosom with her arms.

"A truck with its door opened," he said as nonchalantly as he could, for he had seen more.

He walked over the flagstones and directed the beam at the truck cab where the driver's door was open. He ran the light down and saw the man dangling.

"Should I phone the police?" Jessie called from the doorway. For a moment Lee didn't respond. He stepped closer.

"Yeah," he called back, "I guess you should."

He directed the beam of light over the driver. The man moaned.

"What the hell . . ." Lee knelt down beside him and shook his arm. The man groaned and then started to vomit profusely. Lee jumped up and stepped back to avoid the splatter. The foul odor of whiskey mixed with whatever the man had put into his stomach during the last few hours came up at Lee in undulating waves. Lee fanned the air around him and stepped to the side, directing his flashlight at the cab. He saw the man's feet were caught in the steering wheel and he saw the emptied pint bottle of rye on the seat with a rifle beside it.

The man moaned and began his struggle to right himself, but he had no support and simply flapped about like a fish on land. Reluctantly, holding his breath as he did so, Lee came to his assistance and lifted him so that he could free his feet from the steering wheel. Then he scooped his arms under the man's arms to pull him from the truck as if he were pulling him from a vehicle on fire. He wanted to get as far away from the rancid odors as quickly as he could. He dropped the man gently on the shoulder of the road and ran the beam of light over his face.

The gaunt-looking, unshaven man waved his hand at the light the way he would chase away flies. Lee shook his head in disgust and directed the light back to the truck. That was when he saw the blood, large ruby stains on the street where the man had been hanging upside down.

"Jesus," Lee muttered. He turned back to the drunk and searched his body and face for signs of his wounds, but he found none. He knelt beside him again. The man had turned over and already was snoring. Lee ran the light over his neck and head, but he saw nothing. "What the hell . . ."

He turned back to the stains to be sure they weren't in his imagination. Confirming them, he began to wonder if there was someone else. He got up and walked around the truck, directing his light every which way, but there was no sign of anyone else. Finally he reached in and shut off the truck engine.

"Hey," he said, shaking the drunken man with his foot. "Hey, who the hell are you? Was there anyone with you? Hey?" He shook him again, but the man only groaned.

"Lee," Jessie called from the doorway. "Are you all right?"

"Yeah. It's only some drunk," he replied.

"I called the police; they're on their way."

"Good." He scratched his head and looked around again. There was some other smell here, some horrible odor that didn't seem to be a part of this revolting scene. It trailed off behind him toward the cemetery. He lifted the flashlight in its direction and his light illuminated some of the bone-white tombstones that were close to the road.

Suddenly he thought he saw something moving: a tall, dark shadow. He chased it with his light, but the flashlight was too weak to illuminate at any great distance and the shadowy figure was gone as quickly as it had appeared.

Probably my imagination, he thought. Even so, the image chased him back and he retreated quickly to the house. Jessie had put on her robe and was waiting for him in the doorway.

"What is it?"

"Some guy was drinking booze. He stopped, probably because he didn't know where the hell he was, and somehow he opened his door on the driver's side and fell out, only his feet got caught under the steering wheel, so he was just dangling there. He did me the honor of throwing up most of what he had drunk and eaten during the last few hours."

"Well, where is he?"

"He's sleeping comfortably on the side of the road," Lee said. "I hate to disturb him, much less touch him," he added. He didn't mention the bloodstains.

"Oh." Jessie turned in the direction of the truck. "But I heard such a loud noise, more like a gunshot."

"Since when do you know about gunshots, Jess? You probably heard him screaming for help or something until he passed out." He had seen a rifle on the floor of the cab, but he didn't want to mention it. "Let's wait inside," he said. "I'll make some warm milk so I can fall back to sleep after the police arrive."

Reluctantly she permitted him to turn her away from the door and then she followed him back to the kitchen. Twenty minutes later the police arrived.

Gardner Town was part of a township that consisted of seven villages and hamlets. As such it was patrolled and protected by a township police department, a complement of twenty officers with one full-time detective. The police department had fourteen patrol cars, but usually had only two in operation during the late-evening hours.

The two officers who arrived were local boys. The driver, Burt Peters, was a stout six-foot-two-inch man with curly black hair. He had gone to school in Gardner Town and remained in the community after graduation, working first as a private security guard and then becoming a town policeman. His partner, Greg Daniels, was a lean, muscular, six-foot black man who grew up in one of the neighboring hamlets, Hurleyville, and had come to the police force directly after his stint in the army.

Lee and Jessie greeted them at the outside door. Lee saw that they already had picked up the drunken truck driver and placed him in the back of their patrol car. He sat with his head against the window.

"Sorry you were disturbed," Burt said. "It's Tony Benson; he's sorta famous for this kind of thing."

"He doesn't even have a license to drive anymore," Greg added, shaking his head. "Lost that last time we picked him up."

"Someone will come by in the morning to pick up the truck," Burt said, and nodded. The two patrolman started to turn away.

"Just a minute," Lee said. He looked at Jessie and then

stepped forward. He had kept it from her as long as he could. "There may be someone else out there."

"Sir?" Burt said.

"I saw bloodstains on the street, but I didn't find any wounds or gashes on the driver."

"Bloodstains?" Greg said. He looked at Burt, but Burt shrugged.

"You wanna show us, Mr. Overstreet?" Burt Peters asked.

"Sure," he said, and led the patrolman off the porch and down the street to the truck. Their flashlight was a great deal more powerful than his. It washed the darkness off the pavement. Lee went to the spot and stopped. He knelt down and felt the road. There was nothing there.

"But I saw it," he said quickly, looking up at the two policemen.

"You sure it was here, Mr. Overstreet?" Greg asked.

"Positive. And they weren't little stains either. It looked like gobs of blood had been spilled."

The two patrolmen nodded sympathetically. Burt ran his flashlight over the road alongside the truck.

"Don't see anything now, sir," he said.

"I know," Lee said, standing. "I can't understand it."

"Well, the night plays tricks on you, sir," Burt said.

"Maybe it was just some spilled booze," Greg said. Both policemen laughed.

"No, no, this was blood," Lee said, "and there was a stench."

"Well, there still is, sir," Burt said. "Only we have it in the back of our car." They laughed again.

"No, this was different. It wasn't just the booze and all; it was . . ." He recalled Jessie's telling him of her smelling something rotten and dead an hour or so before he had come home from work. "This was something dead."

"Dead?" Burt looked at Greg. "Well, sir, we don't smell anything now."

"Yeah, I know," Lee said. He looked off toward the cemetery.

"We'd better get Tony Benson to the station," Greg said.

"Right."

"Benson," Lee said as they turned to go back. The possible significance of the name had occurred to him. "He wouldn't have a teenage son in Gardner Town High, would he?"

"Yes, sir. Paul Benson. Great little play maker on the basketball court," Burt said.

"Say," Greg said, pausing, "you wouldn't be the new coach, would you?"

"Yes, I would," Lee said. "That's Paul's father?" he asked, shaking his head. No wonder the boy is the way he is, he thought.

"Yes, sir," Burt said. "He wasn't always like this, though."

"Oh?"

"Went downhill after his wife died. He happens to be an excellent carpenter, only I don't think he's held on to many jobs lately." Burt Peters smiled. "Small town, sir. Everybody knows everyone's business. Sorry you were bothered. Thanks for calling us."

The two policemen got into their vehicle. Lee watched them drive off, Tony Benson still not moving in the rear. He turned to look back at the truck and then he joined Jessie, who waited in the doorway.

"Why didn't you tell me about the blood?" she asked as soon as he stepped up.

"I didn't want to worry you. Fortunately I made the right decision."

"What do you mean?"

"There weren't any bloodstains. I guess I imagined them," he said. "I would have worried you for nothing."

"How can you imagine bloodstains, Lee?"

"I don't know, honey," he said, although he couldn't understand it. He had knelt down and confirmed it the first time. But what other explanation was there? They weren't there now. "I got down on my hands and knees to check again."

"But I heard a gunshot," she insisted.

"Jess, it's late as hell. I'll be as limp as a wet noodle as it is."

She nodded and they headed back to their bedroom. Just after he put out the lights and joined her under the covers, she turned to him sharply.

"Lee?"

"What now?"

"How could old man Carter sleep through all this? He didn't come out; he didn't try to find out what was going on."

"I don't know, honey. Maybe that's a benefit in being old. You don't hear all the nonsense that goes on around you and you have a good night's sleep.

"Boy oh boy," Lee added as he turned over, "and here I thought life in the rural world was going to be too peaceful to stand."

He closed his eyes. He knew Jessie was lying there thinking, but he couldn't stop her.

He couldn't even stop himself, for over and over he saw the image of that dark shadow threading itself around the bone-white tombstones before it disappeared into the depths of the cemetery.

He fell asleep when he finally concluded that the night was a magician casting out illusion after illusion, overwhelming him and making him a victim of his own imagination.

— 4 —

Lee sat in the physical-education office thumbing through Kurt Andersen's old purchase orders and correspondence. Despite the warm welcome he had received from most of the staff, he couldn't help feeling like an intruder. His predecessor hadn't had time to clean out his personal things and no one had bothered to do it for him and his family afterward. Andersen's entire career history still lingered on the walls in the form of congratulatory letters and plaques, as well as pictures with local dignitaries and school personnel. The correspondence in the files included many personal letters from other coaches, parents of former students, and former students themselves. After Lee had perused some of this, it was not hard for him to understand why the man had been something of an institution to the people of Gardner Town.

From the letters Lee could appreciate how much personal interest Andersen had taken in his students. Some had kept in touch with him as long as fifteen years after graduation, and many had still been asking his advice as recently as a week before he died. Obviously he had had more than their respect, he had had their affection, too.

As Lee read through a dozen or so of these letters, he began to experience the particular sort of nostalgia only someone who had been teaching a long time feels. Without ever having had these students, he longed for the likes of them. From the tone of the letters and the references to events and memories, Lee conjured up a picture of an altogether different sort of school and community. There was a closeness, a comradeship, a sense of extended family that simply didn't exist today.

He had to smile at what the boys in the letters considered their difficulties. They were mostly insignificant compared with what occurred in present times. Absent were any references to problems with drugs and alcohol. Only an occasional letter here and there mentioned a broken family. These letters were written before the age of divorce.

Apparently Kurt Andersen had had a nice singing voice and, especially during his younger days, had often been persuaded to sing at school dances. Lee was sure Andersen had had far more than his share of teenage girls with crushes on him, but even back when he was a young teacher, he had probably handled the problem with a fatherly maturity. Lee saw it in the way the girls had written to Andersen years later, thanking him for his advice and his sensitivity.

What large shoes to fill, Lee thought; and yet Kurt Andersen had been the kind of teacher Lee had always wanted to be. From the records on Andersen's discipline problems and the way he had handled them, Lee could surmise that he had been a firm man, but a fair man. Not that he had had many problems up until the last year or so. About then there was a dramatic change.

The file marked *Discipline* was much thicker for the last couple of years, and the problems cited were far

more serious. Andersen had caught boys selling dope
in the locker rooms; he had caught boys stealing, not
only from each other, but even from him. Reading the
report on one such episode, Lee could sense Andersen's
shock and outrage. Students were crossing lines hereto-
fore thought inviolate.

When Lee reached the record of the last six months,
he noted an increasingly frustrated Andersen, frustrated
not just with his pupils, but with his administration, especially with his principal. The correspondence between
them had become quite heated. Andersen was not only
disappointed in Henry Young's handling of the cases he
had referred to him, but in the dispositions, which, Lee
had to admit himself, were far too lenient.

Students who had committed rather serious breaches
of conduct were let off with mild warnings. Everyone
seemed to receive probation or a gentle slap on the
wrist. The most severe punishment Lee could find, even
for physical violence, was a day's detention, and even
that was set up at the boy's convenience. Apparently
Andersen had reached the point where he had decided
not even to bother referring his disciplinary cases to the
principal; he handled them himself by meting out detention and remaining after school or having the boys do
things like police the school grounds, whitewash walls,
clean equipment.

On one occasion, however, it appeared as if Young
were reprimanding Andersen for doing just these things.
After being assigned a task as punishment for defacing
a locker, a boy had complained to the principal and the
principal had informed Andersen that having the boy
clean the locker room was too severe. He claimed he
had given the boy a good talking to and that would
suffice.

In his angry but tempered reply, Andersen reminded Henry Young that the gym and the locker rooms were his responsibility, and as long as he was the head of the department and the coach, he would, in effect, rule his own kingdom. Henry Young simply returned his note with one line added.

Don't mean to give you a history lesson, but the gym and its environs are like a state in the union, and I am like the president.

Lee grew angry just reading the correspondence. How infuriating it must have been for a man like Kurt Andersen. At the end of this folder, he found Andersen had started writing a letter of grievance to submit to the superintendent and eventually, the school board. His general complaint was the lack of support he was getting from the principal. He had started to list some specific cases, but for some reason stopped after three.

Perhaps this aggravation and tension had a great deal to do with his surprising heart attack, Lee thought. Lee closed the files and sat back in his desk chair. Henry Young had certainly not given him any indication that there had been any bad feeling between himself and Kurt Andersen. If anything, Young had led him to believe he had lost a close, dear friend. And why did so many of the other members of the staff rave about Young as an administrator. Even Bob Baker thought highly of him. It didn't make any sense.

A knock on his opened door snapped him out of his reverie. He had been doing all this reading during a free period just before lunch, one of the two periods a day he had for administrative work. He looked up quickly and saw a very pretty brunette, whom he knew to be an English teacher. She was about five feet three inches tall with soft, rich-looking hair she kept brushed down and curled up at her shoulders. Beneath the bangs that were trimmed just an inch or so over her forehead were the two most alluring almond-brown eyes he had ever seen. All her features were diminutive, almost doll-like. She had a very fair, smooth complexion so clear and perfect it looked like alabaster.

Dressed in a rather tight pink sweater and black skirt, she reminded him of girls in the fifties with their hard, pointed bras exaggerating their bosoms. Her narrow hips were well defined in the snug skirt as she entered his office. Her smile went a few steps beyond simply friendliness; it was almost licentious, enticing. He felt a slight tingling begin in his chest and shoot down through his thighs. His first thought was how the hell does she stand in front of a classroom filled with the sort of boys he had and try to teach English literature and grammar?

"Hi," she said. "Do you have a few minutes?"

"Sure."

She snuggled into the small chair across from him and placed a folder on his desk.

"I'm Monica London, Miss Monica London," she added raising her eyebrows, "and I'm the orientation committee chairperson."

"Oh. Hi," he said, and leaned forward to extend his hand. She looked at it first as if it were nearly obscene and then took it into her small one, her soft fingers not squeezing so much as rubbing up against his. Never had a simple handshake been so sensual and pleasurable. He couldn't help being reluctant to let go, but she seemed to understand and held on to him a moment more than anyone would expect. Then she sat back, drawing her shoulders up. Her bosom lifted as the bra hoisted her breasts like two cannons fixed on him.

"Hi," she finally said, nearly mouthing the word rather than actually pronouncing it. He couldn't take his eyes off her wet lips until she widened her smile. "Anyway, I've brought you all the information you need about the teachers' union, dues, meetings, etcetera, and I've brought you information about our sick-leave bank. We ask everyone to contribute two days of their own a year toward it. Are you familiar with the concept?"

"Oh yeah, sure. We had it at the school I was at on Long Island."

"Good. I just hate having to explain every little thing. Anyway, I've also brought you a copy of the grievance procedures, should you ever need to bring one against the administration. No one has, this year anyway," she said. He thought about Kurt's letter in the folder on the desk.

"What about last year?" he asked quickly.

"Oh, there was something," she replied, "but it didn't go far. I'm not on the grievance committee. I'm sure you know all about the dental and medical plans. We just got eyeglass benefits added, so you might want to read about it. It's all in there," she said, indicating the folder. "But should you have any questions about anything, I'm always available." The way she said this and twisted her shoulder made his eyebrows rise, but she didn't seem to notice or care.

"You teach English, right?"

"Yes. Ninth grade." She smiled. "It's the roughest year because both the boys and the girls are really moving quickly from adolescence into young adulthood. Their hormones are screaming," she added. He started to laugh.

"I'll bet."

"But you know all about that, I'm sure. I have an apartment in the Oakwood Gardens," she said as if the information had some relationship to the previous statement. "I understand you live by the cemetery."

"Yes, in the DeGroot House. Are you from Gardner Town?"

She laughed as if to say, "How could you ask such a silly questions?"

"Oh no. I'm from Westchester."

"What brought you up here?"

"I was going with someone at the time and he lived in Fallsburg, the next town over, so I started working here."

"Oh." He didn't want to sound as if he were prying, but she seemed to be comfortable talking about herself.

"He died. We were in a terrible car accident. A tractor trailer jackknifed on us," she said. Her eyes were wide, but her face revealed no personal emotional pain. She could be talking about an event on a soap opera, Lee thought.

"Jeez, that's terrible. I'm sorry. Were you hurt badly, too?"

"I was in critical condition for about a week, but I was very fortunate. The accident happened just outside of Gardner Town and Dr. Beezly was at my side in minutes. They said my heart had stopped, but he gave me cardiac resuscitation"—she pressed the palm of her right hand over her left breast and massaged it slowly— "until my little heart just woke up and started doing its business again. I would have died otherwise."

"I see." Lee felt his own heart thumping.

Monica stood up slowly, drawing herself up off the seat like a puppet on strings unfolding. She stepped closer.

"I don't want to take up any more of your time. I know how busy you are trying to get started."

"That's okay," he said quickly.

"And you've got a ball game only three days from now, don't you?"

"You didn't have to remind me of that," he said dryly. Then he smiled. She stood there staring at him. He had to shift in his seat. The office had gotten so much warmer. He felt beads of sweat break out on the back of his neck.

"I'll see you later," she said. "And don't forget, if you need anything, anything at all, please come see me." She started toward the doorway. His eyes were glued to the movement of her hips and the shape of her small rear end. She stopped in the doorway and leaned against the jamb. "Oh, but I do know about the DeGroot house."

"Pardon?"

"I thought that's what you meant when you asked if I was from Gardner Town."

"No, I . . . what about it?"

"It's famous," she said. "You didn't know? The real-estate agent never told you?" He shook his head. "Understandable. It probably would scare off most people."

"You mean being right next to the cemetery? Unfortunately I—"

"No, I mean about the murder. Kathleen DeGroot killed her husband in that house nearly seventy years ago after she found out he was unfaithful. I think it was the town's first homicide, and a particularly gruesome one. She cut him up afterward and buried him all over the cemetery. Some say in at least ten different grave sites. Now that" —Monica smiled—"is a woman scorned."

"Pardon?"

"You know, 'hell hath no fury like . . .'"

"Oh, yes."

"But it's a nice house. I'm sure you will enjoy living there," she added. "See you later." She twisted so he would have one full look at her curvaceous body before she was gone.

For a long moment Lee could only sit and stare after her. Then he wiped his face with his palms and let out his breath. He was shaking all over. Was it because of the enticing Miss London or because of that gruesome tale? Or was it a combination of both?

He was grateful for the piercing sound of the bell announcing the end of one period and the beginning of another. That was quickly followed by the thunderous roar of student voices as they shot out of their rooms and stampeded down the corridors, some to their next class, some to the first lunch period. The commotion shook him out of his state of anxiety and reminded him it was time to give Jessie a call. He started to panic when she didn't pick up the receiver. Then he remembered this was the morning Tracy Baker was to come by and take her around. He would have to wait until later in the day.

He began to put everything away when he noticed that Monica London had scribbled her home telephone number on the teacher orientation folder she had left with him. The numerals seemed to rise off the page. He felt a titillation. It was almost as if she had left him the key to her front door.

Jessie assured Tracy Baker she would be all right once Tracy guided her to the front walk.

"Are you sure?" Tracy asked, still holding her hand.

"Absolutely, Tracy. I've already committed the front of this house to perfect memory. Lee says I have a photographic memory with or without my eyesight. He credits it to my overworked imagination." She smiled and then, as if to prove her words, began to describe the front. "There are twelve eighteen-inch flagstones from the edge of the street here to the bottom of the porch stairway. The stairway has three steps. To the left are two rocking chairs on the porch. The full-width porch has a round railing running between the massive rectangular masonry supports of the porch roof."

"Yes," Tracy said, laughing. "You know more detail about it than I, who can see, do."

Jessie smiled and released Tracy's hand from hers.

"Thank you for a wonderful day and a great lunch. That homemade apple pie was the best I think I've had. I'll have to tell Lee about that diner."

"It's the only one in town," Tracy said. "Not hard to find. I really enjoyed our time together, Jessie. Like I told you, it's not easy for me to find someone with whom I can hold an intelligent conversation these days, and I don't mean to sound snobby or conceited."

"I understand."

"Not yet," Tracy said. "But you will in time. I think you can count on your fingers how many people buy the *Sunday Times*. Most get all their news and culture from the idiot box. What surprises me," she added, obviously not anxious to end their time together, "is how Bob has accepted all this. Up until last year he was still talking about getting a job closer to the city," she whispered, as though it were one of their personal secrets.

"What changed his mind?"

"I don't know. Oh, I suppose it had something to do with his heart problem. His life changed radically after that."

"What actually happened?"

"He kept ignoring the symptoms and refusing to see Dr. Beezly. Finally one day he collapsed and we had to rush him to the hospital. Dr. Beezly said he had been a walking time bomb for weeks. Just like Bob to have been stubborn and cause himself greater problems.

"After that, security, comfort, and all that went along with it was more important to him than anything else. He and Dr. Beezly have grown especially close. They even have some business dealings together. My husband," she said, not hiding her own surprise, "has become something of an entrepreneur. Far cry from an actor, huh?"

"You don't sound very happy about it, Tracy," Jessie said.

"Well, I don't love him any less, but you already sensed from your first encounter with him how cynical he can be. Funny . . ." she said, her voice drifting off.

"What is?" Jessie asked when the silence lingered.

"How we lose our dreams and ambitions. They're like balloons, firm and full when we're young and optimistic. As time goes by, they lose air, soften; and then one day we wake up and discover some strong wind has taken them off. You're left with a limp string in your fingers and the vague memory of what it was supposed to be."

"I'm sorry," Jessie said softly, reaching for Tracy's hand again.

"Oh no, please. I didn't mean to put a damper on our day. Really, I exaggerate anyway. You mustn't take me seriously. If I ever sound off this self-pity again, shut me right up. Bob gets furious at me when I do that. We do have a lot more than I ever dreamed we would.

"Besides, I'm feeling very stupid moaning and bitching to someone like you. With all you've been through, you should be the one moaning and bitching."

Jessie smiled.

"You should hear me when I get started." She patted Tracy's hand. "I'm looking forward to your dinner."

"I'll phone you tomorrow," Tracy said. "Just in case you need any errands run or want to run some yourself."

"Thank you. Bye," Jessie said, and started down the walk, moving with the self-assurance of someone who had been living there for years and years. Tracy shook her head in admiration and then got back into her car and drove off as soon as she saw Jessie step onto the porch and approach the front door.

But Jessie didn't open it and enter the hallway. She paused because she heard the sound of digging far off to her left. It was coming from the cemetery. Her first thought, of course, was that someone had died and a grave was being prepared. She stood there for a few moments, mesmerized by the rhythmic thud of a shovel stabbing at the earth.

As she listened a horrifying vision began to take form. It was like having a waking nightmare. In it the digging was being carried out by a skeleton who was trying to return to its coffin. Shreds of rotted clothing hung from its shoulders and arms. As it worked, shavings of bone began to peel away from its hands. It fell like dandruff all about it and made it work with more fury. Finally it struck the lid of the coffin and fell to its knees to brush away the remaining soil. It worked its bony fingers under the lid and pulled up with all its might, but the coffin wouldn't open.

The skeleton threw back its skull and opened its jaw. A death rattle emerged. Seconds later the spine snapped, followed by all of its appendages. It fell in a pile of bones on the top of the coffin, and the dirt that had been removed began to fall in over it again.

The grotesque imagery sent her scurrying through her purse for her key. She entered the house quickly and inserted the key into her front door. Not until she had closed and locked it behind her did she feel any sense of relief and security. Then, with her heart still pounding, she made her way to the bedroom to lie down. Lee's phone call from school woke her.

"Are you all right?" he asked.

"Yes. I fell asleep for a little while."

"Oh, sorry."

"No, that's all right," she said. "I'm sure I should be getting up and preparing supper. How are things going today?"

"Better," he said. "How was your day with Tracy?"

"Very nice. We had a wonderful lunch in the village diner."

"I'm glad. I guess you heard them come to take that truck away this morning, huh?"

"Yes, there was the sound of a tow truck. Have you heard anything more about it?"

"No. I see the Benson kid is present, though. Okay, I'll be home on time tonight," he promised.

"Have a good practice," she said, and cradled the phone. She got out of bed and went to the bathroom to dab her face with some cold water. Afterward, feeling somewhat revived, she headed for the kitchen. But as soon as she entered it she heard something that took her to the side window, the one facing the cemetery. She worked it open to hear better and listened.

There was more digging going on, but now it was much closer to the house. How many people could have passed away? she wondered. It was creepy living right beside a cemetery like this, she thought. Perhaps it would be better to talk to Lee about finding them someplace else. She closed the window and went to prepare the dinner.

After she set the table, she went into the living room to listen to the news, but before she turned it on, she heard the patter of footsteps on the patio and then the porch. From the pace of the gait, she knew it was old man Carter. Although they had hardly spoken up to now, she thought it would be nice to have a friendly relationship with their upstairs neighbor. She went to the apartment front door and opened it just as he entered the house.

"Mr. Carter?" she said from her doorway. She could smell the scent of freshly dug earth.

"Hello," he said. He closed the heavy, oak door behind him.

"You had a lot of work to do today?" she asked, smiling. Even though he was only a few feet from her, she couldn't get a sense of him the way she usually could get a sense of someone. It was as if she were speaking to a voice with no body. It unnerved her and she embraced herself quickly, for the pause between her question and his reply seemed endless.

"No more than usual," he finally said. "Some prunin', some trimmin'."

"Oh? I thought . . . I mean, I just assumed you were preparing some new graves today. All that digging," she added.

"Diggin'? I didn't do any diggin' today, Mrs. Overstreet. Nobody new died. Yet," he added.

"But I could have sworn . . ."

"Got enough hot water?" he asked.

"What? Oh, yes."

"Sometimes that damn hot-water heater don't kick in and I gotta go down to the basement and hit the restart button. No sense callin' Charley DeGroot if you don't have hot water. Just call me. He'll only call me anyway," Carter added. She heard him take the first step.

"Oh, thank you. I bet you were wondering what all that commotion was late last night," she said quickly. He stopped on the stairway.

"Commotion?"

"Someone got drunk and fell out of his truck right out in front here. We had to phone the police."

"Never heard a thing," he said. "I sleep better than the dead," he added, and laughed. "I know. I hear them tossin' and turnin' all night out there."

He continued up the stairway. She started to close the door when she caught a whiff of that horrendous stench again. It seemed to move past her, following the old man. In seconds it was gone and all that remained was the lingering scent of freshly dug earth.

Why did he say he wasn't doing any digging? She distinctly heard it. If he wasn't digging in the cemetery, who was?

After she closed the door, she stood there listening to the sound of the old man's footsteps now above her. Yes, she said to herself, there it was again. His footsteps and then that shuffling. There's definitely someone up there with him, someone who could use a bath.

She went into the living room and tried listening to the news, but her mind kept drifting. She replayed some of her conversation with Tracy Baker. She had heard something in Tracy's voice, something more than disappointment or depression, something that had suggested fear. The Bakers had been married nearly fifteen years and they had no children. Jessie had been wanting to ask her about that, but since Tracy hadn't brought up the subject, she thought she would wait until she became better acquainted. Her experience was that people volunteered information about their personal lives freely these days. They didn't need much encouragement. It was the age of exposure and confession.

Jessie was so lost in her thoughts about Tracy and about the things she had heard in the afternoon that she didn't hear Lee enter.

"Well, this is a first," he declared. "You, not hearing me?"

"Oh Lee." She rose and went to him.

"What's wrong?" he asked when he felt how she was trembling. "Something happen since I spoke with you on the phone?"

She told him about the sound of the digging and her conversation with old man Carter.

Lee laughed.

"Jess, I'm sure the old guy is starting to lose it. He probably doesn't remember what he does from one moment to the next. Besides, what would be his reason for lying to you about something like that?"

"I don't know," she said.

"So? Don't worry about it. I'm starving. Let's eat."

"You had a good practice?"

"It was better than yesterday. There was less fouling and other shenanigans and no one complained about my fitness program. Oh, and the Benson kid . . ."

"Yes?"

"He played very well. If his father's behavior is bothering him, he's sure good at hiding it. He behaved as if nothing had happened and his father wasn't in jail. He couldn't have been in better spirits."

"Maybe he just doesn't care about him, Lee."

"Yeah, I suppose that happens. So, tell me about your day with Tracy Baker. I'm sure you have plenty of gossip to relate."

"Now, Lee, you know we don't gossip. We discuss," she said, and he laughed. "You don't have to shower and change for dinner?"

"Naw, I did it at school."

"I guess you're getting into it then," she said happily.

"I guess so. It just takes time. Like anything else, it just takes time," he repeated, and followed her to the kitchen to help get their dinner.

It wasn't until after they had sat down at the table and had begun eating that he noticed the oddest thing.

"Well, I'll be damned," he said suddenly, interrupting her description of the Gardner Town diner.

"What?"

"I just noticed the craziest thing."

"What?"

"After I showered and got dressed in my office . . ."

"Yes?"

"I put on the wrong sneakers."

"What? How could you do that?"

"They were just there in my locker, one of Kurt Andersen's extra pairs. I guess I just grabbed them without thinking and put them on.

"But the oddest thing is they fit . . . perfectly, and I had gotten the impression from his description and from some of the pictures of him in the office that he was a much bigger man than I am."

"He could be taller and heavier and still have the same foot size as you, Lee."

"Yeah, I suppose so. I tell you, honey, I was reading through some of his old correspondence today, and at times I must have been just as angry and frustrated as he had been.

"You pick up where a guy left off," he continued, "almost as if he just passed you the ball, and you continue down the court, even wearing his shoes."

"Just as long as you don't end up the same way, Lee."

"Yeah," he said. "Right."

The long moment of silence between them was unnerving. He was happy when she began to talk about her day with Tracy Baker again. But he couldn't stop wondering what the hell he was thinking of when he put on someone else's sneakers.

— 5 —

"It's a big house," Lee began with enough surprise in his voice to impress Jessie. "And it looks like they have a nice piece of property, too. I'd say a couple of acres."

"How big is the house? Bigger than the DeGroot house?"

"Oh yeah. It's very pretty. Looks recently painted. Wedgwood blue," he continued as he slowed down to turn into the Bakers' driveway. He had made it his business to get better and better at describing things, feeling now that his eyes had to see for the two of them. That, plus his own lingering guilt, made it important that he do anything and everything he could to compensate for Jessie's handicap. "It's a two-story, wood-frame building with a steeply pitched roof. There's a prominent central cross gable on the roof with a very decorative truss at the apex. There are gabled dormers on either side. The windows have a sort of Gothic shape to them. The house has a full-length porch, like the DeGroot house, with flattened arches between the porch supports."

"It sounds very pretty, Lee."

73

"Um. Impressive for a public-school teacher. They must have had some money."

He pulled alongside the immaculate, silver Mercedes-Benz sedan and saw the MD license plates.

"Dr. Beezly is already here," he said. "I don't see any other cars."

"Are we early?"

"Just on time," he said, and shut off the engine.

"Schoolteachers have trouble being fashionably late," she kidded. "You're too used to bells and schedules."

"Occupational hazard."

"What's the front like?" she asked.

"There's a concrete walkway with bordering hedges. Big lawn. Some expensive landscaping. Very, very nice," he added. Then he got out and went around to help Jessie out. She threaded her arm through his.

"How do I look?"

"Beautiful. I don't know how you manage to get your hair so perfect."

She smiled. Jessie did look very pretty and very fresh tonight. He had been worrying about her because she hadn't slept well the past few nights and looked tired and drawn to him every morning.

Jessie hadn't bought any new clothing since the accident. Lee had offered many times to go shopping with her, promising to describe every dress, every blouse, every pair of shoes down to the most minute detail, but she just wasn't interested, or as she put it, she just wasn't ready. She simply didn't have the confidence to try anything new yet. For the time being she felt more comfortable with her present wardrobe. She knew every garment and easily recalled how each looked on her.

For tonight she had chosen one of her Betsy Johnsons, an off-the-shoulder, blue-and-white polka-dot satin dress with a sweetheart collar, a form-fitted waist, and a pleated skirt. It fit her as well as it did the day she had bought it, for Jessie took great care to maintain her figure. She had always been exercise-minded and resumed her routine as soon as she had recuperated enough to do so.

"Step up," Lee said as they approached the walkway.

"It's so peaceful here, Lee. What's the street like?"

"Very wide, tall maples here and there. Most of the homes are as expensive looking and as big as the Bakers'."

"Someday we'll have something like this, too," she said.

"Sure." To him the possibility seemed as remote as their taking a trip to the moon, but he didn't want to sound pessimistic. He knew one of the things that depressed Jessie the most was the fact that she could no longer work and bring in an additional income. He told her that now, with her braille typewriter, she would have more time to work and she would write something that would sell big and have the effect of their winning the lottery.

"Great door," Lee remarked. Jessie ran her hand over the elaborate panels. "And no buzzer. Just this black iron knocker shaped like a hammer. Cute." He let it rap. From the sound of the deep echo, they both knew the entryway was wide and deep. Moments later Bob opened the door. He was dressed in a maroon blazer with a white cravat and dark blue slacks. He held a glass of champagne in his left hand.

"Hi," he said. "Welcome to Castle Baker."

"It's big enough to be a castle," Lee said.

"Lee described it to me. It sounds beautiful," Jessie said.

"Thank you. It's become home sweet home. Come in, come in. Here, let me take your coats," he offered. Lee helped Jessie off with hers and handed it to Bob, who hung it in the deep cedarwood closet.

"Oh, I love the scent of cedarwood," Jessie said.

"All our closets and drawers are done in cedar. Actually we've put a lot of money into redoing the house. It's pretty old, about fifty years or so."

"You wouldn't know it from the outside," Lee said. "How long have you been here?"

"A little over a year. Know what you're thinking, buddy," Baker said. "I didn't get it on a teacher's salary. We had a little money and I invested in an enterprise that's rapidly becoming rather successful. A few of us at the school have, thanks to the wise Dr. Beezly. Maybe we'll get you into it, too."

"Oh? What is it exactly?"

Baker leaned toward him.

"A corporation that owns and operates cemeteries," he said in a loud whisper.

"Cemeteries?" Jessie instinctively brought her hands to the base of her throat.

"Yes, but let's not stand here and talk. Tracy and Dr. Beezly are in the den. We've already started our cocktail hour," he said, lifting his glass. "Know who else is coming?" He gestured for Lee and Jessie to follow him. He brought his mouth close to Lee's ear. "Henry and Marjorie Young. You'll be able to make some quick brownie points tonight," he added in a coy whisper.

Lee didn't reply. He was never able to kiss ass. It was his Overstreet pride. Although he was the first college graduate in the family, his father and his grandfather had both been very skilled cabinet makers. They traced their family lineage back to the Elizabethan age and had documented evidence that their ancestors had built beds and chests as well as chairs and cabinets for the queen. His grandfather had made most of the trick cabinets for Houdini. They never thought of themselves as simple carpenters. They were skilled artisans. If anything, there was a sense of disappointment when Lee decided to pursue a career in athletics and attend college. The Overstreets weren't arrogant, but they never suffered a sense of inferiority. As a result, neither Lee nor his two married sisters were the kind of people who could suck up to anyone.

Growing up with it all around him, Lee had an eye for quality craftsmanship.

"That's a beautiful mahogany balustrade," he said, looking ahead at the stairway. The hand-carved railing curved upward.

"And we never had to do a thing with it. That's the way it was when we first bought the house. To your left," Baker said. Lee turned Jessie gently and they entered the den.

It was a large, cherrywood-paneled room with an oval Persian rug in front of the long, vermilion leather sofa that faced a matching settee. Streams of ruby ran through the rug's design. Like the wall paneling, the side tables and the matching long oval coffee table were cherrywood. The same was true for the bookcases on the rear wall. In fact, the only wood that didn't have some shade of red in it was that used to frame some of the oil paintings, all prints of famous nudes like Botticelli's Venus and Ingres's nudes. There were replicas of nude statues as well, including Maillol's *Three Graces*. All expressed a fascination with the human body, depicted for the most part in a sensual manner, except for an expressionistic painting above the fireplace: Edvard Munch's horrendous rendition of a woman in some agony, her hands on her ears, her mouth a narrow oval as she obviously screamed.

"You can see why we call this the Red Room," Baker quipped. "Lee will explain it to you," he added for Jessie's benefit.

As soon as he spoke, Tracy and Dr. Beezly, who were standing by the fireplace with their backs to the door, turned. Lee was immediately surprised by how young Dr. Beezly appeared. From all he had heard about the man, he had just assumed he was along in his years. But he looked like a man barely in his late forties, perhaps in his early fifties.

More important, Dr. Beezly was physically unimpressive. He didn't stand more than five feet five at the most, with features that were so small as to make him seem almost gnomelike. His black eyes were beady and his mouth was thin and somewhat feminine. He had rather long, thin black hair brushed back on the sides and down his neck with strands disappearing under his collar. Lee thought the man looked like he was drowning in his double-breasted black suit. Perhaps he had borrowed it from someone larger and taller, Lee surmised. Although Lee didn't know all that much about fashion, he concluded the garment was quite old, albeit well preserved.

As they drew closer Lee also noticed that the doctor had a somewhat sallow look made more dramatic by the ebony suit and coal-black hair. His pale skin caused his orange-tinted lips to seem brighter and his dark eyes to appear sharp and luminous, reminding Lee of two small hot coals.

"Lee, Jessie, I'd like you to meet our good friend Dr. Beezly," Baker said.

"I'm very pleased finally to have the opportunity to meet the two of you," Beezly said. He took Jessie's hand first. Lee saw her smile turn quickly into an expression of curiosity.

Actually it wasn't curiosity as much as it was confusion. Shaking someone's hand, hearing his or her voice usually gave Jessie a sense of their identity. Dr. Beezly sounded like a man, but she didn't get a masculine feel. It was as if he were some sort of neuter creature, not male or female, an essence of something, and not something she particularly liked.

Dr. Beezly released her hand from his instantly and shook Lee's. Lee thought he had a rather unremarkable grasp, weak, the fingers feeling as soft as cotton. It was as if the man had bones as thin as those of a fish. A hard squeeze would shatter his palm and knuckles.

"Hi, Jessie," Tracy said, quickly coming up alongside her. They embraced.

"Hi. Lee's been describing your home to me. Why didn't you tell me you had such a lovely house?"

"Oh, I wanted you to see it for yourself. I mean—"

"I am seeing it," Jessie said quickly to spare Tracy any embarrassment. "Through Lee."

"And I promise to take you around myself," Tracy said, "and show you every nook and cranny."

"From the way Lee described it, that sounds like an all-night affair."

Tracy laughed.

"Champagne all right?" Baker asked.

"Fine," Lee said. "Jess?"

"Yes, please."

"Let me escort you to the sofa," Dr. Beezly said, taking Jessie's hand and placing it on his forearm.

Feeling his narrow bony arm, Jessie was immediately reminded of her horrid vision the day Tracy had brought her home. Flashes of that skeleton digging desperately to uncover its own coffin returned. She couldn't help uttering a small moan.

"Are you all right?" Beezly asked quickly.

"Yes, thank you." She forced a smile. He led her to the sofa. "Thank you." She made herself comfortable and ran her palm over the soft leather. "This must be a beautiful piece."

"It is," Beezly said. "So," he continued, taking a seat across from Jessie, "I'm very interested in your impressions of Gardner Town." He looked up at Lee, who moved to sit beside Jessie.

"Well, we haven't been here very long," Lee said.

"Diplomatic retreat," Dr. Beezly said, and laughed. Tracy sat beside him. Bob returned with a tray of champagne and distributed the glasses.

"Small-town life takes a while to get used to," Tracy offered, "especially when you've been brought up close to a place like New York City."

"Both of you?" Beezly turned back to Lee and Jessie. Baker put the tray down, but remained standing.

"I'm from Queens," Lee said. "Jessie's from Westbury on Long Island."

"Where did you two meet?"

"At college," Jessie said, smiling. "I was a cheerleader and Lee was a basketball star."

"Oh, I wasn't quite a star, but I did my share to bring home the trophies."

"Note this carefully, Dr. Beezly," Baker said. "A modest jock. Quite a rare animal these days."

Everyone laughed. The door knocker sounded.

"Must be Henry and Marge," Baker said. "Excuse me."

"So you met in college and got married soon after graduation?" Dr. Beezly pursued.

"A week after graduation," Lee said. He took Jessie's hand. "I had just locked down a job not far from where Jessie lived. We had just gotten started really when I became the victim of a state cutback."

"Their loss is our gain. There's an overall plan at work in the universe," Beezly said, smiling coyly. It gave Lee the jitters, for it was as if the doctor were somehow part of an overall conspiracy, first creating an economic crisis in Lee's former school and then . . . creating an opening here.

"Here, here," Henry Young said, entering alongside his wife. "I heard what you said, Doctor, and I'll second that." Beezly stood up to greet Marjorie Young, a tall woman, almost as tall as Henry. She had short, light brown hair, which was rather lackluster and cropped around her ears unevenly, as if done by an amateur hairstylist. In fact, Lee thought, attention to her feminine appearance was obviously not a priority for Marjorie Young. She wore only a slight tint of crimson lipstick, no rouge, no eyeliner or eye shadow. Her gray-and-blue shift hung on her long body loosely. It had a high collar. She wore no earrings, no bracelets, only a simple wedding band.

And yet she wasn't a totally unattractive woman. Her dull brown eyes were nicely shaped. She had a pretty mouth and a straight, well-proportioned nose. It was her drab complexion and her poor posture—shoulders turned in, a slight lean—that detracted from what must have been former statuesque beauty, Lee thought. She barely

smiled. Her gaze wandered about perfunctorily and settled with only the slightest curiosity on the Overstreets.

"Good evening, Marjorie," Dr. Beezly said. She barely smiled at him, but offered her hand.

The woman looks drugged, Lee thought.

"Let me be the one to introduce you," the doctor
begged. "Marjorie, I'd like you to meet our two newest
residents, Lee and Jessie Overstreet."

Jessie turned and waited. Beezly reached for Jessie's
hand to bring it to Marjorie's. Marjorie's eyes widened with sudden interest as she realized that Jessie
was blind.

"How do you do?" Jessie said when their fingers
touched. Instantly she felt the woman's fingers tighten. It
was a surprising grasp of desperation, a reaching out.

"Hello," Marjorie said. "I'm pleased to meet you."

"And this is Lee, of whom I am sure you have already
heard a great deal. Or doesn't Henry bring his work
home every night?"

"He brings it home," she said with a clear note of
disapproval. "How do you do," she said to Lee.

"Pleased to meet you."

"Henry, step over here and meet Mrs. Overstreet," Dr.
Beezly commanded. Both Lee and Jessie were impressed
with the way he had taken over the party.

"Happy to. Hi there, Mrs. Overstreet."

"Please, call me Jessie. I don't want to sound like the
oldest person here."

Everyone laughed.

Henry Young took her hand and instantly Jessie had
the same impression she'd had when she shook Bob
Baker's hand. It felt as if hers cut through the flesh
and clasped the bones, almost as if the flesh were an
illusion. Because Henry Young was Lee's principal, she

swallowed her distaste and let him hold on to her a moment longer.

"You don't have to worry about sounding like the oldest person here, Jessie. Dr. Beezly has that honor," Baker said. "Let me get these two some champagne."

"Sit here, Marjorie," Tracy said, patting the seat beside her.

"How old are you, Dr. Beezly?" Jessie asked quickly. Lee was surprised at how assertive she sounded.

"Well, my dear," he replied, "let's just say I was old enough to vote for Franklin Delano Roosevelt."

"Yes, Doctor, but which time?" Henry asked, laughing.

"That's my secret."

"You don't sound old enough to have voted for him anytime," Jessie pursued.

"Why, thank you. It's the good life, the simple life."

"Not so simple, from what I hear," Lee said, sipping some champagne. "You've got quite a few patients."

"Yes, but fortunately most of them are healthy."

Baker gave the Youngs their champagne.

"Well, how about a toast, Doctor?" he said.

"Absolutely. I propose we toast our new residents, who I hope to see only on nice social occasions such as this."

"Here, here," Henry Young said. Everyone drank, but Lee noticed that Marjorie Young barely touched her lips to her glass.

"Thank you," Lee said, "and here's to very nice people who have made us feel quite at home." They all drank again.

"Are you enjoying the DeGroot house?" Dr. Beezly asked.

"Well . . ." Lee looked at Jessie.

"We've had a few strange things occur," Jessie said.

"Oh?" The doctor, who was standing beside Bob Baker, stepped forward. "How so?"

"The other night a drunken man fell out of his truck right in front of the house, for one," Lee said.

"Benson. Yes, I heard about that. Unfortunate man."

"What else happened?" Baker asked.

"Living next to a cemetery with the caretaker upstairs hasn't been very pleasant," Lee said. "Especially for Jessie, who is home more than I am."

"Carter. He's a character," Dr. Beezly said. "Don't mind him. That cemetery is his whole life. It always has been. At least as long as I've known him," he added quickly. "But if they're not happy in the DeGroot house, Henry, we should put our heads together and find them something else soon."

"Of course."

"I did sign a year's lease with DeGroot," Lee said.

"Oh, I'm sure we can work something out. We'll look into it, won't we, Henry?"

"Absolutely. I don't want one of my people unhappy for any reason."

"There is never any reason for unhappiness," Dr. Beezly said. "And no reason to tolerate it. That has been my philosophy all my life, even when I was just a boy. In fact, I'd venture to guess that I brought my sense of pleasure and well-being out of my mother's womb with me." He started to laugh, but Jessie spoke up.

"Sometimes events take over and make happiness very difficult for you, Doctor," she insisted.

"Oh, events can discourage us and set us back, but the trick is to turn every sadness into a happiness, every shadow into light, every burden into an accomplishment. I wasn't joking before. Your husband lost his job, but that loss made it possible for him to get this job, and he's going to be far happier here than he would have been there."

"How can you be so sure?" Jessie pursued.

"Instinct. I have been created with a remarkable sense of what makes people happy," he said. "Somehow," he added, turning toward Lee, "I think I know what's going to make your husband happy here." It sounded as if he knew of some sinful interest. Lee felt a tightening in his stomach, but Jessie wouldn't let go.

"To know what will make you happy and to achieve it are two entirely different things," she said.

"Good for you, Jessie," Baker said. "Someone's finally challenging the good doctor, eh, Henry?"

Lee looked at Henry Young quickly. He didn't seem all that happy about this development. Marjorie Young, on the other hand, had suddenly come to life. Her eyes were filled with interest and her face took on a flush of excitement.

"Achieving happiness is only a matter of admitting to ourselves what we are and what we want, and then discarding those things that stand in the way," the doctor replied.

"And what are we, Doctor?" Jessie asked.

"Men. Women. Nothing more, nothing less. The more we try to be gods, the more unhappy we become. Our bodies tell us what is pleasurable, what feels good. Why deny it or try for something else?"

"But what about our souls?"

"That's where you have me, my dear. I'm a doctor of the body. But those who doctor the souls never seem very happy in their work," he added. Baker laughed loudly. "Besides, there's enough time to worry about that afterward."

"That all sounds rather selfish," Jessie said. "And from what we've heard about you, you don't sound like a selfish man."

"She's got you there, Dr. Beezly," Baker said.

"My pleasure comes from seeing that others enjoy their lives to the fullest limits."

"Then you contradict yourself," Jessie said. There was a moment of silence. It was as if everyone, including Lee, was holding his breath.

"How so?"

"You just said when we try to be more than men and women, we make ourselves unhappy. But you're trying to be God."

The silence grew deeper for a moment.

And then Dr. Beezly laughed.

"Of all the things I'd never want to be," he said, "that would top my list. I'm afraid I'm just a country doctor, my dear."

"Well, I don't know about anyone else," Bob Baker said, "but that was a most stimulating exchange, which, I'm afraid has made me very hungry.

"Following Dr. Beezly's advice, therefore, I suggest we all adjourn to the dining room and pleasure our palates."

Everyone rose.

"What the hell got into you?" Lee whispered into Jessie's ear. He didn't sound critical, however; he sounded proud.

"I don't know. It just seemed the right thing to do and say," she replied.

"Lee," Dr. Beezly said, "might I have the honor of escorting Jessie? After all, she just gave me a run for my money."

"Jess?"

"Why yes, Doctor, if that makes you happy," she said, and everyone laughed again.

Except Marjorie Young. Lee thought she looked fascinated. It was as if she had never met a woman who could think for herself or had the nerve to voice an opinion.

The dinner was spectacular. The Bakers had caterers who prepared and served the meal: Peking duck. The wine flowed, and expensive wine, too. For dessert they were served baked Alaska. They sat at an enormous oval glass table with a marble base. The chairs were antique French Provincial and the china was Wedgwood. Everyone, even Marjorie Young now, participated in describing things to Jessie. Lee was very pleased at how quickly Jessie had become the center of attention, and how quickly she had won everyone's respect.

Then Dr. Beezly, who sat on her left, asked her about her blindness.

"Unless you mind talking about it," he added quickly.

"No, I don't mind."

"So it was the result of a head injury in a car accident?"

"Yes."

"And I'm sure you've been to the best doctors?"

"Of course." Lee sounded more testy than he had intended.

"Nevertheless I would like to be presumptuous and offer my own meager medical powers to you, free of charge, anytime you want," Dr. Beezly said.

"Dr. Beezly is rather modest," Henry Young said. "He is truly a gifted healer. If I didn't know better, I'd say he has the power of the laying on of hands. You know, like some of these evangelists claim to have. Only difference is, I have seen him in action.

"Why, when Marjorie has one of her terrible sinus headaches, he merely has to touch her temples, massage them someway, and the headaches end, right, Marge?" he said.

Marjorie Young shot a quick glance at Lee and then nodded.

"Yes, Dr. Beezly is remarkable," she said, pronouncing the words in a monotone, as if they had been memorized.

"It's very nice of you to offer," Jessie said. "I might just take you up on it one day."

"Anytime," the doctor said.

After dinner Tracy, along with Marjorie, took Jessie on a tour of the house. They were gone for nearly an hour, during which time Lee, Baker, Henry Young, and Dr. Beezly had an after-dinner drink in the den. They talked politics for a while and then Dr. Beezly asked Lee about his basketball team.

Lee eyed Henry Young before replying. He saw how interested the principal was in what he would say, so he couched his words carefully.

"Well, I found them somewhat undisciplined, which might be the result of the traumatic events—their coach dying suddenly, a substitute, and then a brand-new man. Most of my time is spent on drilling them to be more of a team, working together."

"Their first game under your tutelage is tomorrow night, is it not?" Dr. Beezly asked.

"Yes. A home game."

"Don't be surprised if it's a packed house," Baker said.

"I'm expecting it."

"They'll do well for you, I'm sure," Henry Young promised. "You've given them some new plays?"

"Just stuck to what they know right now. You've got to crawl before you walk."

"Excellent philosophy, Lee," Dr. Beezly said. "You've got a good man here, Henry. Make sure you don't lose him to one of those fancy outlying districts."

"I'll do my best," Henry said, smiling.

"Yes. Well, we all will," Dr. Beezly said. "We all will."

His smile gave Lee the chills again. Funny, he thought, how something that should sound nice sounds threatening when the doctor said it.

The women returned. Bob offered everyone another round of after-dinner drinks. The conversation shifted to lighter subjects—movies, books, and television.

"I'm afraid I'm at a disadvantage when we talk about movies and television," Dr. Beezly confessed. "I hardly watch television and I think the last movie I saw was *Rosemary's Baby*." He laughed. "Quite amusing."

"How do you spend your free time, then, Doctor?" Jessie inquired.

"I read. A lot of boring medical magazines, I'm afraid. But," he added quickly, "I'd be more than happy to read any of your short stories."

"Oh, I'm not that good. . . ."

"Now, now, all this modesty—first your husband, who we know was an exceptional college athlete, and now you, who I am sure are just as perceptive in your writing as you are in conversation."

"Thank you," Jessie said, a slight blush coming into her face. She reached for Lee's hand.

"Well," Henry Young announced, "I hate to be the one to say it, but I have a big day tomorrow."

"Yes, we better be going, too," Lee said.

Dr. Beezly said nothing. He sat back and watched everyone say their thank-you's and good-byes. Then he rose and approached Jessie. She sensed it and turned. Her impulsive move brought a smile to his face.

"I really enjoyed your company, Jessie," he said, taking her hand. Once again she had that strange sensation, that feeling that she was touching something unusual. She pressed on and envisioned a tunnel of fire.

"Thank you. I enjoyed yours, too, Doctor."

"Then let's try to do it again," he said quickly. "Perhaps I will have you all over to my house one night soon."

"I'd like that," Jessie said politely. She tightened her hold on Lee. He shook Dr. Beezly's hand and they started to follow the Youngs out.

As soon as they were out of the door, Marjorie Young let go of Henry's arm and turned, smiling.

"I'll help Jessie to the car, Lee," she offered. "I'd like to say good night."

"Oh." For a moment Lee was confused. This lethargic woman had suddenly come to life. It was awkward, but he released Jessie's arm and moved ahead to join Henry Young, who put his arm around his shoulders and led him down the walk, giving him advice about the crowd that would come to see the game tomorrow night.

Jessie understood immediately that Marjorie Young had some ulterior motive. She let her thread her arm through hers quickly and join hands. Then the two of them began to follow their husbands, Marjorie deliberately walking slowly.

"You're a rather remarkable woman, Jessie," she said softly. Jessie could feel Marjorie's pulse quickening, her palm pressed tightly to hers.

"What is it, Marjorie?" Jessie asked.

Marjorie Young hesitated so long, Jessie thought she wasn't going to reply, wasn't going to say what she wanted so much to say. Jessie held her breath and waited. They were drawing closer to the cars. The voices of their husbands grew louder.

Then Marjorie Young brought her lips close to Jessie's ear and whispered.

"When your husband dies," she said, "don't let them bring him back."

— 6 —

Jessie sat quietly in the car, nervously running her fingers up and down the seat belt across her bosom. Marjorie Young's warning had left her stunned. Even though she couldn't see the woman's face, she envisioned her vividly through her tone of voice. She saw the hysteria in her eyes, felt the utter trepidation in her heart. The whisper was sharp, nearly breathless, as if she thought they were being overheard, as if she thought there was no place safe. And when Jessie felt the woman's fingers, she imagined a block of ice carved into a hand. It seemed as if the woman had no blood.

"Well," Lee said, "I don't know about you, but I enjoyed myself immensely. It was a very interesting evening, one of the best dinner parties I've attended. Dr. Beezly is a fascinating man. He's traveled so much and has so much knowledge at his fingertips."

Lee waited, but Jessie remained quiet. She didn't know how to begin, what to say.

"You all right?" he finally asked. "In there I couldn't get you to shut up," he added with a short, tense laugh.

"I don't know how to tell you this," Jessie finally said,

"but Marjorie Young just told me the most astounding thing . . . warned me, I should say."

"Oh no. He told me to watch out for her," Lee replied, sounding relieved that this was all it was.

"Who told you? Told you what?"

"Bob Baker. Seems Marjorie Young is recuperating from a nervous breakdown, precipitated to some degree by Henry's physical problems and their subsequent marital problems, which involve their grown son," he said quickly.

Jessie turned, incredulous.

"Bob Baker told you all that tonight? When?" she demanded.

"Well, it wasn't all told to me tonight. He mentioned something earlier in school, but I didn't really pay attention to him. I was distracted with my problems with the team and—"

"Why didn't you say anything to me about her? You knew we would meet her tonight," Jessie asked.

"To tell you the truth, Jess, I completely forgot," he said.

"That's a strange thing to forget, Lee." She turned away and nodded. "A strange thing."

"I'm sorry."

"What precipitated her nervous breakdown, do you know?"

"She got into the sauce," he said.

"Alcoholic?"

"I'm afraid so," he said.

"But there wasn't any hesitation on anyone's part tonight when it came to offering her wine. At least I didn't hear it," she said, now unsure of herself.

"They pretend nothing's wrong. I watched her. She was given her champagne, but she didn't do more than bring her lips to the glass. Anyhow, Baker brought it all up again when you women went touring through the house, and he advised me not to pay any attention to anything she might say. I didn't get a chance to tell you before she said something to you apparently," he added.

"What happened between Henry Young and his son?" she asked.

"I don't know all the details, but it involves his joining one of those religious orders. I think the boy wants to be a monk or something. Just dropped out of college and went off singing Latin hymns. There's been a real falling-out. Henry refuses to speak to him. Marjorie got caught in the middle, but she's not siding with Henry and that has put some strain on their marriage."

"Is he their only child?"

"Yes," Lee said. "She had two miscarriages before."

"You learned all this tonight?" she asked, her skepticism rising to the surface again.

"Bob said her failure to have more children was always a part of her nervous condition."

"How come he knows so much about the Youngs' personal life?"

"Good friends, I guess. I don't know, honey, but the point is, whatever she said to you, you've got to disregard it. I guess she's still out of it. Surely, you noticed how strange she was before, during, and after dinner."

"Yes," Jessie admitted. "I did feel some odd vibrations, but I thought they had more to do with her own fears."

"Baker says paranoia is a characteristic symptom of her condition. He's a very bright guy."

"I thought you thought he was a bit weird, Lee."

"Yeah, but I think I like him. He's certainly done real

well for himself and Tracy. Let me tell you about that Red Room," he added, and began to describe it in detail: the colors, the paintings, the statues.

"That painting of the woman screaming—I know it," Jessie said. "It's a horrifying picture by Edvard Munch. It's called *The Scream*. Munch's art is always neurotic and frequently hysterical. Why would they want such a print in their house? And that fascination with the human body sounds very sensuous, sexual, almost lustful. Yet Tracy doesn't strike me as the type of woman who would want these things. It must be mostly Bob's choices," she concluded.

"Yeah," Lee said. "I bet." She could hear his smile.

"But don't you see, Lee? There is something strange here. I felt it in there, and when Marjorie warned me—"

"Strange? Come on. That was a great party. What did she say to you anyway?" he finally asked. She was hesitant. "After all this, honey, you got to tell me."

"I don't know how to tell you," she repeated.

"Just tell me. Jeez."

"She said when my husband dies, I shouldn't let them bring him back to life."

"What?" Lee started to laugh. "My God, that woman is distorted, isn't she? When your husband dies . . . what, did she say Henry had died?"

Jessie was silent a moment.

"Did she?"

"She implied it. He was seriously ill, wasn't he?"

"But he didn't die. For God sakes, Jess."

"How do we know?"

"What? Oh boy, here we go . . . Jessie Overstreet's imagination is on the loose. I'm gonna leave this one up to you, Jess, only don't start it 'Once upon a time,' okay?"

She didn't respond. He looked at her and saw how still she sat, her body stiff, her face like a mask.

"Jess . . ."

"Something's not right," she said softly. "I've been hearing those voices I heard the first night. Something is not right."

Lee nodded.

"I'm going to push Henry and Dr. Beezly to get us out of that house as soon as they can. That's what I'm going to do," he said. "Then" —he turned to her— "things will be right."

She said nothing. The silence unnerved him and he finally resorted to turning on the radio just so there would be some noise.

"Oh, I forgot to tell you," Lee said as they pulled into their driveway, "Bob said he and Tracy would love to pick you up tomorrow night to take you to the game. You did want to go, didn't you?" Even though Jessie wouldn't see anything, her mere presence would be supportive. She had been to almost every one of his games since he had begun coaching, and it always made him feel good to look up in the stands and see her.

"Yes, of course," she said.

"Good. Bob said to tell you he can't wait to practice his play-by-play announcing. I'm sure he'll have you in stitches all night," Lee added.

Late the next morning Tracy Baker did call to confirm her willingness to have her and Bob pick her up. Jessie used the occasion to talk about Marjorie Young.

"Lee told me some of the things Bob had told him about the Youngs," Jessie said.

"And men accuse us of gossiping," Tracy replied.

"It was sad to hear all those things about Marjorie. Is she still drinking?"

"Not as much since Dr. Beezly put her on sedatives. Actually last night was one of her better nights," Tracy said.

"It was?"

"Well, she was civil, spoke to you and me. Why? Did something happen I don't know about?"

Jessie told her what Marjorie had said on the way out.

"Oh no. She did something similar to me—called me one night, in the middle of the night, and told me she was positive Bob was dead. I said, 'Marjorie, he's lying right beside me, breathing rather well, snoring in fact.'"

"What did she say?"

"She said it wasn't Bob. I did all I could to prevent myself from laughing. I said, 'No? Well, when he gets home, he's going to be pissed.'" Tracy laughed. Jessie couldn't help but smile herself. "I hung up and Bob woke up. I told him what she had said and he told me some of the things Henry had told him. Not long after, Dr. Beezly began prescribing sedatives and she calmed down considerably. But apparently, from what you're telling me, she still has a way to go.

"Anyhow, don't worry about it. We'll come by about six-thirty, okay. Bob says the auditorium will be packed tonight. Everyone knows there's a new coach on board and the school we're playing is something of a rival."

"Fine. I'll be ready," Jessie said, and hung up the phone. She spent the rest of the day working on a new short story. She spoke with Lee twice, and each time she could hear the excitement building in his voice.

"Just about everyone from the custodians to cafeteria staff to faculty has come around to wish me good luck," he said. "It's nice how everyone gets involved. I guess working in a small school system does have its advantages."

They had already decided Lee would get a quick bite near the school because he didn't have all that much time between the end of the school day and the start of the game. As head coach, he had to see about the referees for the junior and senior varsity games, be sure the score clock was set up, and arrange for the sale of tickets.

Jessie wished him good luck. She was happy that he was so involved and apparently taking to the new job. Just after she had sat down to eat something herself, the phone rang. It was Dr. Beezly.

"I thought Lee might still be home," he said. "I wanted to wish him good luck."

"That's very nice of you," she said. "I'll tell him when I get to the school."

"Actually," the doctor went on, "I'm glad I have you on the phone. I don't mean to be presumptuous, but I would like to repeat my willingness to examine your eyes. Sometimes a loss of sight is caused by an injury that involves a swelling, and when that swelling recedes—"

"Yes, I know about that, Doctor. We were told not to be optimistic in that regard," she said.

"Well, it's always easy to be pessimistic. We have a natural tendency to look on the dark side, and understandably so. There's so much to make us unhappy in today's world. You don't have to come to my office," he said. "I'll come to you."

"That's very kind of you, but—"

"Let me call you in a day or so and see if we can coordinate time and day, okay?"

She thought for a moment. Something made her hesitate. She certainly had no hope he would be able to succeed where other doctors hadn't, but she felt awkward about refusing such a kindness.

"All right," she relented. "Thank you."

A half hour later the Bakers arrived. Both complimented her on how she looked.

"Actually, with your hair in that ponytail and that sweater and skirt, you look more like one of the high-school students than the wife of the coach," Bob said.

"Thank you."

"I'm starting to get jealous," Tracy said. "He doesn't compliment me as much."

"Now, honey, you know how I feel about you," Bob said.

"Taking me for granted," Tracy muttered. "Just like a man." She laughed, then scooped her arm through Jessie's and they left the apartment.

"Maybe we should see if old man Carter wants to go," Bob jested.

"I haven't heard him all day," Jessie said. "I wonder if he's all right. But who would know? He doesn't seem to have any visitors other than . . ."

"Than whom?" Tracy asked as they neared toward the car.

"Nobody actually. I mean, I hear footsteps other than his sometimes, or what sounds like footsteps. Maybe it's just him sweeping the floor," Jessie quickly concluded.

"Sweeping the floor? What sort of footsteps sound like sweeping?" Bob asked.

"I don't know. It's . . . my imagination, I suppose," Jessie said. She felt the Bakers hesitate.

Then, simultaneously, they said, "We'd better find you guys a new place to live very soon."

As soon as they arrived at the school, Bob commented on the size of the crowd.

"The parking lot is jammed," he said. "They're putting cars on the lawns."

"Does Lee get very nervous?" Tracy asked.

"He hides it well, but he's nervous," Jessie replied. Bob let them out by the entrance and went off to find a space. From the roar of the audience and the sounds of people all around them, Jessie surmised the gymnasium was ready to burst at its seams.

"Henry's saving us seats," Bob said when he joined them in the lobby.

The junior-varsity game had already begun and was in the third quarter. Jessie heard the cheerleaders chanting. As they entered the gymnasium the crowd let out a roar.

"We just scored," Bob explained. Tracy and he guided her to their seats, which were right behind Lee and his team.

"Lee's way over by the scorer's table," Tracy whispered. "He sees us and is waving."

Jessie lifted her hand.

"He's smiling," Tracy said as they arrived at their seats. Henry Young was waiting.

"What a night, what a night," he said, his voice vibrating with enthusiasm. "We're gonna win the junior-varsity game. Good omen, eh, Bob?"

"Yes, sir," Bob said. Jessie sat between him and Tracy.

"Glad you came, Jessie," Henry Young said, squeezing her hand. "It's nice to see wives supporting their husbands." He leaned over to whisper in her ear. "Men need to be stroked. We're all very vulnerable and very helpless, you know." His breath was hot on her ear.

"Yes," she said, smiling. "I know." She leaned toward Tracy. "Is Marjorie here?" she asked.

"No way. She never came to a game, even before her breakdown," Tracy said.

Lee came to their seats before the junior-varsity game ended and kissed Jessie.

"This is one helluva crowd," he said, his voice revealing how impressed he was. "Got to get into the locker room and give the boys their pep talk."

"Tell them to give 'em hell," Henry advised.

"Good luck, honey," Jessie said, squeezing her husband's hands. She felt his sweat and knew how nervous he was. Her heart pounded in anticipation and she wished more than ever that she could see.

"Lee must have gotten to them. The boys look up for it," Bob began when the team entered the court, accompanied by a thunderous cheer. Jessie felt the stands rattle and the floor shake.

"Ooo, this is exciting," Tracy said. "Lee is talking with the referees. He looks very calm and very handsome."

"A good-looking jock," Bob said. "He's got that jock arrogance. Look at how he holds his head."

"Lee's far from arrogant," Jessie said.

"Well, he's swaggering over here," he said when the buzzer sounded. "Our varsity cheerleaders are taking the court. Those are cute uniforms, aren't they, Trace?"

"Um," she replied quickly.

"Could you describe them to me?" Jessie asked.

"I guess they're something like Playboy bunnies with a ball of black-and-gold cotton on their tight rear ends, eh, Trace?"

"I guess that's the best way to describe it," Tracy said dryly. "I'm surprised these uniforms were approved," she said, loud enough for Henry Young to hear. But if he had heard her, he didn't respond.

"Easy, Trace," Bob said, his voice testy.

Jessie sensed a veiled warning. If Tracy was so prudish, she thought, why did she permit such disturbing decor in her home?

"I'm only expressing an opinion. I can still do that, can't I?" Tracy asked.

Bob ignored her question. "The team's gathered around Lee, Jessie, and he's giving them some last-minute instructions. The boys look fierce, don't they, honey?"

"Like they want to tear their opponents to pieces," Tracy said.

The cheerleaders introduced the players, ending each introduction with the phrase, "He's our man. If he can't do it, no one can."

There was another roar from the crowd as the players took the court.

"The referee is tossing the ball," Bob said. "Oh, damn," he exclaimed when the whistle was blown immediately again.

"What?" Jessie heard the crowd groan.

"They claim Hodes pushed his opponent off as he jumped. Can you believe it? They start the game by giving them a free shot. Jesus."

The game continued and Bob did his play-by-play, priding himself on the accuracy of his descriptions. Rather quickly, however, the game degenerated into a shoving match. In the first quarter alone, two of Lee's players and two of the opponents were ejected for fighting. Then the refs began to call foul after foul, mostly on Lee's team. By the end of the first quarter, two more of his starting five were on the verge of fouling out.

Jessie knew enough about the game and Lee's philosophy of sports to be sure that he was furious with his players. He began making blanket substitutions, and the team's opponents took a hefty lead in the second quarter. The crowd began to call for the starting players again. Even Henry Young chanted names like Benson, Hodes, Gilmore. Finally, with two minutes left in the second quarter, Bob put the starters back in, and almost immediately a foul was called on Gilmore. It was an obvious foul, Gilmore jabbing a boy in the ribs as he went up for a shot.

This time Gilmore turned on the ref. Jessie was shocked to hear Henry Young booing. A principal, booing the refs? Moments later Bob said, "Gilmore has been booted out, but he's not getting off the court. Lee's going out there. Benson has just pushed the ref. It's becoming bedlam."

The sight of the ball players losing their tempers appeared to rile up the crowd even more. Jessie heard spectators jumping off the stands and onto the court.

"Oh no," Tracy said.

"What's happening?" Jessie cried, and seized her arm.

"A bit of a riot," Bob said casually. "Some of the opponent's team members are fighting with ours. Lee and a few others are breaking it up."

After what seemed an interminable amount of time, the court was cleared again. The refs went into a conference with the two coaches and then an announcement was made declaring the game a forfeit. The booing became so loud Jessie's ears began to hum. She heard people scrambling madly all around her.

"Oh boy. What a way to lose your first game," Bob said. "I'd better lend a hand." He stepped off the bleachers.

Security had to protect the opposing players from the crowd.

"Where's Lee?" Jessie asked frantically.

"He's going into the locker room with his players," Tracy said, "and he looks furious."

Jessie could hear Henry Young and Bob just below them, encouraging spectators to leave the gymnasium. Finally people began to make their way toward the exits, grumbling and shouting as they departed.

"I'll wait for Lee right here," Jessie said. "He must be so upset."

"All right," Tracy said. "Henry Young's going into the locker room. I'll get him to tell Lee," she said. "Don't worry. I'm sure he's okay."

Almost twenty minutes later, Lee was at her side. The gym had emptied rather quickly once people had begun leaving.

"That's what I would call baptism by fire," Bob quipped.

"I could have done without it. Some of these fans were behaving like wild animals, not that I can say my team acted much better," Lee replied. "I'd say the refs here are vastly underpaid. They should get battle-front bonuses."

Bob laughed.

"You want to go someplace maybe? Have a drink?" he asked them.

"No," Lee said quickly. "I just want to go home."

"Sure. Hey, don't take it badly. Look at it this way—things can only get better," Bob joked. Lee didn't respond. Jessie felt his tension in his hand.

"Are you all right?" she asked softly.

"I will be when I get out of here," he said. "What a madhouse," he added.

"I told you those boys were undisciplined," he said when they got into their car. "I chewed them up and down and in and out, but they looked at me as if I'm the one who's undisciplined. Some of them actually think they did good. Can you imagine? But the worst part is Henry Young didn't help. In fact, he added to it."

"What do you mean?"

"He came in there and interrupted my bawling them out to tell them he was proud of their aggressiveness, proud of their grit, proud they showed what they were made of. 'From now on,' he said, 'you're the team to fear.' Can you imagine? He and I are going to have a big talk tomorrow. Right now I feel like resigning," he concluded.

Jessie was silent. She could feel Lee's anxiety, his insides tied into a knot.

"I'm sorry," she said finally. "I know how disappointed you must be."

"Disappointed? I'm not disappointed. I'm . . . terrified," he said, and suddenly she realized she was, too.

7

Jessie awoke to the distinct sound of someone digging, but recognized that it was some distance away and probably imperceptible to Lee. He was in a dead sleep anyway. She heard his rhythmic breathing. The digging continued. As quietly as she could, she slipped her legs over the bed and found her slippers. Then she went to the open window and listened harder. The digging seemed to get more frenzied. It was coming from somewhere toward the rear of the cemetery. She didn't move; she remained still, her ears attuned to the sound of the shovel lifting and dumping dirt. And then she heard that clear clack of metal against wood.

In her mind's eye, she envisioned that a grave was being dug up. The image put a finger of ice on the base of her neck and sent it tracing along her spine. She shuddered. Grave robbers? Was that it? She thought she even heard the sound of a coffin being pried open. She started to gasp and put her fist into her mouth. Lee stirred, but didn't awaken. He turned on the bed and then his regular breathing began again.

She listened. Now there were footsteps and they were

coming this way, toward the house. Instinctively she backed away from the window. Then she walked toward the bedroom doorway and paused to listen again. Eventually she heard the front door of the house open and close, so she moved forward and attuned her ears to every sound.

Someone was going up the stairway. Mr. Carter? This late at night? And then there was that shuffling. She had to wake Lee. She just had to wake him so he could hear it. She started to turn when the sound of laughter stopped her. It wasn't coming from upstairs; it was coming from outside. She returned to the window and listened. For a moment there was only the sound of the wind playing on the leaves, and then . . . laughter, but laughter that seemed caught up in the wind. It carried over the house and was gone.

All was suddenly very quiet, deadly quiet. It was too late to wake Lee and he wouldn't believe her now if she told him what she had heard. She made her way back to the bed.

"Jessie?"

"Yes."

"You all right?"

She hesitated. Should she tell him anyway?

"I'm all right," she said.

"Good." He turned over. She lay there listening. The voices were starting again, only louder this time, sounding like a crowd of people complaining about something. They were . . . frightened. She put her hands over her ears and pressed hard.

What is it? she wondered. Why doesn't it stop?

When sleep returned, it was truly an escape.

In the morning it all seemed like it had been a dream. Lee was already up and dressed. She sat up and tried to remember every detail. Had it been a dream or had she gotten up out of bed and gone to that window to hear the digging and then the laughter? The answer didn't come until she accompanied Lee to the front door after they both had had breakfast and he was on his way to school. He kissed her good-bye in the doorway.

"I'm sure there will be lots of chatter about last night," he said. "The first thing I'm going to do is get myself an appointment with Henry Young and let him know what I think of what he did last night." He sighed. "I guess we won't be staying here too much longer after this year, Jess."

"I don't care, Lee. I'm beginning to wish we had never come," she said firmly. She felt his surprise, felt it travel through his fingers and into her shoulder, where he still held her. It made him laugh. Then he kissed her again and turned to go.

"Jeez," he said just outside their doorway. She was closing the door and stopped.

"What?"

"You should see the mess out here. Old man Carter must have tracked in fifty pounds of mud. I don't know when the hell he did that," Lee added. "It wasn't here when we returned from the game last night, if I can call that farce a game."

"Mud?"

"Don't worry about it. I'm sure he'll clean it up. He probably does this often." Lee walked out the front door before she could tell him about last night. She held the door open a bit longer. A moment later she heard a door open upstairs. Its hinges squeaked. But Mr. Carter didn't come down.

He's standing up there with his door open, she thought. Why?

"Mr. Carter? Is that you?"

There was no response, but she was sure she sensed another presence . . . someone, maybe at the top of the stairway. Her face flushed. It was as if she had opened the door of a stove. The heat washed over her, driving her back into her apartment. She closed the door quickly, making sure it was locked. Her heart was pounding. She pressed her right palm against her breast and took a deep breath.

What was going on here? What was really going on here? she wondered.

She tried to keep herself busy all day. One of the remarkable skills she had relearned since her accidental blindness was housecleaning. She went about the vacuuming with a geometric precision, crossing and recrossing carpets. She had no trouble envisioning the floor plans of each room. Anyone watching her would be hard put to confirm she was blind. She looked like a woman cleaning her apartment but thinking of ten thousand other things as she worked.

She polished the furniture and then washed the windows, mopped the kitchen linoleum, and washed down the counter and cabinets. The housework had its hoped-for therapeutic effect. By the time she sat down for lunch, she was tired, but grateful her mind had not dwelt on the events of the evening before.

Lee called during his lunch break.

"I've got an appointment with Henry at the end of the day," he said.

"Don't lose your temper, honey," she admonished. "Just explain it calmly, but firmly."

"Don't worry. I've calmed down a lot. There's been a steady stream of people—faculty, custodians, everyone—stopping in to tell me how last night's fiasco wasn't my fault. Seems there was an away game just before I came on that wasn't too much different. It didn't end in a forfeit, but six players had fouled out by the time the game ended.

"Now here's the strange thing about it all," he continued. "I've seen some of the boys in regular gym classes already, and they are all acting remorseful, ashamed. It's almost as if . . . as if they couldn't help themselves. Individually they act okay, Jess; but when they're together on that court, even at practice, they're . . . wild animals."

"What do the other teachers say about them?" she asked.

"Other teachers? I don't know. Why?"

"Find out how each of them behaves in class, or at least how your top boys behave. Maybe competition does something to them, excites them so much they lose control," she suggested.

"Hmm. That's a thought. Hey, you might want to go back to school and study child psychology," he jested.

"First I have to study my own psychology," she said. Lee's silence was tacit agreement. She didn't, as she thought she still might, bring up the digging that had awakened her in the middle of the night.

"All right," he finally said. "I'll try to be home early. See you later."

"Okay," she said, and cradled the receiver.

After she washed the dishes and silverware she had used for lunch and put away the food, she went back to working on her short story for the rest of the day, becoming so involved with her characters, she lost all track of time. She nearly jumped out of her seat when she heard the front door open and close.

"Jess," Lee called.

"Lee?" She reached for the clock and felt it. "Oh no," she muttered. She got up quickly and went out to greet him. "I was working and didn't realize—"

That sixth sense stopped her. It was as if a cold wind crossed between her and Lee. She felt his distance and the bad vibrations. He hadn't rushed forward to embrace and kiss her; he was standing before her, silent.

"What happened? You and Henry Young got into an argument?" she asked.

"I never got a chance to see him," Lee said.

"But I thought you had an appointment."

"I did, but he had to leave school early. Marjorie Young nearly killed herself," Lee said.

Jessie felt her legs turn to straw. She reached out for the arm of the nearest chair and pulled herself around and into it.

"What happened?"

"Seems she was taking a bath with a blow dryer plugged in and the damn thing fell in the water," he said.

"Oh my God."

"Yeah, very stupid and careless. The electrical system in their house isn't that up-to-date. It's one of these restored homes. So the circuit breaker didn't go off immediately."

"How did Henry find out? Was someone in the house with her?" Jessie asked.

"Luckily Tracy Baker was going there, doing Henry a favor and bringing some pills to Marjorie. She came to the door moments after the accident and saw the lights flashing. As soon as she found Marjorie, she called Dr. Beezly, who rushed to the scene. He performed CPR and brought her back."

Jessie raised her head. It was like being stabbed in the heart with a sword made of ice.

"It's all right now," Lee said. "She's going to be all right," he added, coming to her to seize her hand and reassure her. She pulled her hand from his quickly.

"No," she whispered. "It's not going to be all right. Don't you see?"

"See? See what, Jess?"

"She was dead. He brought her back from the dead," she said.

Jessie couldn't calm down enough to make dinner. Lee proposed that they go out to eat.

"I should get you out of this house anyway," he said. "You've got cabin fever."

She didn't resist his suggestion. They went to the Gardner Town Diner and both ordered roast-beef dinners. Many people recognized Lee and stopped by to comment on the game. Jessie didn't hear them complaining about the boys' behavior as much as she had expected. Instead she heard comments like, "They're just full of grit," "It's good they're aggressive," "I guess we showed them what our kids are made of, huh?"

"These people seem so angry, so full of antagonism," Jessie commented.

"I know. We've always been told people are belliger- ent in the cities, but I'm beginning to wonder about these small towns. It's as if we've entered the Dark Ages or some time before morality had any significant influence on the way people think and behave. You can't see the faces of those people who made those remarks, but they looked like they wanted to replay the game and go after the other kids with axes and hammers.

"Whatever happened to sportsmanship, for crying out loud?" he muttered.

"Let's go home, Lee," Jessie suddenly said.

"Huh? I just started to eat."

"No, I mean home, back to the Island. Next week," she said more aggressively. "We'll stay with my parents until we find our own place and you get another job," she said.

"Quit. Just like that. Jeez, Jess, they'd have my head. Why, Young could complain to the state education department and get my teaching license revoked."

"But you can leave a job if you want to, can't you?"

"Yeah, after giving them proper notice, but—"

"So give them proper notice. Please, Lee," she said, reaching across the table. "There is something about this place. I don't like it here."

"Sure it's just not the house and being practically on top of a cemetery?" he asked.

"That's part of it, but not all of it, Lee. It's just a feeling I've had ever since the first night."

"Still hearing those voices, huh?"

"Yes," she said, and described what she had heard the night before. "And you said there was mud in the hallway," she quickly added when she was finished.

"Grave robbing? Carter?"

"I'm not saying it's that."

"Well, what else could it be? That's ghoulish. Maybe the old geezer loses track of time, or maybe he just likes to work late."

"Lee, do me a favor," she said quickly. "See if there's been a death in town and if there was a funeral and burial today."

"Jess . . ."

"Please."

"All right, but I don't know what it's going to prove."

She reached across the table and found his hand again.

"You want to leave, too, don't you, Lee?"

He hesitated.

"Yeah, I guess. Maybe you're right," he concluded. "I'll give Henry Young notice tomorrow and we'll start again someplace else."

"I'm glad, Lee." Jessie smiled and suddenly her appetite returned.

"Of course," he said softly, "it's sure going to look like I've been overwhelmed and I'm a quitter."

"Who cares what these people think, Lee?"

"Right," he said, but not with a great deal of force. As if he somehow had overheard their conversation, a tall, gaunt man with thinning brown hair, strands of which lay matted over his forehead, got up from the counter and stopped at their table on his way out.

"Coach," he said, "you don't let last night throw ya. Those boys are like wild horses right now, but before long you'll turn them into Thoroughbreds and channel all that energy. Good luck," he added, and patted Lee on the shoulder.

"Who was that, Lee?" Jessie asked quickly. She had felt a sudden chill in the air. It was as if they were in the dead of winter and someone had opened a door. She couldn't help but embrace herself.

"Paul Benson's father," he replied. She couldn't see him shake his head, but she felt he wanted to say more. Then she realized who the man was.

"Paul Benson's father? Wasn't he the man you found drunk in the truck that night?"

"Yes."

"The night you thought you saw blood, blood that disappeared."

"It didn't disappear, Jess. I probably imagined it. I'm sorry I ever told you those things. It only fanned the fires of your imagination."

Jessie was silent for a moment. Lee began to eat again. Then she reached across the table and found his forearm. He stared at her.

"What?"

"Tomorrow," Jessie repeated, "give Henry Young your notice."

The following morning, shortly after Lee left for work, the phone rang. It was Tracy Baker.

"I suppose you heard about Marjorie," she began.

"Yes, Lee told me. Thank goodness you were there," Jessie said.

"I know. Anyway, I'm going over to see her in a little while and I wondered if you wanted to come along. She's home; she's all right. I could use the company," Tracy admitted.

"Sure. I'd love to."

"I'll be at your house in fifteen minutes, if that's all right."

"Fine," Jessie said.

She went to the front of the house to wait for Tracy, and when she heard the car drive up, she was out the door before Tracy reached the front entrance.

"You continually amaze me," Tracy said. "How did you know it was me?"

"Sounds have become very distinct. When you're blind, you depend on that a great deal more than you did when you could see. There's something about your car, some rattle, some sound in the engine that identifies it," Jessie explained.

"I thought it might be the click of these stupid shoes with the little metal tabs on the heels. I don't know why I wear them," Tracy said. She escorted Jessie to the car and helped her in.

"How's Lee been since the game?" she asked.

"He's still very upset."

"I bet. Things will get better, though," Tracy promised. "You'll see."

It was an opportunity to bring up the subject of leaving, but Jessie let it pass. She didn't want anyone to try to talk her and Lee out of it. Ever since Lee had agreed to give notice, she had begun to feel relief. She couldn't help believing they were escaping from something terrible. For them this move to Gardner Town had simply been a mistake. People change jobs continually in America nowadays, she thought. There was no reason to feel guilty about it, and especially no reason to be ashamed.

"So how is Marjorie today? I can imagine, with all her other problems—"

"She seemed okay when I spoke with her on the telephone, and for the first time in a long time she sounded happy about having people visit. She became a terrible loner, practically a hermit, since her breakdown, which is hard on poor Henry. He's such a social animal, loves people, parties, crowds. Bob says he can't pass up a gathering of four people on a street corner," she added, laughing.

"He didn't seem all that upset about what had happened at the game," Jessie remarked. She was fishing for Tracy's real opinion of Henry Young. Maybe she would say something that Jessie could bring back to Lee.

"Oh, it takes a lot to upset Henry these days. Bob says it's self-preservation."

"How's that?" Jessie asked.

"There's so much to upset educators these days—student misbehavior, the lack of interest in their studies, the failure of parents to live up to their responsibilities, apathy in our society when it comes to our schools . . . all of it. Bob says Henry could lose his temper every other minute if he didn't have good self-control, and you know what stress like that can do to someone.

"Look what it did to poor Kurt Andersen, the man Lee replaced."

"What was he like?" Jessie pursued.

"A very nice man, a distinguished man, loved in the community, but a man who bottled up his frustrations and let them fester, until one day they just burst his heart. So," she sang, "I think my husband's right—keep your sense of humor, don't take things too seriously, and always find the bright side to anything, no matter how discouraging it might seem on the surface."

"And you think that's why Henry Young didn't chastise the boys more or lose his temper at the game?"

"Exactly. Don't misunderstand me. Henry's not happy about what happened, but he'll correct it in his own way and not add on a pound of gray hair. That's what Bob says," she added.

Jessie was silent. Were they overreacting? Was Tracy right? Maybe she was doing the wrong thing in urging— no, practically demanding—that Lee give his notice. Maybe they hadn't given things a real chance here. Maybe a lot of what she felt was her own imagination.

When they pulled into the Youngs' driveway, she asked Tracy to describe the house. Tracy said it was a turn of the century Queen Anne, a two-story with a steeply-pitched roof. It had bay windows and a full-width porch one story wide and extended along the east wall.

"The Youngs have reshingled the roof and put on aluminum siding. All of the shutters have been replaced as well and Henry has done extensive landscaping, put

in new flower beds and fountains. Next summer he's
putting in a pool just beyond the gazebo."

"Sounds very nice," Jessie remarked.

"It is and it's located in a very scenic part of Gardner
Town. I wish you could see," she said, and then immediately regretted her words. "I mean—"

"That's all right. Describe it to me," Jessie said quickly.

"Well, from the front you have an almost unobstructed
view of the Catskills, and in the rear there are acres and
acres of rolling hills. There's a forest filled with hickory
and birch on our left."

"Aren't there any neighbors?"

"Not for a half mile on either side. This place was the
summer home of some wealthy New York businessman
once. Henry keeps finding wonderful things hidden in
the attic. Ready?"

"Oh yes."

Tracy got out and helped Jessie. Then they made their
way over the walk, up the steps, and to the front door.
Just before Tracy rapped the brass knocker, however,
the door was opened and Jessie was surprised to hear
Marjorie Young greet them exuberantly.

"I've been waiting for you two," she said. "I thought
something might have happened."

"We're not late, Marjorie," Tracy said, laughing.

"When you live out here and you're expecting guests,
they're always late. That's because you're so anxious for
company. Come in, come in," she coaxed. "Hi, Jessie.
It's so nice to see you again. I've made some of those
cakes you love, Tracy," Marjorie said.

"You baked today?" Jessie asked incredulously. "But
I would have thought . . ."

"Of course I baked today. Why shouldn't I? Henry

has a sweet tooth. I can give you tea, or"—she paused
and leaned toward Jessie—"we can sample some of my
homemade elderberry wine. Wouldn't you like that?"
She squeezed Jessie's hand. Jessie tried to lift hers out
of Marjorie's fingers, for they felt as cold as ice, but
Marjorie held on.

"I can't wait to show you everything, Jessie," Marjorie
said. "We've made quite a few changes, haven't we,
Tracy?"

"Practically rebuilt the place," Tracy agreed.

"Well, why not? We can afford it now." Marjorie
finished with a short, light laugh.

Her voice gave Jessie the chills. She remembered
this woman; she remembered her vividly because of
the things she had said and how she had behaved at the
Bakers' dinner party. This wasn't any sort of hysterical
reaction to what had almost happened to her. This was
different. She wore the same perfume, her voice was the
voice Jessie had heard, but it was as if . . .

As if there were someone else inside Marjorie Young's
body, someone very different.

— 8 —

There was a sound in Marjorie Young's laughter that not only rang untrue, but also filled Jessie with a sense that she was in the presence of someone rather promiscuous. Her voice was full of abandon. She sounded as if she had been into her elderberry wine for some time before Tracy and Jessie had arrived, and Jessie detected its scent on her breath, but there was also something about the way she rubbed her body up against Jessie that made Jessie feel very uncomfortable. Never had another woman pressed her breasts so firmly and fully against her, nor had any woman rubbed her hips this way as they walked and talked. Marjorie's hands groped a bit, too, her embrace over Jessie's shoulder slipping down under her arm, the fingers finding the sides of Jessie's breast as she led her to a seat in the living room.

Marjorie babbled incessantly from the moment they all entered. She talked about the weather, the wine, her sweet cakes, and kept repeating how nice it was that they had come to visit. When Jessie commented on how comfortable the sofa was and asked about the material, Marjorie went into a detailed description of her home, going over each and every valuable piece, speaking about the house as if it were a national treasure. Occasionally she would pause to ask Tracy to verify something she had said.

"She isn't exaggerating, not one bit," Tracy remarked at one point. "This vase on the table here must easily be worth—what, two thousand dollars?"

"If we wanted to sell it, Henry says we could get twenty-five hundred without a bit of haggling," Marjorie replied, and followed her words with her thin, high-pitched laugh. There was something terribly familiar about that laugh, Jessie suddenly thought. She tilted her head and played back her most recent memories . . . something.

Then it came to her. That was the same laugh she had heard last night, the laugh in the wind that seemed to fly over the house after she had heard the digging in the cemetery. Realizing the connection made her feel as if icicles were dripping down her spine. Were all these strange events causing her to lose her mind?

"You look a bit pale," Marjorie said. "A glass of this will warm you up and put some color back into your face." She took Jessie's hand to wrap her fingers around a glass filled with the sweetly scented liquid. She practically brought it to Jessie's lips.

Reluctantly Jessie took a sip. It was richer, thicker in texture than any wine she could recall. It did taste good, but it felt like she was swallowing blood. The liquid lingered so long in her mouth and over and under her tongue. It felt . . . sticky.

"There now, aren't we all comfy cozy," Marjorie said. "Oh, I'm so happy you two came to see me," she squealed.

"How are you feeling, Marjorie?" Jessie asked. Seeing how that had been their motive for visiting, she didn't see any reason why they had to pretend nothing had happened or nothing was wrong.

"Exhausted, if you want to know the truth," Marjorie said.

Jessie nodded.

"I can just imagine," she said.

"Oh, can you?" Marjorie said, and laughed again. "I suppose maybe you can. It depends on what sort of a lover Lee is."

"Lover?"

From the moment of silence and the stifled laughs, Jessie sensed Marjorie and Tracy were smiling at each other.

"What in the world does that have to do with anything?" Jessie asked.

"It has everything to do with everything," Marjorie replied quickly. "That's why I'm so tired today," she continued. "Henry was a beast last night, an insatiable beast."

"I don't understand," Jessie said, smiling with confusion.

"Henry is a bit oversexed," Marjorie said, and then laughed again.

Jessie kept her smile of confusion, but said nothing. It had always been embarrassing for her when other people described their intimate relationships. She was never one to compare notes, even when she was going to high school and the girls' room was a conference hall for sexual discussions. Her friends used to tease her about how red-faced she would get, and others were always after her, prying away at her secrets. But she had always felt talking about intimacy was a kind of betrayal. Love required trust, a dropping of the normal guards, a revelation of souls. To expose someone who had been that way with you and share the intimacy with others who would only be titillated and amused was a kind of treachery, a treachery of the heart. Maybe she was old-fashioned about it, but that's the way she was and always would be.

"Usually," Marjorie continued, her voice filled with an eager excitement, "Henry is one of those slam-bam-thank-you-ma'am lovers. You know, spends himself and then turns over to snore. But not last night. Last night he was at me like a caveman. He insisted on holding my arms behind my back and had me pinned down, so I could barely move. Why, it was as if I were being raped," she said, lowering her voice to a whisper.

Jessie felt the heat rise into her neck.

"Unbelievable," Tracy said. "Henry?"

"Yes, and then, once that was done and I thought it was going to be as always, I turned over to go to sleep, and wouldn't you know it, in moments he was at me again, coming at me from behind. He pressed my face down so hard into the pillow, I almost smothered to death. But," she added, laughing again, "it was wonderful. I think I had seven orgasms, before he was finally through, groaning and moaning like some teenage boy.

"So," she concluded, "you two can understand why I'm a bit tired today. He was even amorous this morning. Why, the moment his eyes opened, he—"

"That isn't what I was referring to," Jessie interrupted sharply. It seemed this carnal tale would never end. "We came here because of your accident, to see how you were doing."

There was a strange moment of silence. Jessie tilted her head and lifted her ear.

"Accident?" Marjorie finally said. "What in hell is she talking about, Tracy?"

"Oh . . ." Jessie heard the hesitation in Tracy's voice. "Jessie is just confused," she said quickly. "On the way over here I was telling her about the time you fell off that stepladder and fractured your ankle. She must have thought it had happened recently."

"Oh," Marjorie said. "That stupid time. Well, isn't it true that household accidents are the most common? Do you like the wine, Jessie?"

"What?" What was going on? Jessie wondered.

"The wine, my homemade wine," Marjorie cried. "It takes so long to make a mere quart and I use only the best berries."

"Oh, yes. It's very good."

"Then why don't you drink it?" Marjorie laughed again. "Let me get the sweet cakes. I just took a fresh batch out of the oven and I'm sure they're cool enough now. I'll be right back." She rose from her seat, stopped in front of Jessie and took hold of the hand that held the wineglass, then raised it toward Jessie's lips, just as before. "Drink up, Jessie. There's plenty where this came from," she added, and stood there until Jessie took another sip. Then she left.

Jessie listened keenly to her footsteps disappearing down the corridor and then she turned toward Tracy.

"What's going on? Why did you say I was confused about her accident?" she demanded. "What was all that about falling off a ladder?"

"Obviously Marjorie's had a lapse of memory," Tracy said quickly. "Dr. Beezly told Henry it's very common in cases like this. Part of her mind wants to reject what has happened, refuses to remember. It's sort of a self-defense mechanism. It won't do us any good to try to remind her, and it may do her some harm."

"But she's acting so strange, so different. Telling us

about her sex life like that and laughing after everything. Don't you think she's radically different?"

Tracy lowered her voice.

"Yes, but I think I like her better this way. There's no doom and gloom in her face and she's not telling us all that weird stuff. She looks happy. Maybe we should be happy, too, and just leave well enough alone," she said. "Don't you like her wine, though?"

"What? Oh yes, it's nice. Maybe a bit sweet. I can't drink a lot of it. It's heavy and I think it's already going to my head."

"That's all right. Don't worry. She won't remember how much you've drunk. If she keeps insisting, I'll tell her we had another glass while she was gone."

"Is this house really filled with so many expensive things?" Jessie inquired.

"Absolutely not," Tracy said. "It's one of her fantasies. The vase we were talking about is brass."

Jessie shook her head.

"How sad," she said.

"Here we are," Marjorie suddenly announced. Jessie nearly jumped in her seat. She hadn't heard her returning footsteps. Had the woman tiptoed back?

Marjorie placed a tray on the table and then brought a cake to Jessie.

"Thank you," Jessie said.

"Now, if you don't like it, you don't have to eat it," Marjorie said.

Jessie bit into the soft dough. At first it was absolutely without taste, almost like chewing flavorless gum, but then there was a surge of flavor, a strange taste that flowed over her tongue and filled her mouth. The closest thing she could think of was clove.

"Interesting," Jessie admitted, nodding.

"What a nice way to say you don't like it," Marjorie said, and she and Tracy laughed.

"It's not that I don't like it exactly. It's so different from anything I've eaten that I'm a bit surprised," Jessie explained. She didn't want to add that she couldn't eat much of it, just as she couldn't drink much of this wine. "What's in it?"

"Oh no. I never give away my recipes. Which is much nicer than what an aunt of mine used to do. She would give away her recipes, but she would always leave out an ingredient, or change a proportion so that whoever made the food would never get it as good as she could."

"No, I wouldn't make it," Jessie said, surprised herself at how frank she was. Was it because of the effect this wine was having on her? Her tongue seemed free of inhibitions suddenly.

Marjorie laughed.

"That's being honest. Don't worry, dear. You don't have to eat any more of it," she said. "Now Tracy here is just gorging herself."

Jessie couldn't help smirking skeptically. How could she be?

"Um," Tracy said, her mouth full, "I just love this. What do you call it, Marge?"

"It's my own special devil dog," Marge said, and laughed again. Was it the wine? Jessie wondered once more. This time Marjorie's laugh became thick, heavy, deep, like the laugh of a man. "I do hope you really like my wine, though," she said to Jessie. "Otherwise I'm a total disaster," she moaned, sounding on the verge of tears.

"Oh no, it's good. Really," Jessie said, and demonstrated by taking another long sip. Then she put the glass of wine down and sat back.

"So how has Lee been since his first game?" Marjorie asked. "Henry told me what happened."

"He's very upset," Jessie said. "He's going to speak to Henry about it today."

"Oh?"

What's wrong with me? Jessie wondered. I didn't want to tell them that, especially not Marjorie.

"And what is he going to say to Henry?" Marjorie pursued.

Jessie felt herself struggling to think of something other than the truth. Her mind did somersaults. Words came and went.

"He wants . . ." She felt a little warm and, suddenly, a bit dizzy. It was as if the sofa were beginning to spin. She clutched her thighs.

"Yes? He wants?" Marjorie coaxed. "What does Lee want?" she asked, sounding a bit impatient.

"To tell him how unhappy he was with the way Henry spoke to the boys afterward in the locker room," Jessie said. The words just flowed out. She tried biting down on her tongue afterward, but her mouth snapped open again. "He thinks Henry should have reprimanded them instead of complimenting them."

"Oh? What else does he want to say to Henry?" Marjorie demanded.

"He wants to give notice."

"Give notice? You mean, Lee wants to quit Gardner Town High School?" Tracy asked quickly.

Jessie swallowed and nodded. She couldn't help it; she couldn't hide the truth.

"Yes," she said, and then, for no reason she could imagine, she began to cry.

She bawled like a baby, sobbing about bad things that had happened to her in her past, going back as far as the

time Sarah Feinberg took her rag doll and ran off. On
and on she went, recounting her life until she reached
the accident. And all the while Tracy and Marjorie sat
listening, occasionally comforting her, consoling her as
if she were only five years old.

Finally, exhausted, she lay back. Marjorie got up
quickly and came to her side to embrace her and stroke
her hair softly.

"There, there," she said, "everything will be all right
now. You're safe now."

Her words were soothing, soft, like a lullaby. Jessie
felt herself drifting, sinking, falling through a fleshlike
dark tunnel with walls that oozed a cool, slimy sub-
stance, which made it impossible for her to slow or
stop her descent. She fell into a pool of icy darkness,
shattering it so that it exploded around her like bolts of
lightning, and then all grew quiet and darker.

Suddenly there was a tiny pinpoint of light above her
and she began to ascend, rising out of the pool and shoot-
ing toward the surface to gasp air. Her heart pounded and
a rush of blood filled her face with heat. She felt like she
was stifling. A surge of panic flowed through her body
as she groped at the air in front of her.

And then, as suddenly as it had come over her, it all
began to ease off. She began to breathe more regularly.
She had been submerged, come up from under whatever
cloud had fallen over her. Marjorie had returned to her
seat. Jessie realized she was lying back on the sofa and
sat up quickly. She had no idea how long she had been
lying there like that.

"What?" she cried as if someone had said something.

"Is something wrong, dear?" Marjorie asked.

"Yes, I . . . what were we talking about?" she asked.
Thoughts were so jumbled.

"The PTO dinner dance," Marjorie replied. She continued in a nonchalant tone, as if nothing had happened. "As I said, it will be a pot luck supper and so each of us is making something. What do you want to make, Jessie? You said you would make something."

"I did?"

"Yes," Marjorie said, still laughing. "Don't you call me absentminded, Tracy. We have a new champ."

"I'm sorry, I . . . I don't know what's wrong with me. Maybe the wine. I . . ."

"We're talking about the PTO dinner," Marjorie repeated. "What do you want to contribute?"

"Oh. I . . . what about potato salad?"

"Excellent," Marjorie said. "Tracy?"

"That's great," Tracy said. "It's always a nice affair, Jessie. You will enjoy it and it will give you the chance to meet a great many more residents of the community."

"People who really care," Marjorie emphasized. "People you would want to meet."

"Exactly," Tracy said. They heard the doorbell.

"Oh, another visitor," Marjorie cried. "Please excuse me."

"I feel so strange," Jessie said as soon as Marjorie had left the room. "Like I lost consciousness or something."

"It must have been the wine," Tracy said. "You were right about not being able to drink too much of it."

"What happened to me?"

"You started babbling and crying."

"I did? Oh, I'm so ashamed."

"It's all right. The way Marjorie is, nothing surprises or upsets her. We calmed you down, you stopped, and we started talking about the upcoming PTO affair. I knew you were drifting in and out of the conversation a bit."

"That's an understatement," Jessie said, rubbing her cheeks. She turned toward the doorway when she heard Marjorie's laughter.

"Look who's here," Marjorie exclaimed as she returned to the room. "Our own good Dr. Beezly."

"Well, I didn't mean to interrupt anything or intrude," Dr. Beezly said. "I just stopped by to see how Marjorie was doing."

"Oh, Dr. Beezly," Tracy said, "you could never be accused of intruding."

"Thank you. Hello, Jessie. How are you?"

"I'm all right," Jessie said quickly.

"Um, you look a bit flushed."

"I think I drank a little too much wine," Jessie confessed.

"Oh," Dr. Beezly said. "Marjorie's famous elderberry wine, eh? Yes, I've been known to imbibe a bit too much myself. It's addictive."

"I've discovered," Jessie said. Dr. Beezly laughed.

"Well, it's very nice of you two to stop by. I'll just borrow my patient for a few minutes if you don't mind."

"It's all right, Doctor," Tracy said. "Actually we have to be going."

"Yes," Jessie said firmly. She was so anxious to leave, she stood up abruptly, but the quick move, on top of how she felt, caused her to become dizzy and lose her balance. Dr. Beezly was at her side first, practically flying through the room. He seized her around the waist.

"Are you all right, my dear?"

"Yes, I just had a little dizzy spell. I don't know. . . ."

"I guess you did have a little too much wine. Marjorie, you should be ashamed of yourself," Dr. Beezly chided.

"Oh, I'm sorry. I didn't mean to—"

"No, I'm all right now," Jessie said. "Please, don't make a big thing of it."

"Just sit down for a moment more," Dr. Beezly advised, and firmly guided her back to the sofa. He continued to hold her hand. She felt the heat from it travel up her arm and over her shoulders, a warm pulsating glow that soothed and relaxed her muscles. But then suddenly his touch changed: his fingers felt rough and scaly and he seemed to have long, sharp fingernails. Jessie grimaced and he quickly released her. Instantly the heat retreated down her shoulders and her arm, leaving her chilled for a moment. She shuddered and took a deep breath.

"All right?" he asked.

"Yes. Thank you," she said quickly. She didn't want him to touch her. "I'll try again. We really have to be going," she said.

"Oh, really, I don't mean to break anything up. Please, stay," Dr. Beezly implored.

"No, we do have errands," Tracy said. Jessie was grateful when Tracy came to her side and helped her to stand. "All right?" Tracy asked.

"Yes, I'm fine."

"Well, okay then," Dr. Beezly said. Jessie knew he was still standing very closely to her. She could feel his hot breath caress her face. "Now, Jessie, I don't want you to think I've forgotten about you. Can I come by your place tomorrow afternoon, say about two o'clock."

"Oh, I don't know. I—"

"I won't be there long. I promise. I never overstay my welcome."

"That's very nice of Dr. Beezly," Marjorie said. "You should take advantage of his generosity," she added in what sounded like a threatening tone.

"Of course I wouldn't do anything or recommend any treatment without first consulting with the physicians who originally treated you," Dr. Beezly added.

"You don't have to be afraid of Dr. Beezly," Marjorie said, leaning in to whisper in her ear.

"She's not afraid of me, are you?" Dr. Beezly asked.

"Of course not." Jessie paused, but sensed that they were all waiting for her to respond. "Fine," she finally said. "Two o'clock will be fine."

"Great. I'll put it in my appointment book immediately," the doctor said. "Now, as for this wine thing, take a couple of aspirins right away and lie down; otherwise you will wake up with a real hangover, I'm afraid."

"Okay," Jessie said. "I will. Thank you." She turned toward Tracy, who began to guide her out.

"Well, we'll be going then," Tracy said. "Marjorie, you call if you need anything, anything at all."

"Thank you, dear. And thank you, Jessie, for stopping by. I'm sorry about the wine."

"I'll be all right. Really. I feel so silly." Suddenly she giggled. She couldn't help it.

"Don't forget now, you're down for potato salad," Marjorie called as they started toward the front door.

"And don't forget the two aspirins," Dr. Beezly added.

"I won't forget," Jessie said. The moment the door was closed behind them, she took a deep breath of relief. "I really do feel so stupid. I must have made such a fool of myself."

"No, no, believe me, it was nothing. It took Marjorie's mind off her own problems."

"She doesn't seem to have any problems anymore," Jessie said. It came out like a complaint.

"Well, maybe this accident was a good thing, then. She's outgoing again and eager to participate in community affairs. Her face is full of life and excitement. Maybe," Tracy suggested, "having that hair dryer fall into the bathtub was like an electric shock treatment. You know, a treatment they give mentally ill people. It ripped her out of her depression. Don't you think that's possible?"

"I don't know. Right now I can't think too straight. I want to go home and take those aspirins and lie down. I'm sorry."

"Don't be sorry. I'm glad you were able to come along. And just think—if you hadn't, you wouldn't have run into Dr. Beezly and arranged for him to see you tomorrow."

"Wait a minute," Jessie said. "If Marjorie doesn't remember her accident, why wouldn't she wonder why Dr. Beezly has come by to see her?"

"I don't know," Tracy said, and then laughed. "I guess he comes by so often, she just accepts it. What else could it be?"

"I don't know." Jessie's head continued to spin. "I don't know anything right now," she added, "except I want to go home."

— 9 —

The intercom buzzed in Lee's office just as he came in from his last morning class. It was Henry Young's secretary.

"Mr. Overstreet, Mr. Young wants to know if you can meet with him after your regular basketball-team practice instead of at the end of the day," she said.

"He'll be here that late?" Lee responded.

"He has a meeting with the board of education's building committee at the end of the day and he anticipates it will last at least that long. Do you think it will be all right?" she asked.

He thought about it a moment. He didn't like the idea of coming home late, especially because of Jessie's state of mind these days, but he didn't want to postpone this meeting with Henry much longer either. That would make her even more upset, he thought.

"Okay. Tell him I'll step up as soon as I shower and change," he said. "If there's any earlier opening . . ."

"I'll call you," she promised.

As soon as he turned off the intercom, he went to his telephone and dialed home, but Jessie didn't answer.

He let it ring nearly ten times before he recalled she was going with Tracy to visit Marjorie Young. Still, he thought, gazing at the clock, he would have expected her to be back by now. Maybe Tracy and she went someplace for coffee, he thought, and put it out of his mind.

He was preoccupied with his new strategies for basketball practice anyway. He had decided to concentrate on the team's behavior on the court. After they went through their basic drills, he began the scrimmage by telling them he wanted to get them to change priorities for the next few games.

"We don't worry about preventing the opponents from scoring points as much as we worry about fouls," he lectured. "Here's the deal—you get a foul called on you, you come out and sit ten minutes, just like hockey players who get put into the penalty box, understand?"

"Hey, Coach," Gilmore said, smirking, "what happens if so many of us get fouls in ten minutes that you don't have enough substitutes?" He started to laugh, the others joining in with smug smiles.

"So we'll play with four players," Lee said, shrugging. It wiped the smirks off their faces.

"You're kiddin', Coach. You wouldn't do that," Benson said.

"Let's just see if I don't," he promised, his eyes narrow and determined.

Reluctantly they played more carefully, pulling back instead of intimidating their opponents with their bodies. Hodes didn't jab anyone, and Lee had to call really slight fouls to call any at all.

"See that," he said, after blowing the final whistle. "You guys can do it. You can play gracefully, using your skills instead of your fists. The team that has the most points wins in this game, not the team who has the most fouls. If you want your opponents to fear you, beat them soundly on the scoreboard, not on the court. Understand?"

They were silent and sullen, but they obeyed. Most, with their heads down, went off to shower and change to make the late bus.

Lee smiled to himself and retreated to his office to shower and change for his meeting with Henry Young. As he stripped off his shirt he went to call Jessie to let her know he would be a little late. Once again he let it ring and ring, and still, she didn't answer. Worried now, he called Tracy Baker.

"Oh hi, Lee," she sang.

"I've been trying to reach Jessie, but she doesn't answer. I knew she had gone with you to see Marjorie Young, so . . ."

"Oh, dear," Tracy said. "You're making me tell tales out of school."

"What is it?" he asked quickly.

"Jessie had a little too much of Marjorie's homemade elderberry wine. I took her home a little while ago and saw that she went into the bedroom safely to lie down. I'm sure she's sleeping it off."

"Wine? Jessie?" He smiled incredulously.

"It sort of crept up on her. Don't tell her I told you or she'll hate me. I'm sure she's embarrassed enough as it is," Tracy said.

"No, no, I won't. I was just concerned." He shook his head. "Can't let you women go anywhere, it seems."

"At least we go right home," Tracy responded, "when we know we've had enough."

"All right, all right, no battle of the sexes. Thanks, Tracy."

"You're welcome."

He hung up and laughed to himself. Jessie with a hangover, he thought. She's not going to be happy about that. He slipped off his pants and his underwear and went into the bathroom to turn on the shower. Just as the water began to feel warm enough he heard his name called and peeked around the door to look. It was Monica London.

"Oh hi," she said. "I didn't mean to disturb you."

"No, no, that's all right. One minute," Lee said, and turned off the water. He wrapped the towel around himself and came out of the bathroom. Monica had come in and closed the door behind her.

As usual, she was dressed in a skirt that was so snug it outlined her bikini panties. She wore a light, cable-knit sweater that did little to conceal the uplift bra. Its deep V-neck collar exposed the enticing shadow of her cleavage and the light raspberry tint of her nipple. Lee couldn't help thinking that she had a waist so narrow he could probably touch his fingers spanning it.

Most of the female teachers he knew usually looked a bit frayed by the end of a teaching day. Strands of hair broke loose from the firm settings, clothing looked wrinkled, shoes scuffed. And their faces, even the faces of ones who were heavily made up, looked drained, tired. Voices were strained from lecturing and reprimanding all day. Those who had boosted their energy levels with caffeine highs throughout the day were practically dragging their rear ends over the parking lot to their cars. Anyone who believed teachers had it easy should appear at the end of the day to see how stress and mental fatigue took its toll, Lee thought.

But Monica was different. Despite the hour she looked as if she had just arrived, fresh and sparkling. Her eyes were bright, her hair perfect. Her lips, shaded with a wet pink, were enticing. Her complexion was rosy. It was as if a gust of cool, refreshing air had come into his office. She pulled her shoulders back, lifting her breasts, and smiled. How did she get her teeth so white? he wondered. And then he thought, What is this girl doing here? She was too beautiful to be buried in a little high school in upstate New York. She should be somewhere being discovered, movies, modeling.

"I'm sorry to appear so late," she said, "but you were the last name on my list."

"List? Hope it's not a hit list," he joked. It was kind of corny, but he couldn't help it. She made him feel younger, threw him back to his teenage days when it was important to impress the girls with how cool you were.

"Ooo," she said, hugging herself like a Marilyn Monroe impersonator. It had the effect of pushing up those already spilling-over breasts. The raspberry tops rose to reveal a line of creamy whiteness. He couldn't help but envision what it would be like to press his lips to that inviting bosom. The image flashed through his mind quickly, but it lingered enough to send a shock of warmth through his thighs. His penis began to grow erect. Like a mutinous crew member, it surged on until it was clearly outlined against the towel, something Monica London didn't miss.

He reddened and turned his body so he could cloak the rebellious organ from sight.

"No," she said, "it's not a hit list. It's a list of teachers I was to see about the upcoming PTO dinner dance." She stepped forward, her right hand sliding up from her waist and settling just under her bosom.

"Dance?"

"Yes. It's so important," she continued, elongating the "o" sound so that her lips remained opened a bit longer, "for us to have a good faculty turnout."

"Oh. Sure, sure. I'll put it down on my calendar," he said, and looked toward his desk. He wasn't sure he could walk there. She was standing between him and the desk and to go past her seemed an impossibility.

"It's next Thursday night," she said. "Seven P.M."

"Okay, I'll remember," he said. She didn't move.

"You're so lucky to have your own personal shower," she said, stepping closer. "You can just hop in and out and get refreshed anytime you want."

"Well, we do work up quite a sweat down here," he said.

"I love to see a man break out in a sweat," she murmured. "The sight of that wetness, that silvery, slippery wetness over his skin . . . it does something to me," she added, and shook her body, her breasts jiggling. "Like the way your shoulders are shining now," she continued, stepping closer.

"Well, if you stepped into a men's locker room after a ball game, you wouldn't feel that way, believe me."

"Oh," she assured him, "I think I would go mad. It would be like a sexual smorgasbord."

He had to laugh.

"Sexual smorgasbord. That's good."

"Yes." She was standing right in front of him now. "Your arms are so muscular," she said. "So few men here have muscular arms. Arms turn me on." She touched his biceps and ran her fingers up to his shoulder.

"Um, I think . . ."

"It's all right," she said quickly. Then she winked. "No one's here."

"Hey, wait a minute. I'm a married man," he told her, but it was a weak protest, his voice already cracking.

"When you're with your wife."

"Pardon?"

"You're a married man when you're with your wife. When you're not, you're not," she recited, and jabbed her right forefinger in between his towel and his stomach. He flushed. She lifted her head and fixed her eyes on his, drawing him to her with their magnetic and hypnotic power. He felt as if he were falling into those enticing orbs filled with erotic promise. Her finger tugged gently and then more firmly on the towel until it unraveled and dropped to his feet. She didn't drop her gaze; she continued to hold his eyes on hers. While she did so he began to feel her hands traveling down his hips, her palms sweeping over his thighs until her fingers found his erection and gently squeezed and lifted.

He couldn't keep his lips from hers, and when they kissed, he found it almost impossible to pull his lips away. He was gripped by the taste of her. She clutched his buttocks and backed up toward the desk, pulling him with her. When they reached it, she stepped back just enough to lift her sweater over her head. He stood there dazzled by the sight of her bosom when she flung off her bra. Her breasts remained firm, the nipples pointed up at him, calling to his mouth. In seconds she had unzipped and dropped her skirt. Her panties seemed made of air. With a quick gesture, they were gone and she was pulling him down onto her. Her legs were lifted and he settled over her, his mouth on hers.

Vaguely, somewhere deep under the blanket of sexual pleasure, he heard a tiny voice crying out warnings and criticism, but it was as if he had been shrunk to an inch of himself and no longer mattered. All that mattered now was driving himself deeper into that pocket of ecstasy she had opened for his entry and gratification. On and on he went, unconcerned that he was making love on the top of his desk, that anyone could walk in on them at any moment, that he was committing adultery. None of those concerns seemed to be part of the world he had entered. This was a world of fantasy, of erotic dreams come true.

She moaned and twisted herself beneath him as if nothing he did or could do would ever satisfy her. It made him feel challenged and he became more aggressive, lifting her legs higher and pushing himself deeper, driving, grunting, fueled by his male ego. I'll show her, he thought. I'll show her.

Why this suddenly mattered he did not know. He was drunk on the act, inebriated from the scent of her perfume, the taste of her lips and soft skin. His body was enveloped in a pocket of warmth that caused him to imagine he had literally fallen into her vagina. She had absorbed him, but he loved every moment, every ecstatic second.

Finally she cried out and he exploded in long, delightful bursts, now his body feeling attached to hers, as if they had turned into some mutation, a male-female creature that experienced both male and female orgasm simultaneously. He grunted and withdrew, turning over his papers, his pens, pencils, and calendar and knocking his telephone over the desk. It bounced with a ring, the receiver sliding off the cradle.

She sat up and dropped her legs over the edge of the desk as she began to brush back her hair with her hands. Her recuperation was instantaneous, which was something that annoyed him. He was still breathing hard. What was going on here? He was supposed to be the athlete.

She turned and smiled down at him.

"You were wonderful," she said, "just as I expected you would be." She brought the tip of her right forefinger to his chest and touched him. His skin seemed to sizzle under her and it actually stung.

"Hey!" He sat up, thinking she had stuck him with her fingernail.

"I'm sorry," she said, and leaned over to kiss his chest. Then she stepped off the desk and gathered her clothes.

Still a bit dazed, he shook his head and watched her dress. She moved quickly, and in seconds she was standing before him, looking as together as she had when she had first entered the office. He remained sitting on his desk, naked. She leaned over to place a quick kiss on his lips.

"Don't forget the PTO dinner," she said, smiling. Then she added, "Now I can cross your name off my list." She started out and stopped at the doorway. "Whenever you have any questions, don't hesitate to call me," she said, and smiled widely. "You know how to call me, don't you, Lee? You just let your imagination run wild. I'll be sure to hear it." She laughed, opened the door, and was gone like a dream evaporated at the sound of an alarm clock.

He felt like a man who had been unconscious and just returned to consciousness. Suddenly he realized how stupid he looked. He was still sitting naked on his desk. He had knocked everything about. The phone still lay on the floor. He jumped down quickly and put it back. Then he moved toward the shower, not quite sure that what had just happened wasn't really just a dream. The sight of his towel on the floor in the bathroom reinforced the reality of the erotic episode and he could detect the scent of Monica's perfume on his body, everywhere he had touched her and she had touched him.

Monica had been here. He couldn't deny what had just occurred.

Who would have thought that in seconds he could be seduced into being unfaithful to his wife? he thought. A surge of panic swept over him. Jessie will know. This damned second sight of hers, this extraordinary power to sense and know things beyond what people with sight sensed and knew would tell her, would expose him. She would hear it in his voice, feel it in his hands. She would probably smell Monica.

That thought drove him into the shower. He ran the water as hot as he could endure and scrubbed and scrubbed himself until his skin was red, especially around his prick. But it was the spot on his chest where she had touched him with her finger after they made love that still bothered him. He examined it in the mirror, but saw nothing. The pain was imaginary, he concluded, caused by his guilt. He practically bathed himself in cologne and powder to cover any lingering scent of Monica and the lovemaking. Even so, he didn't feel very confident and that made him shake in anticipation of a horrible scene.

How could he betray Jessie after all she had been through and all of it because of him? She had been so forgiving, so sensitive, so loving. No man could ask for a more dedicated and faithful wife. This new guilt piled onto the guilt he already carried because of the accident and her blindness was unbearable. He sat at his desk and shook his head. What was he going to do?

The worst part of this was that he couldn't shake off the ecstatic memories. Despite his regret and his remorse, he couldn't deny that making love to Monica had been spectacular; and the promise of it happening again, her suggestions and willingness as she left, filled him with erotic excitement. He felt torn by two opposing feelings and thoughts.

I'm a sinner; I'm no good, he thought.

But oh, it was so good and it doesn't mean anything. She wasn't looking for any meaningful relationship. What had she said? *When you're with your wife, you're married. When you're not, you're not.*

The evil part of him laughed. What eyes she had and those breasts . . .

Jessie, he thought.

Damn myself, damn.

He stood up abruptly and then rushed from his office like a murderer fleeing the scene of his crime. It wasn't until he was around a corner and heading toward the parking lot that he remembered his appointment with Henry Young. He wasn't in the mood for this, but it had to be done.

Henry's secretary was gone, of course, and there was no one else around. Apparently Henry's meeting with the board-of-education people had ended. Lee approached his office. The door was open. He peered in and saw the principal at his desk scribbling notes. He knocked and Henry looked up and smiled.

"Come in, come in. Sorry it had to be this late, but I figured you had something serious on your mind or you wouldn't want to meet today. Have a seat." Henry pointed to a chair in front of his desk.

"Thank you, Henry." He settled himself quickly. Henry sat back and folded his hands over his stomach.

"So what can I do for you, Lee?"

"Well, I . . . I guess it's no great secret that I was very upset over the game."

"No," Henry said, laughing. "That's no great secret."

"Yeah, well, to tell you the truth, Henry, I was even more upset about the things you told the boys in the locker room afterward. I felt we should be reprimanding them for their behavior and even thinking of punishing them. Certainly not telling them they were on the right track by the way they behaved. Getting the opponent to respect you is one thing; getting him to fear you . . . that's not sportsmanship and sportsmanship has always been an integral part of athletics, a reason for it."

"I see," Henry said, nodding. "You have a good point, Lee. I guess I've gotten caught up in this rivalry thing myself. Everyone puts so much emphasis on it. I'm sorry." He nodded again and then put up his hand like a man taking the witness stand in a courtroom. "I swear, from this day on, I will stay out of your face when it comes to the team."

"That's fine, Henry. I appreciate your saying that and I appreciate your apology, but Jessie and I have been talking things over and we think it might be best for us to move on as soon as we can. I think I want to give you my notice," Lee said.

"Oh no," Henry said, sitting forward. "You can't mean that, Lee. Everyone's impressed with you. No one has started work here with such overwhelming approval. I don't know anyone who doesn't like and respect you. Please reconsider this. You're making a tragic mistake. This situation with the team will improve in time and you'll mold them into the sort of team you want them to be. I assure you."

"Well, it's not just that . . . it's—"

"I know, I know. Jessie's uncomfortable at the DeGroot house. Well, good news. I've spoken to Charley DeGroot on your behalf and you're out of the lease as of the end of the month. Furthermore Dr. Beezly called me late this afternoon to tell me about an apartment now open in the Courtyard Gardens, a first-floor apartment with an attached garage. The rent, believe it or not, is less than what you're presently paying. And it's closer to the school."

Henry sat back, smiling.

"Actually you'll find out anyway, but Dr. Beezly owns the Courtyard Apartments. Perhaps, with that sort of news, you can cheer up Jessie and get her to reconsider. What do you say?"

"I don't know, I—"

"At least sleep on it, Lee. You have a lot going for you here," he added.

"Yeah, maybe," Lee said.

"Of course." Henry stood up and came around his desk. "Why, you've hardly had a chance to get to know people, including some of the other members of the faculty," he said. Lee looked up sharply. He had certainly gotten to know Monica London.

"Right." He stood up. Henry extended his hand.

"You're a fine young man. I'm proud to have you on our team."

"Thank you," Lee said. He started away. "Oh, how's Marjorie doing?"

"Better. Much better. And it was very nice of Jessie and Tracy to visit her today. She called to tell me they had been there and she was very up because of their visit. Tell Jessie I appreciate it. She's really a remarkable woman, your wife. With her handicap, she does so much. An inspiration, truly. Another reason why I'd hate to see you two go."

Lee nodded again and walked out. His mind was reeling with confusion.

Maybe he should give it all just one more chance. After all, he had hardly had a chance to try to make a difference. Look what sort of progress he had made with the boys today, and as far as some of this other nonsense went . . . well, now he could promise Jessie they would be moved out of that old house and away from the cemetery by the end of the month. Surely that would make things much better. Her imagination would calm down. Maybe they could make a life for themselves in this community yet, he thought. Really, where were they running away to anyway? What sort of a job could he get? He didn't want to go back to driving a cab. He was a teacher, a coach, a professional. He had an opportunity here. The people in authority liked him. Why throw all this away?

Just as he stepped out to the parking lot, a door slammed and Monica London emerged from a side entrance. She crossed the parking lot farther down and went to her car. Before she got in, she turned and looked his way. His heart began to pound. She waved and he waved back. Then he waited as she got into her car, backed out, and drove off.

He hesitated at his own car because he felt like he was being watched. He spun around, but there was no one there. Then he lifted his eyes toward Henry Young's office windows. Because of the way the late-afternoon sun hit the building, those windows looked dark, almost like two black eyes gazing down at him. Then a curtain was pulled open and Henry Young appeared.

He waved and nodded, smiling. A moment later he was gone and the windows were dark again.

Lee got into his car and started away. What would I ever tell Jessie if she found out what had happened between me and Monica London? he wondered. Like a fugitive covering his tracks, he groped about mentally for excuses and reasons, leaving a trail of deceit and lies behind him as he fled from the truth.

— *10* —

Jessie was still sleeping when Lee arrived. Without a light on, the apartment was dark and gloomy. The sun had fallen behind mountains and trees, so that long, deep shadows flowed through whatever windows had their curtains open. Lee turned on a lamp and started through the apartment. Not hearing her in the kitchen, he went directly to their bedroom, where he found her sprawled on her side, in the fetal position, her right hand cupped just under her chin.

She looked so peaceful, so content, he didn't have the heart to wake her. Seeing her this way brought an ache to his heart because it made the memory of his adultery that much sharper and more painful. In so many ways she was so helpless. What a bastard he was.

He had to turn away and get his mind on something else, so he decided to prepare their dinner. Twenty or so minutes after he had begun, she came to the kitchen door. She had walked so softly, he had never heard her approaching. One moment there was no one in the doorway, and the next there she was.

"Hi," he said. "I didn't hear you get up. Feeling okay?"

"Yes," she said, even though she was still so groggy she had to lean against the doorjamb. "I can't believe I didn't wake up when you came in."

"I tried phoning you a couple of times today," he said quickly, unable to filter out a note of defensiveness. She didn't appear to notice.

"I never heard it ring. How long have you been home?"

"Oh, awhile," he said. "You were sleeping so soundly, I didn't want to bother you."

"I'm sorry." She pressed her palms against her forehead and then ran them over her hair.

"Hey, no problem. I have things under control. The table's set. What were you, tired from visiting Marjorie?" he asked, pretending he didn't know. Lies, little lies, he thought. Why not just admit he called Tracy and she told him about the wine?

"Oh Lee," she said. Her lips began to tremble.

"Hey." He put down the pot he was using and rushed to embrace her. "What is it, honey?"

"I drank too much of her wine," she cried.

He started to laugh.

"No, don't laugh," she said, pulling back. "It wasn't funny. It wasn't like wine; it was like a drug to make you tell the truth."

"Huh?"

"I want to sit down," she said, and he guided her to the kitchen table. He sat beside her and still held her hand.

"What are you talking about, Jess? What drug?"

"I didn't want to say anything about your meeting with Henry today. It wasn't anyone else's business."

"So?"

"After I started drinking the wine, I just babbled away, telling everything," she moaned.

"Hey." He patted her hand. "There's no harm done; and as far as the wine being a drug . . . well, a lot of people open up when they drink alcoholic beverages. It's no big deal."

"Oh Lee, I can't help feeling I told them the most intimate things."

"What sort of things?" he asked softly.

"Events, feelings, I don't know. It's all a blur now."

"So maybe you really didn't say anything you thought you did. Maybe you just imagined it," he suggested. She shook her head.

"No. I don't think so." She took a deep breath.

"Apparently Marjorie was feeling all right then?"

"Feeling all right? Didn't I tell you on the phone?"

"We didn't speak on the phone, Jess," he said. "I told you I tried to call, but—"

"Oh, I'm so confused. Marjorie's fine; Marjorie's even better than she was. At least according to Tracy."

"What do you mean?"

"She's bright, animated, laughing, baking cakes, and telling risqué stories. You wouldn't think it was the same person we met at the Bakers' dinner party. Tracy says the accident had the effect of an electric shock treatment. She thinks it was good."

"Hmm." Lee sat back, folding his arms across his chest. "Maybe so. Who's to say no? Just her doctor, I guess."

"He was there, too," Jessie said quickly. "And he's coming here tomorrow to examine me. I couldn't get out of it."

"Is that so? Well, maybe he can do something, suggest something."

"What can he do? Lee, you know it's a waste of time. We've been to the biggest doctors and the best hospitals. What's a country doctor going to do that they couldn't? I don't even know why he wants to examine me. It's . . . it's weird, just like everything else around here."

"Now, hold on, honey. This doctor does seem to have performed near miracles here. Don't forget, medicine is an art, too. There are physicians who are more talented than others. Maybe he's one of them."

"You're not serious?" she said, and then the look on her face changed. "Lee, what happened with Henry Young? You gave him your notice, didn't you? We're leaving, right?"

"Well, not exactly," he confessed.

"Oh no." She brought her hands to her face.

"Just listen for a minute, Jess. I did go there to resign, just as we discussed. I began by bawling him out for his behavior with the team after the game."

"So?"

"He didn't get upset with me. In fact, he admitted he had been wrong. He said he had gotten caught up in the rivalry and excitement just like everyone else. He promised not to have anything more to do with the running of the team."

"And you believe that?"

"I don't see why he would lie about it, Jess. Then, contrary to what we thought, he was terribly upset about my leaving. He went on and on about how well I was doing and how quickly and enthusiastically the other staff members have taken to me."

"Lee, he was just saying these things because it will be hard for him to find a replacement," she insisted, but he couldn't quell his new feeling of pride.

"I don't know; the school family has been very congenial and I have received a number of compliments from other teachers, secretaries—"

"Lee," she cried. "I can't stand it here. I can't!"

"I know, and that's another thing Henry told me. He's spoken to DeGroot on our behalf and the lease can be broken. He and Dr. Beezly have found us a new apartment in a much nicer area and cheaper rent, too. We're moving at the end of the month. You won't hear any more of those imaginary noises or be spooked by old man Carter. How's that sound?"

"Did you see if there was a funeral today?" she demanded.

"I looked in the paper during lunch hour. Nothing, Jess," he said.

"I didn't imagine the digging. I heard it," she insisted.

"All right. So maybe there are grave robbers out there at night. Who knows? At least we'll be moving away from it."

She sat silently for a moment and then leaned back in defeat.

"What about all the things that disturbed you? The team, the community . . ."

"I had those boys turning today, Jess. It took a lot more effort, but they were different. I think they're beginning to understand, and once I change their behavior, I can mold them into a halfway decent squad. I'm not saying we'll break records or even be contenders, but at least I'll bring back a semblance of normalcy and . . ."

She shook her head.

"No, you won't, Lee. You're just deluding yourself. Something's happened," she said perceptively. "Something's changed you, blinded you."

"What are you talking about?" he replied guardedly. Before she could reply, he took the offensive. "Look, Jess. Where are we running to anyway? Do I have another position waiting for me in the wings? What were we thinking about when we decided to hightail it out of here? Hightail it to where? To live with your parents or mine? Me going back to driving a cab or some other such job while I wait to find another opportunity like this? I'm a teacher, a coach; I want to do what I'm supposed to do."

He realized he had made his hands into fists and pounded his own thighs for emphasis. Jessie said nothing for a moment, sensing the tension in his voice; then she nodded.

"Okay, Lee," she said, relenting. "We'll do what you want."

"Once you're in a nicer apartment in a more pleasant atmosphere, it will all change for you, and you will see it's what you want, too. It was a mistake to jump to take this place just because it was so large and inexpensive. I regret that now, but thanks to Henry and Dr. Beezly, we can correct it shortly. Listen." He reached across the table to put his hand over hers. "Do you think we would have people so willing to help us in the more urban areas? Small-town life has its advantages."

"Your hand feels so hot," she said. Instantly he lifted it from hers.

She's going to sense it, he thought. She's going to know.

"I'm probably still overheated from practice."

"Didn't you shower?"

"Sure. Well, I'd better get back to our dinner. I'm working up one of my special meat loafs, the recipe that won your heart."

She didn't smile.

"Okay?" he pursued.

"I don't know, Lee," she said firmly. "Is it okay?"

"Sure . . ." He stood up quickly. "Sure, it's okay. You'll see. We'll be fine."

"I'm going to go wash my face," she said, standing. "I'll be right back."

"Everything's under control," he repeated. He watched her walk away. She looked twenty years older, her shoulders slouched, her steps short, ponderous.

"It'll be all right," he whispered to himself. "It has to be."

Jessie didn't eat much for dinner, even though she said everything tasted good. He managed to get her to smile a few times, but the veil of sadness and depression over her face didn't lift. She complained of still being tired. He tried to make light of it by joking about her having a hangover, but she said it wasn't like a hangover.

"It's more like I've been drained, invaded," she insisted.

"If you still feel this way tomorrow," Lee said, "you should tell Dr. Beezly while he's here."

She raised her head. The way she was sitting, face forward, her shoulders and back stiff, she looked hypnotized. Then she shook her head softly, the lines in her mouth relaxing.

"You don't think it's odd then, his coming to see me?" she asked.

"Oh no. From all I have heard and from what I've seen of him myself, he seems to be a bright, compassionate person, a holdover from another time when life was less complicated. People take each other more seriously in these small towns, Jess. Don't you think that's all it is?"

"I don't know," she said. "I want to feel that way, but I don't. Instead I feel . . . frightened."

"Oh Jess. Afraid of a doctor? After all you've been through?"

She hesitated for a moment, thinking. Then she nodded softly.

"Perhaps you're right," she said. "I'm just tired." She stood up like one accepting her fate. "You want any help with the dishes?"

"No, no. Just go lie down. I'm going to do some reading and watch a little television. There's a game on cable I want to see."

"All right," she said, starting away. "Oh." She turned in the doorway. "I almost forgot. Check to be sure we have at least ten pounds or so of potatoes. I've got to make potato salad."

"Potato salad? What for?"

"The PTO dinner dance," she replied. Then she almost smiled. "You know about it, don't you?"

For a moment he couldn't speak.

"Er . . . yeah. It was mentioned to me today."

She nodded as if confirming a suspicion. It had to be his own guilty conscience making him imagine things, he thought. There's no way she could have guessed what had happened. No way, he chanted to himself.

It was more like a prayer.

He lost himself in the televised game. The Knicks were playing the Lakers. While he watched he fantasized himself becoming an NBA coach someday. Why not? He could do something here and then move on to a college, and from there . . .

A few weeks ago coaching a high-school basketball team again seemed like a near impossibility. Now he was imagining all sorts of possibilities. His wounded ego had rebounded. He felt invincible, full of potential and promise, as eager and enthusiastic as he was when he played college ball. After all, he was just outside that circle of players who were contenders for professional ball. If he had been another three or four inches taller . . .

Making love to Monica London seemed to have restored his youth. He had been living under the gloomy clouds of defeat and anguish too long. Sure, it was wrong to be an adulterer, especially to betray a woman like Jessie and especially at this time in her life, but the erotic incident had come just at the right time, he thought. He rationalized that it was more like a treatment, a psychological boost, than an immoral act. He would be an even better husband to Jessie now because his confidence had been restored.

These thoughts lifted the weight of guilt from his conscience. He promised himself it would never happen again. It served its purpose and it was over. The end justifies the means, right?

There was a time-out and a beer commercial broke in. He would barely have listened or watched, only suddenly the girl at the pool table in the commercial looked just like Monica London. The close-up confirmed it. He shook his head and covered his eyes. When he looked at the set again, the girl was different.

He laughed at the workings of his own imagination.

"I'm getting as bad as Jessie," he muttered, and sat back to watch the remainder of the game. It ended late because there were two overtimes and he couldn't pull himself away from the set. Finally, a little after midnight, he turned off the TV. Just as he reached over to turn off the lamp, he thought he heard whispering.

He spun around, expecting to see Jessie in the doorway, but the room was empty. He listened again and then turned slowly to look toward the front window. He nearly jumped out of his skin.

It was Monica London.

"Jesus," he muttered, his heart pounding. She smiled and beckoned for him to come out. "Oh damn," he said, and stepped into the hallway. He listened for a moment to see if Jessie had awakened, but it was deadly quiet. Then, as silently as he could, he slipped out of the house, closing the door gently behind him. When he stepped onto the porch, he saw no one and for a moment thought it had been his crazy imagination at work, just as it had been with the commercial. Then a shadow moved and became Monica.

"What the hell are you doing here?" he whispered loudly. "Are you crazy?"

"I couldn't sleep," she said, smiling. She was wearing a jacket over a sheer nightgown. In the yellow light of the porch fixture, he could see her legs and triangle of pubic hair clearly. "I kept thinking about you, about us," she added.

"You've got to get out of here. My wife . . ."

"She's asleep, isn't she?"

"Yes, but . . ."

"So," she said, giggling. She reached out and seized his hand firmly. "Come on," she coaxed. "There's something I've always wanted to do." She tugged. He tried to resist, but it was as if his legs heard different messages. As she pulled him along he felt like his head and heart were merely passengers on a runaway body. All the avenues of communication between his brain and his limbs were shut off. The lines emanating from his conscience were down.

It was a partly cloudy night with just enough moon-light filtering through and in between the clouds to provide a dimly lit pathway through the darkness. The trees that were silhouetted against the night sky looked like morbid observers, bent and twisted sentinels guarding a fortress of evil. Nothing moved except Monica and he. Even the bats seemed to have fed and gone contentedly to sleep. It was as if he were being dragged into a painting, a tableau created out of the nightmare of some brooding and macabre artist.

Monica pulled him through the entrance of the cemetery. As if the moon followed orders, it broke free of the wispy clouds that had surrounded and trailed it. A wave of bone-white light washed the tombstones. Monica stopped before a large monument and a long marble slab.

"Isn't this kinky?" she whispered, and giggled. She sat on the slab and pulled him down with her. He wanted to resist. He kept telling himself this wasn't really happening; this was a dream. He was back in the house, in the living room, asleep in his chair while the television played on. But Monica's hands were all over him, unbuttoning, unfastening. And when he gazed down at her, he saw her beautiful body shining as softly as the marble slab. She was as smooth as polished stone. He couldn't keep his hands away.

He slithered out of his pants and underwear like a snake shedding its skin, and in moments he brought his erection to the mouth of her vagina. She wrapped her right hand around the back of his head and pulled him down until his lips met hers and then he entered her and they began to make love on this grave. Monica didn't complain about the hard slab. In fact, it seemed to get softer and become as comfortable as a mattress. She moaned softly, her fingers digging into him and driving him to be more passionate. When he opened his eyes, he and Monica were drowning in a sea of moonlight.

The lovemaking became more and more frenzied. It was more than erotic; it was as if his body was in turmoil, maddeningly pursuing some impossible orgasm. He felt as if his head would explode and fly off his neck. He envisioned his body turning into liquid and pouring down toward his loins until it did burst and flow through his erection, his entire being rushing into her. He thought she screamed, although he couldn't be sure it wasn't he who had screamed.

Finally it ended and he turned over, his back against the cold slab. He lay there, struggling to catch his breath, his eyes closed. When he felt her rise, he opened his eyes. She gazed down at him, her body seemingly gigantic, statuesque, carved from granite.

"It was wonderful," she said. "Wonderful." Then she laughed softly and fled into the night, her nightgown flying up behind her, making her look like a fugitive ghost.

He closed his eyes again; his heart was pounding so hard, he was sure he would have a heart attack and be found dead on this gravestone with his pants still down. He struggled to pull up his garments. Finally his heart slowed and he was able to sit up.

Where was she? He heard a car engine start and then saw the headlights go on. Moments later she was driving away. This wasn't a dream; it had happened, he thought, and scrubbed his face with the palms of his hands. Leaning against the tombstone, he pulled himself to a standing position. Still in the moonlight, he was able to read the monument. It was the grave of someone named Frederick Hardenburg, but it was the birth and death dates that brought a shudder to him. The man was his age when he died. Just coincidence?

He stumbled away. The moon, behaving once again like a stage light, slipped behind a heavy cloud and the darkness grew thick once more. Just as he stepped onto the road and turned toward the house, he heard a strange sound and paused.

Christ, there it was. Jessie hadn't imagined it after all. Someone was digging out there, digging in the grave-yard. The sound seemed to grow louder and draw closer. He stepped back, tripped, and fell on his rear end. He scurried to his feet and ran all the way back to the porch steps. There, he paused to catch his breath. Can't go bursting into the house, he thought. He was sure to wake Jessie.

Calmly and as quietly as he could, he tiptoed up the steps, aware that they as well as the porch floorboards squeaked. The hinges of the damn front door squeaked, too. It was as if the house was determined to expose him. He reentered the apartment and stopped in the hallway to listen for signs that Jessie had awakened. All was quiet. He returned to the living room and turned off the lamp. Then he hurried down the corridor and slipped into the bathroom as quickly and as quietly as he could.

His face was a sight—all red and streaked with mud. He washed quickly and then just stood there with a cold cloth on his neck. Finally he made his way to the bed. There was just a little moonlight coming through the window, but it was enough to reveal that Jessie had embraced his pillow in her arms, twisting and turning it as if she had been in some struggle with it and finally had subdued it.

He didn't want to wake her, so he left the pillow in her arms and tried sleeping without it. In the morning the alarm clock jerked him out of a deep sleep. When he turned around, he saw that Jessie was already up and his pillow had been placed under his head. He sat up and threaded his fingers through his hair. Last night seemed so much like a dream now that he thought he could tell himself it had been.

What was he thinking of? How could he let her pull him off like that? And to make love on a tombstone . . . let it be a dream, let it be a nightmare . . . anything. He rose from bed and went to the bathroom to shower. Hot water, a good breakfast, the prospects renewed his optimism. Sometime today, he would put an end to this Monica London business. He'd go to see her and tell her in no uncertain terms to stay away from him. Sure, he thought, that's what he was going to do.

The problem was he felt like a smoker who had stopped a thousand times, deluding himself each time that he could stop anytime he wanted to stop.

Maybe it was because of this house, he thought. There's a curse on it; it puts a spell on its inhabitants. It makes me sin, he rationalized. Sure. What was that story Monica London told him—the story about the DeGroot ancestor who killed her adulterous husband and cut his body up to spread over the cemetery. Wasn't it ironic, though, how it was Monica who told him the story and then tempted him into adultery?

In the bathroom, he paused before the mirror and studied his face. God, his eyes were so bloodshot. In a way he was lucky Jessie couldn't see him this morning. He was about to turn away and start the shower when something on his body caught his eye. He paused and then brought his hand to the spot on his chest.

It was where Monica had touched him that first time in his office. He had thought she had jabbed him with a fingernail, but this blemish . . . it looked more like the scar from a burn, and it seemed to be growing larger even as he stared at it.

It felt hot to his touch. It even felt as if it were burning into his body as well as around his chest. He stepped into the shower as quickly as he could and ran a stream of ice-cold water over it. It appeared to help. The burning sensation ended, and when he gazed at himself in the mirror again, the spot was nearly gone. After he dressed, he opened his shirt and checked once more. It was barely visible.

Relieved, he went to start his day, but the memory of that scar was so vivid that he had to check periodically to be sure it hadn't reappeared. Sometimes it looked as if it were returning, and sometimes it looked like it had completely gone. It was as if it had a mind of its own and was determined to tease and torment him.

He felt sure that the moment he cut Monica London out of his life it would all end. If it didn't, he might have to pay a visit to Dr. Beezly himself. He didn't know how he would explain it, but something told him he wouldn't have to. Dr. Beezly would know.

— *11* —

Jessie sensed Lee was very different this morning. He had been aloof, kissing her quickly when he entered the kitchen and then moving away as if he were afraid of her touch. He wasn't as talkative either, and when he did speak, he sounded tired. She wasn't sure when he had finally come to bed last night. All she knew was she had awakened sometime during the night, realized she was clutching his pillow in her arms, and returned it to him without waking him.

She had had such horrible nightmares. Once again she heard those strange footsteps, only this time in her dream she was able to picture something making those sounds. She had to refer to it as something; it wasn't a person and it wasn't an animal. Not exactly an animal. It was more like a giant insect, something with a hard shell instead of a back, something that stood on two feet, if you could call them feet. They were scaly, fishlike appendages, slabs of meat, and they left this trail of slime as the creature moved through the hallway and up the stairs to old man Carter's apartment.

In her dream she had opened the door just as it was

halfway up, and it turned. It had no head, just a swollen lump with two slits that housed pale yellow orbs, each dripping a green, syrupy liquid that flowed down the black sides. Suddenly, what she thought was solid softened to form a sort of toothless mouth, and instead of a tongue, a triple-headed snake emerged, each head spitting and hissing. Her gaze dropped quickly as an enormous phallus sprang out from the creature's crotch. The tip of it was as red as a hot coal.

The first thing that was odd about her dream was the fact that she could see the horrible thing. For a short period, when she had opened the apartment door to see what was making the sounds, her sight had returned. The second was that she didn't appear to be surprised. It was as if she knew, as if she were merely confirming her suspicion. The creature seemed to understand. It smiled and then continued up the stairway, moving with what looked to be a limp.

At breakfast she wanted to tell Lee about the dream; it had been so vivid. But she knew he would simply chastise her for indulging these horrible images and thoughts. He would blame it on her wild imagination or simply on the wine. He certainly wouldn't see any significance in the dreams, nor would her relating them to him change his plans in any way.

In fact, she concluded that his standoffish behavior this morning was the result of her complaints and sometimes hysterical behavior. Maybe she had been unfair and unrealistic to expect him to understand and appreciate her second sight, if she could call it that. Maybe he had been right all along—maybe her accident and the trauma of becoming blind had left her mentally unbalanced, her thoughts often distorted, her imagination unhinged.

Apparently no one else had complained about late-night digging in the cemetery. Lee never heard the strange footsteps, and he certainly never heard the voices. As far as he was concerned, she had permitted Marjorie Young, a woman who had suffered a nervous breakdown, to spook her, to feed her frenzied imaginings and nurture her distortions. No one else heard strange tones in people's voices or felt their bones through the flesh when shaking hands. No one else heard skeletons crumbling in the night or laughter in the wind.

If you took away those things, what did you really have? One night a man got drunk and fell out of his truck in front of their house? The police had come promptly to take him away, and apparently he had done things like this before. Lee's team got into a free-for-all and the school and community had become excited over it? Well, as Tracy had said, these were small towns with traditional rivalries. People don't have all that much to entertain and distract them up here. Marjorie Young had nearly electrocuted herself and as a result had a radical change of personality. Well, maybe she was a schizophrenic. Maybe everyone was right—she was a nervous, hysterical woman.

Calmer minds had to rule the day, Jessie reluctantly concluded. Lee wasn't all wrong about that. Where were they running to? What would he do? If he thought he could turn things around and was willing to give it another try, why shouldn't she support him and give it another try herself? They were moving out of this spooky place; things had to get better.

Feeling guilty now, she tried to cheer Lee up before he left for work.

"How about my making chicken Kiev tonight?" she asked him at the door. It was his favorite dish. "I'll call the grocer and have everything I need delivered."

"Sounds great."

"And I might just make a chocolate cream pie for dessert," she added.

"Fantastic. You feel up to it?" he asked.

"Yes. I'm in the mood to drown myself in domestic duties today," she replied, smiling. "We won't have any wine at dinner, though," she added. He laughed. "I don't care if I ever have wine again."

"Okay, Jess. Oh, what time is Dr. Beezly coming to see you?"

"Two o'clock," she said, and laughed. "I nearly forgot."

"I'll call you in the afternoon to see how it went." He leaned over to kiss her on the lips. Once again she sensed his kiss was perfunctory, which left question marks dangling in her mind. She stood there listening to him depart. The quickness in his footsteps made it seem as if he were fleeing. Moments later she heard him drive off and all was quiet. She shook herself out of the pensive mood before it could settle over her and return her to her previous state of depression, and then she went off to make a list of groceries and plan the dinner.

She wanted it to be something special, romantic. It had been a while since they had made passionate love, or since they had simply been truly loving to each other. Most of their time had been spent mulling over these problems, real and imaginary. It was time to turn things around, and nothing did that better than a gourmet meal, soft music, and fervent lovemaking. She longed for it and for the moments of satisfactory, sweet fatigue that would follow. Tonight, for sure, she would have an easeful, trouble-free sleep. She was determined.

She was surprised to receive a phone call from Marjorie
Young later that morning.

"Tracy and I were just talking about you," she said,
"and I thought I would call to see if you were doing all
right."

"Yes, I'm fine, thank you. I'm sorry about yesterday,
about the way the wine went to my head, but—"

"Oh, don't think anything of that. It was my fault,
really. I shouldn't have pushed so much of it on you.
It's just that I so enjoy watching people enjoy what I
make. Aren't you a little like that?"

"Sometimes, yes," Jessie admitted, but she couldn't
help wondering why Henry permitted Marjorie to make
elderberry wine if she had been having trouble with
alcohol.

"Anyway, I wanted to be sure you weren't nervous
about Dr. Beezly coming to see you. You seemed anxious about it, but you won't find a sweeter, more gentle
doctor anywhere," Marjorie insisted.

"I'm not nervous; I'm just not very optimistic," Jessie
confessed.

"Well Dr. Beezly will change that attitude," Marjorie
replied quickly. She sounded like a grade-school teacher
reprimanding an insolent child.

"I hope so."

"He did it for me," Marjorie emphasized. "And he did
it for Henry and he did it for Bob, and he will do it for
you," she predicted firmly.

Jessie didn't know what to say. If the woman could step
physically through the telephone to drive that conclusion
into her, she would, Jessie thought. One moment she had
been apathetic, depressed, even fearful of everything and
everyone, and now she was a major cheerleader. The way
she and some of the others spoke about Dr. Beezly, they

sounded more like disciples than patients.

"I'm willing to give him a chance," she finally said.

"That's all he asks for, a chance," Marjorie sang. "If you need anything, please don't hesitate to call. We're all a happy little family here."

"Thank you," she said. She was tempted to bring up the frightening comments Marjorie had made to her when they were leaving the Bakers' dinner party. She just wanted to see what the woman would say now, but she was also afraid it might do some psychological damage, set Marjorie back, and then everyone would blame her.

"Well, good-bye and good luck with Dr. Beezly," Marjorie said.

"Bye. Thanks."

A short while later Tracy phoned to see how she was doing, too.

"I wanted to phone earlier, but I was afraid of disturbing you. Do you have a bad hangover today?"

"Actually, no."

"Dr. Beezly's advice was on the money, huh. He's amazing. The way he just seems to know what's best for everyone. Even if he can't help you physically, he'll offer you good advice. He seem to have a prophet's wisdom."

"It surprises me he's not the mayor of this town," Jessie said. The words came out a lot harsher than she had intended, but there was something annoying about the way they all praised Dr. Beezly. No man should be thought of in such extravagant terms, she mused. It's almost sinful.

"What do you mean?" Tracy asked.

"Everyone thinks so highly of him."

"Oh." Tracy laughed. "I suppose we do sound like

idolaters or something, but it is rare to find someone with all his qualities. Most of the doctors I've known were kind of narrow. When they look at you, they see kidneys and glands, not people. Dr. Beezly sees you for what and who you are."

"I'm not so sure I want someone that perceptive looking into me," Jessie said thoughtfully. Tracy laughed again.

"Don't worry. He's discreet."

"Sounds more like a clergyman than a physician," Jessie muttered.

Tracy giggled.

"That's what Marjorie used to say."

"Oh? She called earlier," Jessie said. "She apologized for force-feeding the wine."

"How nice. I know she felt bad about it."

"Tracy, why does Henry let her make wine if she has had a problem with alcohol? Or for that matter, why doesn't Dr. Beezly say something about it?"

"Well . . ." Tracy said. Jessie sensed her hesitation.

"What?"

"I'm sure it might have been because you had some on a relative empty stomach or something, but it's not very strong. The only thing it does to me is make me nauseous because it's too sweet. Of course, I wouldn't tell Marge that, but—"

"Not very strong? It hit me like a brick."

Tracy laughed.

"Maybe you're just allergic to elderberries. Believe me, if Dr. Beezly thought it was dangerous for Marjorie to make it, he would speak up. He's not one to keep his opinions in a trunk, as you will soon learn," she added, and laughed again. Only this time Jessie felt as if Tracy knew some secret, some secret Jessie was about to have revealed to her. Tracy, too, wished her luck before ending the conversation.

The groceries were delivered a little before noon. Jessie put them away and prepared the chicken Kiev after she made herself some lunch. By the time she had finished and cleaned up, it was close to two o'clock. Anticipating Dr. Beezly's arrival, she went to the front of the apartment and listened for his car. Oddly, though, she never heard him drive up.

Suddenly, as if he had materialized out of thin air, he was knocking on her apartment door. The sound took her by such surprise, she literally jumped in her seat. Then, for a moment she couldn't move. He knocked again. She took a deep breath and rose from the chair. When she opened the door, she was first greeted with a whiff of that now-too-familiar stench. It passed quickly, however.

"Hello, Jessie," Dr. Beezly said. She smiled and extended her hand. He took it slowly, his fingers curling around hers. Once again she had the sensation that she was shaking hands with a corpse. Her fingers cut through his smokelike flesh and she felt his bones. He held on and then entered the apartment when she said hello and stepped back.

"I didn't hear you drive up," she said.

"Really? My Mercedes is a diesel and makes far too much noise for my taste," he said.

She stood there smiling incredulously. Her hearing was keen. Even if he had driven up with his engine off, she would have heard the crunch of gravel under the tires. Surely she would have heard him step up to the porch. She hadn't even heard the front door open and that door squeaked so loud, she could hear it when she was in the kitchen. Maybe she had been too deep in thought, she mused.

"This is a roomy apartment," Dr. Beezly commented as he walked farther in. "But you will be much better off in the new one," he added quickly. "It's too isolated out here. You should be around people, activity. I don't mean noise," he said, touching her shoulder. "I imagine it's deadly quiet here. No pun intended," he said, laughing.

"You'd be surprised how noisy it gets," she replied. "At least in my mind or my imagination, as Lee puts it."

"Oh?"

"I hear digging all the time, it seems, and when I ask Mr. Carter about it, he claims he's not doing any digging. Lee and I are both wondering now if there aren't some grave robbers."

"Oh my. Perhaps I should have the police look into it," Dr. Beezly said. "I'll see about it."

She shrugged.

"I don't know anymore. I'm the only one who seems to hear it happening."

"Uh-huh," he said. "Why don't we sit on the sofa here," he suggested. "I've brought my bag along and I'd like to do a few tests quickly. Nothing complicated."

"All right." She sat down and folded her hands on her lap as he placed his bag on the coffee table. She heard him unzip it.

"So," he began, "tell me a little about the accident."

"I don't remember it well," she said quickly.

"Yes, that's very common with serious accidents."

"Like what happened to Marjorie," she said.

"Exactly. The mind blocks out details. It's too painful to remember, especially if someone you love is killed or seriously hurt. Or someone you love causes the accident," he added. She felt herself tighten into a fist inside. "Was it a one-car accident?"

"Yes. We went off the road and hit a tree."

"I see. You and Lee had been coming from a party late at night?"

How did he know that? she wondered. She certainly hadn't mentioned it to Tracy, or to anyone else in Gardner Town for that matter, and she couldn't imagine Lee having done so.

"We were going home, yes."

"People never realize how much they've drunk, do they?" he said.

"No." What did this have to do with the examination of her eyes? she wondered. Is he just trying to make small talk? If so, he's chosen the wrong subject.

"I'm sure he feels bad about it. Guilty," he added. For a moment she didn't respond. "These things are difficult to face up to," he added.

"I don't blame him. Accidents happen. It wasn't something he wanted to happen or something he did deliberately," she said. She couldn't help sounding testy, but if he was going to continue on this subject . . .

"Oh, I know you don't hold him accountable, but that doesn't mean he won't blame himself, I'm sure. I suppose we're all sinners of one sort of another. It's in our nature to be so. Drunk driving is what I would call a sin of weakness, as opposed to a sin of passion or a sin of greed. Do you agree?" he inquired.

"It's not something I enjoy talking about, Doctor. I'm sorry," she said. She almost snapped at him.

"Of course." He sat beside her and took her hand into his for a moment. "Now, you just try to relax," he said, patting her hand softly. "I'm not going to do anything that would cause you any pain."

"All right." She took a deep breath. Then she felt his fingers on her forehead and his thumbs pull up on her skin so her eyes opened wider. She heard him snap on a small light and imagined he was pointing the beam directly into her pupil, her dead pupil.

"Uh-huh," he said. Suddenly there was that putrescent odor again. It seemed to come from his mouth. How could a physician have such halitosis? she wondered. He has to get so close to people all the time.

The fingers of his right hand moved to her left temple and the fingers of his left hand moved to her right. She sensed him standing directly in front of her now, holding his hands on her and gazing closely at her face as he did so. The odor grew stronger, sharper, more difficult to tolerate. She squirmed.

"Easy," he whispered.

"I think it's a little stuffy in here," she said, trying to be polite about it. "Maybe we should open a window."

"The windows are open," he replied. He began to massage her temples slowly, softly. The bony feel of his fingers changed until it was more like something wet. It felt like some cold liquid was emanating from the tips.

"You do see something, don't you, Jessie?" he suddenly asked, only the question sounded more like an accusation than an inquiry. "You see more than people know. You have a deeper vision, one that penetrates surfaces, passes through words and sounds, a vision that comes to you through your sense of smell and touch and hearing. Even through taste, a vision that is sharper, clearer, and far more accurate. A vision that is prophetic, clairvoyant."

His voice was soothing, mesmerizing. She felt as if he were hypnotizing her. Her mind began to reel. His words were adrift on her sea of understanding, floating, probing, seeking. She couldn't resist him.

"Yes," she admitted. "I do."

"I think," he said, "that you are the only person who can see me. If you want to, if you permit yourself to, that is. Go on, Jessie. Do it. Open those inner eyes of yours."

She shook her head.

"Go on."

"No," she said, her voice small. She started to back away, but his fingers were glued to her temples now. Whatever that putrid fluid was, it cemented her to him and it created new paths, new synapses into her mind. Down his arms his identity flowed. Through his wrist and hands, into his fingers and into her mind, where her vision was clear and vivid.

She gasped.

First she saw the beetlelike creature. It had taken the place of Dr. Beezly. Suddenly it metamorphosed into a giant fly, its eyes red, and then it changed into a man with a cadaverous face, sunken eyes, yellow and pale skin. He was naked, which revealed how lean he was. He had a humped back and was covered with coal-black body hair, a trail of it moving down from his chin to his chest, and flowing over his stomach to join with his thick patch of pubic hair, out of which emerged a thick, red, pulsating penis, its opening dilating as it swelled. With her inner vision, she saw that his legs were like the legs of a goat with cloven feet. Hanging down under his crotch and just visible was a thick, hairy tail.

She screamed and backed away with all her strength, breaking his hold on her temples. Even so, the picture that had been sent into her mind remained vivid. She screamed again and lifted her arms protectively over her face, but his hands, with their long, crooked fingers and strands of hair growing out of the palms, caressed her breasts. Some drool fell from his thick, wormy lips. His teeth were black and his tongue writhed like a small, pink snake.

She screamed once more, this time her voice reaching a shrill, high pitch that was painful to her own ears. It didn't drive him back. It seemed to bring a smile to his raw face, a face that appeared skinless, the blue veins drawing road maps over his cheeks and forehead.

She wanted to push his hands off her bosom, but when she touched his arms, they felt revolting, sticky and wet like flypaper. Her fingers became attached, rendering her helpless. His fingers unfastened her blouse and peeled it away from her breasts. They unclipped her bra and lifted it up and over her bosom, and then he lowered those twisting, squirming lips to her nipples and the snakelike tongue slithered over them, first the right and then the left.

She wasn't screaming anymore, at least not aloud. Her screams were turned inward and trapped in an echo chamber in her mind. It made her dizzy. She passed out and regained consciousness a number of times while her skirt was being lifted and her panties lowered. She felt herself being shoved and adjusted so that he could bring that thumping phallus to her vaginal lips. There, it rested, throbbed, waited, poised for entry.

Trapped beneath this slime, her arms and hands rendered helpless, her body in a viselike grip, she waited, anticipating a most horrible violation. But he was still. The only movement was the rhythmic nudging of his gross penis against her, an erotic prying, urging her to open and welcome it. She held herself tight, her body locked in firm resistance. The drool that fell from his lips

splattered on hers and some of it found its way into her
mouth, leaving a sweet and salty taste. She gagged, but
she couldn't prevent it from flowing down her throat.

While his body remained pressed down on her she
could feel the black hairs tickling her skin. His breath
was so hot, she felt she was on the verge of being
burned.

"Jessie," he finally said. The word echoed in her mind
as if it had bypassed her ears, as if it had emerged from
someplace within her. "Jessie."

She shook her head to deny it, but it wouldn't be
denied. It demanded her attention.

"Jessie, I can offer you restored sight. I can heal you.
I can make you a whole woman again, beautiful and
bright. I can give you health and happiness for as long
as you want. All you have to do is want, want me, open
to me, welcome me. I'll bring you to a height you've
never before reached."

The pulsating phallus thickened between her thighs. It
pressed and pried harder, but she held on.

"NO!" she screamed.

"Jessie, Lee will soon be mine. You don't want him
to leave you behind. Join him; join us. See again. Live
a full life. Open to me," he pleaded. "Open to me."

"Open to him," a chorus of voices within her chanted.
"Open to him."

"No," she said weakly. She was opening. The tip
of that thick penis grew warmer and warmer. She felt
herself softening. His drool fell faster; the stench of
him crawled up her nostrils, making her mind spin.
Her legs were starting to part. Her spine was relaxing.
He brought his mouth to her breasts again and sucked,
that reptilelike tongue extending and lifting. Her head
was falling back.

"Surrender and you will see again," he promised. "Surrender."

The penis was crawling in like a plump little rodent, twitching from side to side, squirming, thickening. . . .

"NOOOOO!" she cried with one desperate surge of resistance. "JESUS, NO! JESUS, HELP ME! HELP ME!"

The words washed him back. The grotesque phallus shrank rapidly and retreated. His body lifted from hers and her fingers broke free of his sticky and pasty skin. She screamed again and again until all the lights that had been turned on inside her mind went out. Wave after wave of soft, gauzelike light replaced it. It drifted over and over her. It made her feel safe and she relaxed.

All was quiet, still. It had ended.

— 12 —

The ringing of the telephone awakened her. She sat up slowly, unsure for a moment where she was. Her groping hands informed her she was in the living room on the sofa. The phone rang on. She leaned over to grasp the receiver and ran her right palm over her forehead at the same time.

"Jess?"

It was Lee. For a moment she couldn't speak. It was as if the wires running from her mind to her tongue were burned out. The words were stuck somewhere in between. Her lips began to tremble and then finally she made a short, guttural sound.

"Jess? You there?" Lee asked.

"Yes," she croaked. At least that's how it sounded to her. She had been turned into a frog. The thought put her into a panic and she dropped the receiver and began running her hands up and down her body, confirming that she still had legs and arms and breasts. She was still a woman, but after what she had just been through, nothing would have surprised her.

Lee's voice cried out in mechanical tones. For a

moment she hallucinated him as tiny and trapped in the receiver. She clutched it quickly and brought it back to her ear and mouth.

"LEE!" she cried.

"What is it, honey? What's going on?"

"LEE!" She started to cry.

"Jessie, talk to me, honey. Is Dr. Beezly still there? What's going on? Jessie?"

"Lee," she said in tones more recognizable. Her voice was returning. "I was almost raped. Maybe I was. I'm not even sure." There, she had gotten it out. The horror was put into words.

"What? When? How? I'm hanging up," he added quickly. "I'll be right there. Have you phoned the police?"

"The police can't help," she said softly, and shook her head. In fact, the thought of the police coming suddenly made her laugh.

"Jessie?"

She laughed again and again. Tears began streaming down her cheeks.

"The police?" she said, and laughed on until she had to drop the phone. Once again Lee's voice sounded tiny, mechanical. Then her laughter turned to sobs, long, hard sobs that made her draw in air so quickly it brought an ache to her lungs. She embraced herself and crouched over to stop the pain, but it wouldn't end.

Lee's voice stopped, and after a few moments there was a monotonous hum coming from the receiver in her lap. She threw it off, the hard plastic implement bouncing on the rug, away from her.

Suddenly it occurred to her that she might not be alone. That he might still be here. He could even be in the room, sitting across from her, smiling and watching.

The thought sent a chilling wave of fear through her body. Her limbs grew soft and weak. She listened. Was that the sound of heavy breathing?

"Are you here?" she asked, but there was no reply. Slowly, fearfully, she stood up. Her legs wobbled. Where would she go? What was a safe haven? Surely no place in the apartment was.

She took her first steps, nearly tottering as she did so. She clutched herself tightly and waited for the dizziness to pass, listening keenly. That was definitely the sound of heavy breathing; he was still here, watching her, waiting.

Flustered, she spun around, indecisive about what direction to take. Once again she thought it wasn't safe anywhere in the house, and so she groped her way to the front door and seized the knob. Was that laughter? She didn't wait to find out. She turned the knob and stepped into the entryway. The moment she did so, she heard the shuffle, those horrible footsteps. Now he was coming down the stairs . . . slide, step, slide, step.

She lunged ahead and ran her hands over the large front door until she found the knob. In moments she turned it and burst out, forgetting the distance between the door and the steps. Unfortunately she missed the top step and went tumbling down, slapping her shoulder hard on the slate walkway. The fall left her stunned for a few moments. Then she distinctly heard the front door being opened again.

She got to her hands and knees quickly and thrust herself forward until she was on her feet again. In her panic, however, she had lost her sense of direction, lost the image of the front of the house she had memorized so well. Terrified she would run into something or fall off of something, she froze after going only a few feet.

She heard him behind her on the porch. She heard him take the first step and then the second.

"HELP!" she screamed, and turned. "HELP! SOME-ONE, HELP ME!" She spun around and extended her arms. The spinning caused her to lose her footing and she fell on the grass. For a few moments she simply lay there crying. She heard him coming toward her, but she was too tired and too confused to flee. She lay there, waiting, sobbing. He was right beside her. For a moment he just stood there looking down at her. Then, to her surprise and relief, he continued on, away from her, moving toward the street.

She pressed her face to the grass and relaxed her body. That was where Patrolmen Burt Peters and Greg Daniels found her when they arrived. Lee's panicked phone call had brought them running. Siren blaring and bubble light spinning, they were at the DeGroot house minutes later.

"Mrs. Overstreet?" Burt said, taking her arm and urging her to try to stand. "It's the police, Mrs. Overstreet."

Jessie raised her head from the grass.

"Your husband will be here any moment, ma'am," Greg said. "Why don't you try to stand and we'll go into the house, okay?"

"Is he gone?" she asked.

"Who, ma'am?" Burt asked.

"Satan," she said.

The patrolmen looked at each other.

"Yes, ma'am," Greg said quickly. "There's no one here but us."

She let them help her to her feet.

"Are you hurt, ma'am?" Burt asked. "Can you walk?"

"I can walk," she said. They led her to the steps. Just

as they reached the front door Lee pulled up. He charged out of his car and ran up the walk.

"Jessie!" he cried, coming up behind them. She turned and threw her arms around his neck. Immediately she began to sob. He began to comfort her by kissing her forehead and cheeks and stroking her hair.

"We found her outside, lying on the lawn, sir," Burt said. "She doesn't appear seriously injured."

"Let's go inside, Jess," Lee coaxed gently. "Come on, honey. Inside." He tried to pull her arms off his neck, but she wouldn't relinquish her hold, so he scooped her up and carried her through the door. Greg opened their apartment door for him and Lee carried her to the sofa. Burt Peters surged forward and put the telephone back on the side table. After Lee lowered Jessie gently to the sofa, he sat down beside her and held her hand.

"I'll get a wet washcloth, sir," Greg said.

"Down the corridor on the right. Thanks."

"Maybe I should just look around a bit," Burt suggested. Lee nodded.

"Jessie," he said. She looked unconscious. Finally her head turned and she took a deep breath. "It's all right now, honey. It's okay. Tell me what happened, Jess."

Greg Daniels returned with the washcloth and Lee wiped the grass stains and mud off her face. Then he folded the cloth and placed it over her forehead. She seemed revived.

"Nothing looks unusual in the apartment," Burt reported. "No windows broken, nothing messed up."

Lee nodded and turned back to Jessie.

"Honey, the police are here with us. Tell them what happened."

"Dr. Beezly," she muttered.

"Yes? What about Dr. Beezly, Jess?"

"He turned into . . . he is the most horrible, ugly . . ."
She brought her hands to her face.

"Dr. Beezly?" Burt Peters exclaimed. He looked at
Greg Daniels, who shook his head in disbelief.

"Maybe I should phone the doctor and see what happened," Lee suggested. "He was supposed to visit her
today and examine her eyes."

"Good idea," Burt replied.

"I've got his phone number here," Greg said, and
pulled a small pad out of his back pocket. He flipped
it open and showed Lee the number.

"Thanks." Lee lifted the receiver and punched out the
numbers. Dr. Beezly answered the phone himself. Where
was his receptionist? Lee wondered.

"Doctor's office," he said.

"Dr. Beezly, it's Lee Overstreet."

"Oh, hello, how are you? I was going to phone you
later when I knew you would be home."

"The police and I are with Jessie now," Lee said
quickly.

"The police?"

"Yes. She's hysterical; she claims she was almost
raped."

"Oh no. I'll be right there. Give her some warm tea
and try to keep her calm."

"But, Doctor, she—"

"I'm on my way," the doctor said, and hung up. Lee
turned to the police.

"He's coming over," he said.

"NOO!" Jessie cried. "I don't want him here. NOO!"

"Easy, Jess. Why are you blaming the doctor? What
did he do?"

"He turned into him!" she cried.

"Into him? Who?"

"Satan," she repeated.

"Satan? You mean, the devil tried to rape you?" he asked, unable to cloak his amazement.

"Yes, yes." She nodded emphatically. Lee looked up at the patrolman.

"Just rest here a few moments, Jess. I'll put up some water for tea. You should get something warm in you." He started to get up, but she reached out to seize his wrist.

"Don't let him near me again, Lee," she pleaded. "Please."

"No one will come near you, Jess. I promise. There are two big, strapping policemen standing right here."

"That's right, ma'am," Greg said. "No one's gonna hurt you now."

Jessie relaxed, and Lee pulled away gently and stood up.

"I'll just get you some tea," he repeated. Burt Peters nodded to indicate they would stay by her side. Lee hurried into the kitchen to put up the water. By the time he returned with the cup on a tray, Jessie had drifted into sleep.

"Maybe you just oughta let her rest," Burt suggested. Just then they heard Dr. Beezly pull into the driveway.

"Let's talk to him," Lee said, and put the tray on the table. They greeted the doctor on the porch.

"What happened here?" he asked.

"I phoned Jessie and she was hysterical, claiming she had almost been raped. Said, in fact, that she might have been. She wasn't sure."

"Oh boy." Dr. Beezly nodded at the policemen, who nodded back.

"I phoned the police immediately and started for home."

"We found her right out here, facedown in the grass."

"It's my fault," Dr. Beezly said. "I should never have left her alone afterward."

"What happened?" Lee demanded.

"I examined her and we talked and I told her I was afraid there was nothing I could do to help her regain her sight."

"We shouldn't have gotten her hopes up in the first place," Lee chastised. Dr. Beezly nodded.

"You're right, Lee. It's mostly my fault, my damn arrogance. It's just that sometimes even the best of our profession miss things or misjudge things. And sometimes people's conditions change and there's room for a new evaluation or treatment.

"Anyway," he continued, "she did take it badly. I tried letting her down carefully, but she is a very perceptive and intelligent woman and saw right through my euphemisms. There's no fooling Jessie."

"That's for sure," Lee said.

"I thought she would be all right, even though she began relating some of these hallucinations she's been having lately . . . hearing someone digging up coffins, strange footsteps in the night, laughter in the wind . . . I was going to tell you that I wanted to prescribe some tranquilizers for a while."

"Might not be a bad idea," Lee said, nodding. "Those hallucinations have been getting worse and worse."

"Yes. When I left her, I thought she would be all right until you returned at least. She was calmer, but it's hard to tell what's going on in the mind of someone like Jessie. How's she doing now?"

"She's fallen asleep on the couch," Lee said.

"She didn't hurt herself in anyway, did she? I'd feel just terrible . . ."

"No. Just a few minor scrapes," Lee said.

"I could look at her," Dr. Beezly suggested, and turned toward the doorway.

"No, I don't think you should go in there just yet. She might go right back into it."

Dr. Beezly looked surprised.

"Did she say something bad about me? Am I part of her hallucinations now?"

"She said you turned into a creature and that creature tried to rape her," Lee reported.

"Oh my." Dr. Beezly shook his head. "I am sorry. Probably because I was the last one to see her before she went into it," he mused aloud. He dug into his jacket pocket and produced a bottle of pills. "These are some mild tranquilizers. They will keep her calm and relaxed until she passes through this hysteria. Give her one every four hours, four times a day. If she has a particularly bad night, you can give her one during the night," he added.

Lee took the pills.

"Thank you," he said.

"I'm really sorry I left her alone. I should have realized," the doctor repeated, and shook his head.

"I don't suppose anyone could anticipate something like this," Lee said.

"I'll see her as soon as you think it will be okay to do so," Dr. Beezly offered.

"Thank you, Doctor." After shaking the doctor's hand, Lee and the two policemen watched him go back to his car.

"He feels real bad," Greg said.

"Dr. Beezly hates to lose a patient or make mistakes. That's for sure," Burt said.

"Can't imagine anyone calling him Satan," Greg said,

shaking his head. Dr. Beezly waved and drove off.

"No," Burt agreed. "Funny, though," he added just before Lee began to turn back to the house.

"What is?" Lee asked.

"That night we came by to pick up Tony Benson when he fell out of his truck drunk . . ."

"Yes?"

"He claimed he had come to kill Satan. That's what he was mumbling."

"He came here? To kill Satan?" Lee asked.

"That's what he was saying."

"The man was dead drunk," Greg said. "How can you even repeat what he said?"

Burt shrugged.

"He mentioned it to a few people before he came here," Burt said. "I was just thinking that maybe someone said something to your wife and planted it in her mind."

"I don't know," Lee said. "Maybe."

"Sorry you had some trouble, Mr. Overstreet," Greg said. "But we're glad it wasn't anything more serious."

"Yes, thanks. I appreciate how fast you two responded," Lee added, and they started away. Lee looked out toward the cemetery for a moment and then hurried in to care for Jessie.

She was a great deal calmer after she awoke again. Lee reheated the tea and spoon-fed her a cup. Her emotional episode had left her quite exhausted, however, and he let her remain on the sofa. He sat by her side while she dozed on and off. Whenever she woke, she did so with a jerk and he had to reassure her he was at her side and everything was all right. He made her another cup of tea and some toast and jam and tried to get her to eat a little, but she claimed she was still too nervous to hold anything down. All she would do was sip tea. He fingered the bottle of tranquilizers in his pocket and wondered how he would get her to take any. He would have to sneak them into her food for a while, he thought. She became terrified again when he told her Dr. Beezly had returned and had spoken to him and the police.

"Just relax, Jess. He's gone. Now just take your time and tell me again what you think happened. He came to examine you, right?"

"Yes," she said, pulling herself into a sitting position. She swallowed some tea and continued. "I came out here to wait for him, to listen for his car, only I never heard him drive up. Suddenly he was at the door. It was as if he had been here all the time."

"Maybe he had come earlier, Jess. Maybe he was upstairs with Mr. Carter."

Her face froze, her arm stiffening so that the cup remained a few inches from her lips, and she nodded, a smile of realization forming.

"Yes," she said in a whisper. "That's it. That's why I hear the shuffling sound. He is often upstairs with Mr. Carter. Don't you see, Lee?"

"See what, Jess? What are you talking about?"

"He and Mr. Carter . . . they're doing something in the graveyard . . . digging up graves."

"Oh, come on, Jess. Listen to me. Listen to me!" he demanded, seizing her free hand. "Dr. Beezly was here. He examined you, right?"

"He started to."

"And he saw there was nothing he could do for you, and when he told you so, you became upset, right? Isn't that true, Jess?"

"No," she said, shaking her head. "I never really

believed he could do anything. You knew that."

"I'm sure you hoped, Jess. You had to have hoped. It would only be natural. Jess, you've been having many hallucinations. This isn't the first time."

"Hallucinations? You don't believe me? You don't believe he tried to rape me!"

"Jess . . ."

"You don't!" she screamed, and put the cup down quickly. Then she got off the sofa.

"Jess . . ."

"No," she said, holding her hand out to keep him away. "You believe him. They've gotten to you. You've done something," she said in a cold whisper, "and they've gotten to you."

"Jess, please . . ."

"Keep away from me, Lee. You believe him. You do," she said, shaking her head and backing up. She turned and made her way out of the living room and down the corridor toward the bedroom.

Lee lowered his head. What was he going to do? She was out of control. All this had gone too far. He checked the time. He either had to call the school and have his basketball practice cancelled or get someone to stay with Jessie. Their next game was tomorrow night. Damn bad time for all this to happen, he thought. Not that there would have ever been a good time. He decided to try Tracy Baker. He didn't have to go too far into an explanation before she understood.

"I'll be right there, Lee. It's no problem, really."

"Thanks, Tracy. I appreciate it."

"Don't worry. She's going to be all right," Tracy assured him. After he spoke to her, he went to the bedroom and looked in on Jessie. She was lying down, her hand on her forehead.

"Honey," he began, "I'm sorry. You have to appreciate how hard it is for anyone to believe your story. You're an intelligent woman. You can see that, can't you?"

"Yes," she said, but she sounded defeated. "It's all right, Lee. I'll be all right."

"Sure you will." He sat on the bed and took her hand into his. He patted it reassuringly. "Once we move out of here and—"

"It won't matter where we go in this town anymore, Lee. He knows I know. I resisted him. I realize that now. Do you know what he offered me? He offered me restored sight," she said.

He stared down at her. That made sense; it made perfect sense she would hallucinate such a thing.

"That was the deal for me not exposing him—restored sight."

"How can you expose him, Jess?"

"I'm the only one here who can see him, see who he truly is. I don't know why. It's just something that happened, some power I gained. The voices I hear are not imaginary, Lee." She turned her head toward him. "They're the voices of the dead. I heard them the first night we moved in here and I've heard them on and off ever since."

"All right, Jess," he said, relenting. "Suppose I believe you. What are the devil and Mr. Carter doing? What does it have to do with the digging up of graves? And people dying and being reborn?"

She was silent, thinking. He shook his head and started to get up when she reached out to seize his hand.

"He's bringing them back," she said.

"Bringing them back? Bringing who back?"

"The evil souls."

Despite his skepticism, Lee felt the back of his neck grow cold and that chill spread quickly down his spine.

"He's resurrecting them," she said in a whisper. "He's finding them new bodies and resurrecting them." Still holding on to his hand, she pulled herself into a sitting position. "That's why Marjorie was so different. Don't you see?"

"Jess."

"And why the real Marjorie told me not to let them bring you back once you died. Marjorie had found out, too, so they arranged the accident. That's it; it makes sense. Now you believe me," she said quickly. "Now you understand, don't you?"

"I don't know. It's a very frightening idea." Maybe it's best to placate her, to humor her at this point, he thought. Later, when this passes, she will come to her senses.

"Of course it is, Lee. Oh Lee," she said, clutching his hand with her other hand, too. "Let's get out of here. Tonight. Let's just pack up and go. Please."

"Take it easy; take it easy. Let me think," he pleaded.

"There's no time to think, Lee." She started to get out of bed. "I'll start to pack."

"Jess . . . all right, all right," he said, holding her back. "I'll make some arrangements. I do have a few responsibilities, you know."

"They're not important. Not anymore."

"Not to you and me maybe, but to other people, good people, they are. Everyone in this town isn't a reborn evil soul, right?"

She hesitated.

"If we do bad things to them, we'll work right into the devil's hands," he said. Where did I get that from?

he wondered. I'm getting to sound like her.

"All right," she said. "Do what you have to do to make our leaving painless, but do it quickly."

"I will. I promise," he said. They heard the doorbell. "That's Tracy," he said quickly when she reacted with instant fear. "I asked her to stop by and stay with you while I go to practice. All right? She's one of the good guys, right?"

"I don't know," Jessie said.

"You never had any bad vibrations from her, right?"

"No."

"So she's clean. And while I'm gone, try to eat something, Jess. You're only going to make yourself sick. Okay?"

"All right," she said, lying back. "All right. As long as you get us out of here soon."

"I'll be back as quickly as I can," he promised, and went out to let Tracy in.

"How is she?" she asked immediately.

"Rambling, going on and on with this hallucination. Just humor her, keep her calm. Get her to eat something, and if you do," he said, taking out the bottle of tranquilizers, "get one of these into the food. They're tranquilizers Dr. Beezly gave me."

"Oh, sure. If Dr. Beezly wants her to take them, they must be good." Tracy smiled. "Don't worry, everything will be all right."

"Thanks again," he said, and hurried out.

As he pulled away and down the road he looked to the right through the old stone arch of the cemetery, and in the rear in one of the older sections, he thought he saw old man Carter standing with a shovel. He just had a glimpse of him while he passed, but it looked like he was preparing to dig in front of a tombstone, dig up a grave.

See how easily weird ideas can be planted in your mind, he told himself. No wonder poor Jessie had so many planted in hers. Her blindness had imprisoned her in a chamber of horrors and left her to be victimized by her own nightmares. It added to his weight of guilt for drinking too much that fateful night and driving them into a tree. He had hoped so much that Dr. Beezly would perform a miracle.

Even if he were the devil and were able to offer her sight, Lee mused, I wonder if I would have blamed her for taking the deal. He had grave doubts that he would hesitate if it were offered to him on her behalf. He rode on, pursued by demons he had himself resurrected and now lived in his own heart.

— *13* —

As if his boys sensed that his level of toleration was low, they all played exceedingly well. There were no fights, no arguments, and there was evidence of a great deal of teamwork. It encouraged and excited him, and like a devoted jock addicted to sports and the love of the game, he lost himself in the activity. For nearly an hour and a half he thought about nothing else. At one point he substituted himself for one of the players and scrimmaged a bit with the boys. He felt younger. The boys cheered when he made his jump shot from the corner. His teamwork—the way he passed the ball sharply, screened for another player, and sacrificed personal glory to make a play work—inspired them and they began to move like a well-schooled squad instead of wild and independent individuals.

I'm making a difference, he thought. I'm finally getting through to them.

At the end of the practice, they were smiling and congratulating each other as well as saying nice things to him, thanking him, wanting to shake his hand or have him pat them on their backs. As they left the court to

shower and dress, he thought they were finally turning
into a team, his team, and maybe one of his best.

How am I going to desert them at this point? he
wondered sadly, and retreated to his office to shower
and dress. After a few days, after we move out of the
DeGroot house, maybe Jessie will get better, he thought
hopefully. He figured if he could only find new ways to
distract her, get her mind off these weird thoughts, he
might turn this thing around.

He sat behind his desk and untied his sneakers. Then
he phoned home to speak to Tracy.

"How's she doing?" he asked.

"She's fine, Lee. I got her to eat some hot cereal and
I opened one of the capsules and mixed it in. I sat with
her until she ate it all. Now she's resting," Tracy said.

"Oh, that's great, Tracy. I don't know how to thank
you."

"No need."

"Did she tell you what she thought had happened?"
he asked.

"Not really, no. I didn't push it either."

"Maybe she's getting better; maybe she's snapping
out of it," he said.

"Oh, she will," Tracy promised.

"I'm just cleaning up here. I'll be there soon."

"Don't rush. I've already spoken to Bob and he's
decided to make us dinner tonight. I can't wait to see
what that will be like. He hasn't cooked for years."

"If he poisons you, I'll feel it's my fault," Lee kidded.

"I promise I'll haunt you forever," she replied. He
hoped Jessie hadn't overheard that or she would hallucinate something else, he thought.

He showered, dressed quickly, and hurried out to the
parking lot. His was the only faculty car left tonight.

The late-fall afternoons had grown shorter and shorter until it was nearly pitch-dark by the time his basketball practice ended. As far as he was concerned, it was the most depressing time of the year because he rose in the dark and went home in the dark. Early evening was much colder, too. He had to remember he was in upstate New York now; it was a colder climate. It was time to wear a thicker coat. This old university basketball jacket wouldn't suffice. He actually shuddered as he reached into his pants pocket to search for his car keys.

Just as he opened the door he thought he heard laughter, a woman's laughter. He turned and looked back at the building, but all was quiet; all was still. There wasn't a person in sight. The custodians had all the corridor lights on and some of the rooms were being cleaned, but other than that, the building looked deserted. He listened again and imagined it had been only the wind whipping around a corner, that and his fragile imagination.

He got into the car and started the engine. The laughter reminded him of Monica London. All day he had looked for an opportunity to seek her out and tell her in no uncertain terms that he wanted to end their sexual shenanigans, but whenever he was free, she was in class or simply nowhere to be found. He didn't want to go around asking for her because he was afraid of calling attention to himself. He returned to the gym, thinking he would try again tomorrow.

He backed the car out of his space. When he checked his rearview mirror out of habit, he thought he saw someone move out of the shadows. He stared for a few moments, but the figure turned into a shadow again. He shifted his car into drive and shot forward, driving like one escaping. Imaginary laughter, figures in the shadows, it was all getting to him. It wouldn't be much longer before he would be in as bad a shape as Jessie, he thought. How did this happen? How did it all somehow go wrong?

He couldn't help recalling their first days together, meeting after a ball game and rushing off to be alone, parking up on Angel Cliffs to neck, their passion for each other becoming overwhelming until they made love in the back of his Oldsmobile. Thank goodness for that big backseat, he thought, smiling. Then there was the first night they got up enough nerve to go to a motel. What was it called . . . the Pit Stop? Jessie had gotten cold feet; she was terrified someone would see them go in and out. Finally they came up with that silly disguise—she dressing like a man. How they laughed about it afterward.

He had never dreamed he would be a heavy drinker. Of course, he had had his beer-drinking days at the fraternity and with his teams afterward, but then he got into the habit of joining the other coaches during his first two years as a teacher and coach. They would scout teams and go off to drink and talk shop. He had been very lucky up to that fateful night. So many times he had come home a bit high, but always managed to manipulate the car.

It's all luck, he thought. One time too many, one missed turn, all a roll of the dice, a spin of the wheel, and you pay for your errors and sins. Only what had made it worse was he hadn't been the one permanently damaged; he hadn't been the one punished. How many nights would he go off alone someplace in the house or even out of the house and rant and rave at himself? How many times would he curse the God who had decided to make his punishment more severe by punishing the one person Lee loved more than himself? He longed for

Jessie to be angry, for her to hate him, because the pain he suffered was made more intense by her forgiveness.

Maybe that's why he had started up with Monica London, why he had succumbed to her advances. He wanted to hurt Jessie again, hurt her so badly that she would finally hate him. He needed to do penance; he longed to be whipped. Instead she pitied him and gave him more love and affection. If she only knew how passionately he had made love to Monica, how eagerly he had accepted her kisses and sought her touch.

Just recalling it stirred him. He couldn't prevent it. Monica loomed in his mind like the ultimate male fantasy, *Playboy, Penthouse,* Christie Brinkley, Kathleen Turner, Madonna, all and any of them rolled into one. It had been like making love with a dream. His body shook with the memory.

And suddenly, just the way she had predicted when she had said, *You know how to call me, don't you, Lee? You just let your imagination run wild. I'll be sure to hear it,* she appeared. Not beside him, not in the car, but outside the car, her face materializing and then fading, first in the rearview mirror, which made him spin around and look in the back, and then on the windshield. She smiled and beckoned. There she was on the front passenger's-side window. There she was in the outside mirror. He jumped when her voice came over the radio.

"Hi, Lee. I knew you would call me again and again and again."

He reached for the on-off knob frantically, but the radio wasn't turned on. Her face began to flash faster, appearing in every piece of glass. She filled the rear window. Her voice began to echo and grow louder and louder.

"What is this?" he screamed. "Get out; get the hell away from me!"

"Lee, oh Lee . . ."

He didn't realize he was pressing his foot down harder on the accelerator, but the more he heard and saw her, the faster he drove. Other traffic flashed by; some drivers, annoyed with his erratic driving, hit their horns, the blaring sounds adding to his own inner commotion. Monica's voice grew even louder. He let go of the steering wheel twice to cover his ears and then seized it again.

Frantic, he decided to pull over, but instead of hitting the brakes, he hit the accelerator even harder. It made no sense, but the car shot forward, Monica's face now filling the windshield and blocking his view of the road. He never saw the turn, but vaguely, as the car left the highway, he recalled the route and realized this turn had come up. His automobile seemed to lift off the road like a single-engine plane off a runway. It flew a few feet over the embankment before striking a very large old maple that absorbed the blow as if it had been growing for years and years in anticipation of being struck just this way. Its long, gnarled, and crooked branches shuddered and the last few dried leaves of late autumn rained down in a mist of yellow, orange, and brown.

Lee's body slumped forward over the steering wheel, his chest pressing down on the horn. The damaged automobile cried like a wounded beast, its yowl reverberating through the night. Squirrels scurried for protection, a fox foraging nearby fled down a ravine, its tail floating like an afterthought in some celestial mind. A trickle of blood began to run out the sides of Lee's mouth, the drops dripping slowly onto his hand and lap. His body lifted as though he were preparing to utter a deep sigh and then it settled against the steering wheel again. The radiator hissed steam and a wheel lifted off the ground and spun on as if the car had a mind of its own and was trying to find footing so it could continue.

Finally the wheel spun to a stop like the wheel of fortune Lee had been imagining earlier. The tree ceased shaking and dropping dried leaves, and the horn grew lower as the battery began to short out. A dark silence fell over the scene; it was almost as though the car had been there for decades. The frightened squirrels tweaked their noses and after a few more moments began to reappear. They peeked out of the shadows with eyes made ghoulish by the light of the emerging moon. One of the braver ones leaped onto the roof of the car and, after concluding it held no promises of food, leaped off and chattered his disappointment into the night. Then, as quickly as it had been noticed, the car and its inhabitant were ignored.

Jessie lay vaguely awake. She had been fighting to remain conscious, but any sounds she heard seemed distant and thin, making her wonder if she wasn't really asleep and dreaming. Then she heard the voices, the whispering. It grew louder, longer, closer. It was coming from outside the bedroom, just down the corridor, toward the front of the apartment. Was it Lee?

She moved her lips and wondered if she had made any sound. It seemed to her she had; only no one came; no one heard her. She tried again and again. Finally she was sure she had called out. The whispering stopped. Someone was listening for her. She garnered all her strength and called once more. Now she heard footsteps; it was more than one person. Lee had come home. Thank God, she thought. She tried to sit up in anticipation, but her body felt so heavy, she didn't seem to have the strength to lift it.

"Lee?"

"No," Tracy said. "It's me and Bob."

"Bob?"

"Hi, Jessie," Bob said.

"Bob? Where's Lee? What time is it?" She found the strength to reach for the clock to feel the numbers. "Where's Lee?" she repeated with a note of hysteria creeping into her voice as soon as she confirmed the time.

"I'm afraid there's been an accident," Bob said.

"Oh no." Jessie stuffed her fist between her teeth and bit down. She shook her head frantically. Tracy was at her side, embracing her.

"He went off the road . . . lost control," Bob continued. "For some reason, he was driving very fast and missed a turn. Henry Young phoned me just a little while ago and asked me to come over here."

"Is he dead? Did he die?"

"He's not dead, but I'm afraid he's in a coma, Jessie," Bob said.

"He'll make it; he'll be all right," Tracy said, tightening her embrace. "Gardner Town Community General is a good hospital."

"He didn't die yet," Jessie said softly. "Then it's not too late. Please take me to him. Please," she begged.

"Now, Jessie, from what Tracy tells me, you've had a very bad day," Bob began. "You're far too weak and this can only make you weaker. It's best you just rest here. There's nothing you can do. Dr. Beezly has been called and is on his way to the hospital now."

"NOOOOO!" Jessie screamed. "NOOOO!"

"Jessie, easy. Please take it easy," Tracy pleaded.

Jessie fought to escape her grip, and with a surge of desperate energy tore out of her arms, but Bob was there to keep her from rising to her feet. He placed his hands on her shoulders and drove her down. She couldn't continue her resistance. She was too weak and so tired. Why was she so tired?

"Please," she begged. "Please. If I don't get there, he'll take him."

"Take him? Who'll take him?" Bob asked.

"I told you," Tracy said. "She's been having some terrible nightmares and hallucinating."

"I'm not hallucinating. . . . I knew this would happen; I knew it," Jessie cried.

"All right, Jessie. All right," Bob coaxed. "You just rest here and we'll keep you up to date."

"We'll stay with you. I promise," Tracy said. Her hands replaced Bob's and pressed down on Jessie's shoulders hard, forcing her to lie back. "That's better. You rest. As soon as you're strong enough, we'll take you to the hospital. Right, Bob?"

"Absolutely," Bob said.

"No, you won't," Jessie said, shaking her head slowly. "No you won't," she repeated, but she couldn't keep awake. She couldn't resist. The darkness outside her crept in over her thoughts and in moments she was asleep.

She had no idea what time it was or how long she had been sleeping when she woke up again, regaining consciousness with a shudder that traveled up her spine. It was as though someone had stuck a finger in her ribs. This impression was so vivid that she sat up and reached out to see if anyone was sitting beside her.

"What?" she asked the darkness. There was no sound, no sense of anyone else's presence.

She was awake, but there was a thick veil of grogginess over her. Every move, every gesture was ponderous, difficult. She felt like she had a weight on her chest, and she groaned with the effort to sit up. It took all her concentration and strength just to swing her legs over the side of the bed. The moment she did so and pulled herself upright, her head began to spin. She started to dry-heave, pressed her hands into her diaphragm, and took deep breaths to drive the urge back down. Even so, she had to lie back again and regain her strength.

Gradually, in wave after wave of resurfacing thoughts and memories, she recalled what had happened and where she was. Realizing how desperate the moment had become, she worked her way into a sitting position again and drove away the dizziness long enough for her to reach for the clock and feel the time. Only an hour and ten minutes had passed.

I have to get to the hospital, she thought. I have to get to Lee before it's too late. She listened keenly for Bob and Tracy. They were still in the house. The murmur of their voices could be heard on the other side of the wall. They were sitting in the kitchen.

As quietly and as carefully as she could, she found the telephone and dialed the operator.

"NTE," the operator sang. The voice was so mechanical, Jessie feared it might be a recording.

"Operator, I'm a blind person," Jessie began. "I need to call a taxicab company. It's an emergency."

"Just a moment, please, and I'll connect you with information," the operator recited. A moment later an almost identical voice came on.

"Information. How can I help you?"

"Operator, I'm a blind person," she began again. "I need to phone for a taxicab. It's an emergency."

"What town are you calling from, ma'am?"

"Gardner."

"Just one moment. I have a Gardner Town Cab Company. Would that be all right?"

"Yes, yes," she said frantically. How can these people stay so calm? she wondered.

"Just a moment." A few seconds later a recording played the telephone number. Why didn't the operator simply dial it for her? She had to listen to the second reciting to get the number memorized. Then she tapped it out slowly to be sure she was accurate.

"Gardner Town Cabs," a gruff voice answered.

"I need a cab right away."

"Address?"

"I want the driver to pick me up in front of the Gardner Town Cemetery," she said. "I'll be at the stone arch in front."

"You're kiddin'?"

"No, sir. Please. It's very important. Tell the driver I'm blind."

"You're blind and you'll be standing at the entrance to the cemetery?"

"Yes, please, please believe me," she begged. He was silent a moment and then in an increasingly skeptical voice continued.

"All right. Where are you going?"

"To the hospital."

"What's your phone number?" he demanded.

"Please," she said. "Don't call me back. My name is Jessie Overstreet. My husband teaches at the high school."

"The new coach? Yeah, that's right. I heard his wife was blind," the dispatcher said as if he were talking to a third party and not to her.

"Yes. My husband's the basketball coach," she said, finally finding a reason to be grateful they were in a small town.

"All right, ma'am. I'm sending someone right out."

"Thank you," she said, and hung the phone up quietly. She listened again. The rhythmic murmuring of Tracy and Bob's voices continued unabated.

Jessie found her shoes and slipped them on. Then, with her heart pounding so hard it nearly took her breath away, she started out. Almost immediately she had a spell of vertigo and nearly fainted. She hugged the wall and battled desperately to remain conscious. The spell passed and she made her way out of the bedroom and into the corridor. She moved as stealthily and as quickly as she could toward the front door, but every few moments the vertigo threatened to return and she had to pause to take deep breaths.

At one point she heard Tracy's laugh and then silence, so she stopped and waited to be sure they weren't getting up. They began to talk again. There was the clink of dishes. She continued on. She nearly forgot the small table in the hallway by the door and almost bumped into it, which would surely have sent the vase on it crashing to the floor. She stopped just in time, felt for it, and then made her way around. When she reached the door, she hesitated, listened again, and then turned the knob in tiny increments so the click of the lock would be unheard.

Everything squeaked in this house, she thought as she started to open the door. She had to wait for them to raise their voices. Fortunately Tracy laughed again, and at that moment Jessie opened the door and slipped into the hallway. The moment she did so, terror filled her heart because images from her nightmare returned. Was the creature on the stairway? What about old man Carter?

She listened and waited in anticipation, half expecting some cold wet hand to seize her by the neck and pull her down. However, the dank stench wasn't strong. Nothing happened. All was still. Relieved, she moved to the heavy oak door and, just as before, took her time opening it. She no longer could hear Tracy and Bob speaking, so there was nothing she could do at this point but take her chances with the squeaks. They wouldn't be able to hear it anyway, she realized. Even so, she didn't open the door an inch more than she had to in order to slip out and onto the porch.

As soon as she was outside, she hurried to the stairway, took hold of the short railing, and stepped down quickly. A wave of nausea washed over her, nearly bringing her to her knees. Her stomach churned. It felt as if the ground beneath her feet was softening. When she straightened up and began to step forward, she had the sense she was walking over a giant mattress, her feet sinking here and there, each time threatening to topple her anew.

Reciting the map of the front yard over and over to herself, she moved as quickly as she could down the slate walk. Lee had described the road and the surroundings in detail to her. Now she had to recall it accurately. At the end of the walkway she made a sharp right turn and stood up straight. She inhaled the cool night air, gasping like a person just saved from drowning. The chill felt good, felt refreshing, helped to revive her. More confident now, with her head high, she took firm steps down the side of the road, estimating the distance she was covering. Every once in a while she stopped and groped in the darkness to see if she could feel the stone arch. She was terrified she would overstep it, get lost, and the cabdriver would miss her and leave.

Finally, realizing she had to be close, she took a chance, stepped off the side of the road, and waved her hands in small circles until her fingers found the rough granite surface of the stone arch. She was standing at the entrance to the cemetery. She breathed relief and turned back toward the road to wait. Almost immediately she heard it.

The silence of the night was broken by that ghoulish, all-too-familiar sound of the shovel striking the earth, lifting, dumping, and striking the earth again. They're preparing for Lee, she thought. They're coming for him. She cowered against the stone arch. Moments later she heard the sound of an automobile and she stepped forward, hoping and praying it was the taxi and not Dr. Beezly or one of the poor souls he had successfully claimed as his own.

— 14 —

Jessie held her breath as the car pulled to a stop in front of her. For a moment she didn't move a muscle. She heard a door open and someone get out.

"You Mrs. Overstreet?" a deep, male voice asked as the man approached.

"Yes."

"Well, I'm Mickey Levine, the cabdriver. You wanted a cab, right?" he asked. She sensed how the setting and situation had confused and unnerved him.

"Yes, yes," she said, and held her hand out. Mickey hesitated and then took it and led her to the taxi.

"Kind of cool out tonight. Don'tcha have a jacket or nothin'?" he asked as he opened the door.

"I'm fine," she said, and got in. "Please," she said, sensing he was standing there and looking around. "Hurry."

"Right." He walked around the cab quickly and got in. "Community General Hospital?"

"Yes. My husband's been in a car accident."

"Oh," he said. "Sorry." Mickey dropped the transmission into drive and shot off. As soon as the car began to

211

move, Jessie sat back in relief. She had made it; she had gotten away. Now she would be able to help Lee, she thought.

"Was it a bad accident?" Mickey asked.

"Yes. He's in a coma."

"Oh boy. That's serious stuff. I know your husband," he added quickly. "I mean, I don't know him personally, but I know him. I was to that ball game the other night, the one with all the fights."

"So was I," she said. "It was horrible."

"Yeah. So how come you was waitin' all alone by the cemetery?" Mickey asked.

"It's a long story," she replied. She certainly wasn't going to start telling it now, and if she did, he might think her crazy and not take her to the hospital.

"I'll bet," he said.

They were quiet the rest of the way, the only sounds being those that came over the squawk box. Just before they turned up the drive to the hospital, Mickey radioed his location. He brought the cab to a stop in front of the main entrance and hopped out to help her.

"Please, take me to the receptionist," she asked. He led her into the hospital and brought her to the circular desk in the lobby, presently manned by one of the volunteers from the service organization known as the Pink Ladies because of the pink cotton coats they wore over their dresses and slacks.

"This is Mrs. Overstreet," Mickey announced as they approached an elderly volunteer. A name tag over her left breast read *Rose*. "Her husband was in an accident," he added.

"Oh dear. Let me see. . . ." Rose flipped the pages of her directory.

"He's the high-school basketball coach, Rose," Mickey said as if he expected everyone would know that.

"Yes, he's in the intensive-care unit."

"Well, someone's got to help her," he added before Jessie could speak for herself. She realized Mickey Levine had taken her on as his responsibility. He leaned closer to Rose. "She's blind."

"Oh dear," Rose repeated. Now completely flustered, she began to push buttons on her intercom, finally coming up with another volunteer, who said she would be right there to help escort Jessie.

"Okay," Mickey said, turning back to Jessie. "I hope things go well."

"Thank you," Jessie said.

"I got a ten-dollar fare to collect," he added after a moment.

"Oh . . . in my haste I forgot to take any money."

"You forgot?"

"I'm sorry. I'll get the money to you as soon as I can."

"It don't bother me, but Tony, he's a pain in the rear, if you know what I mean. Maybe someone can loan you some money."

He looked at Rose, but she still looked overwhelmed.

"I don't know anyone here," Jessie said. "I'll get it to you. I promise."

"I'll call Tony and see what he wants me to do." Mickey shook his head and walked off to radio the dispatcher. A moment later a tall, thin black woman in her early thirties arrived to escort Jessie. She took her to the elevator and they went up to intensive care, where she introduced Jessie to Sue Martin, the head nurse.

"How is he?" Jessie asked frantically.

"I'm afraid there's not much of a change. He suffered a serious head injury. You will have to wait for Dr.

Beezly to return in order to get more detailed information," she added. "He's gone to confer with the radiologist."

"NO," Jessie cried, pulling back.

"Pardon?"

Jessie's sudden outburst caught the otherwise efficient and imposing-looking head nurse by surprise. She was a tall, lean woman with sharp facial features.

"I don't want Dr. Beezly near my husband. I don't want him near him. DO YOU UNDERSTAND?" Jessie shouted. She had her hands clenched into fists and pressed them against her bosom.

"Please, Mrs. Overstreet," Sue Martin said, regaining her composure quickly. "Keep your voice down. You're in the intensive-care unit. These patients are critical," she snapped, her voice hard, cold.

"I'm sorry," Jessie said, catching her breath. "I'm sorry. I just want it understood that Dr. Beezly is not to go near my husband."

"It was my understanding that he was your family doctor," Sue replied.

"That's not true. Take me to my husband. Please. Take me to him," she begged.

"I'll take you to him, but I must insist you control yourself. You can easily disturb one of our other patients."

"I'll behave. I promise," Jessie said.

Sue Martin seemed content with her assertion of authority. She took Jessie's hand and walked her down to the end of the intensive-care unit and turned her into a room.

"Please," Jessie said. "Put my hand on his."

Sue did so and then brought her a chair.

"Thank you."

"Isn't someone here with you, Mrs. Overstreet?" Sue Martin asked.

"No," Jessie said, her voice cracking. Lee's palm still felt warm, but the tips of his fingers felt cold. Death was creeping over him slowly, she thought. And then she thought, This is Dr. Beezly's doing. Whatever's happening to Lee now is his design.

"Lee," she whispered. She ran her fingers up his arm until she reached his face and touched his lips. They felt so dry and cool. "Fight back, honey. Don't let them take you from me? Fight them, Lee. Please listen to me, darling, please," she said.

Sue Martin, listened for a moment and then smirked before turning away. She walked back to her station, shaking her head. The escort had remained to talk to Janet Paulet, another nurse.

"How did she get here?" Sue asked her.

"Taxicab. She didn't have any money to pay him either and he's fit to be tied. His boss told him to stay here until he gets paid," Janet said.

"This is ridiculous," Sue Martin said. "A hysterical blind woman wandering about on her own," she muttered, and went back to her reports. Occasionally she looked up to gaze toward Lee and Jessie. Jessie had her forehead on Lee's arm now and looked like she was chanting something.

Sue Martin lifted the phone and dialed radiology.

"Is Dr. Beezly still there?" she inquired quickly. After a moment she added, "Well, would you please tell him Mrs. Overstreet has arrived and has given me instructions not to let him near her husband. The woman looks like she is on the verge of a nervous breakdown."

Sue hung up the receiver. Jessie was standing now and holding Lee's hand against her bosom. She had her head back and looked like she was praying. A moment later the door was opened and Tracy and Bob Baker entered. Tracy spotted Jessie first and the two started toward her.

"Just a minute," Sue Martin said, coming around her desk. "Can I help you?"

"We've come after Mrs. Overstreet," Bob said. "We were looking after her and didn't know she had gone off on her own."

"Oh. I was wondering why a blind woman was by herself like this."

"She's not very well," Tracy said softly. Sue's eyes grew narrow. "She's recently suffered a nervous breakdown and now this."

"I thought so. She came in here quite hysterical and demanded I keep Dr. Beezly away from her husband," Sue said.

"Oh no. Lee Overstreet always had a high degree of respect and admiration for Dr. Beezly. In fact, they've become good friends," Bob said. "I can vouch for that. He teaches with me at the high school."

"Well, I was surprised when Mrs. Overstreet was so adamant. I had never heard a complaint about Dr. Beezly before."

As if he were waiting in the wings to hear his name mentioned, Dr. Beezly came through the door. He exchanged a quick, icy gaze with Bob before smiling at Tracy and the head nurse.

"What seems to be the problem?" he asked, approaching.

"Apparently Jessie called a cab without our knowing and then snuck out of the house and came here. She's made a bit of a scene already," Bob explained.

"I handled it," Sue Martin assured them, "but if she's

having a nervous breakdown . . ."

"We've got to get her out of here quickly and quietly," Dr. Beezly said. "I've been treating her for severe depression. Perhaps," he said, looking at the Bakers, "I ought to have her admitted. At least for a day or so. She needs to be watched. Especially under these circumstances. Her loss of sight is the result of a previous automobile accident," he explained to the head nurse. "And the trauma of her husband being in another car accident . . ."

"There are no other family members?" Sue Martin asked.

"Not in the community. I have both his and her parents' phone numbers and will be calling them soon," Dr. Beezly said.

"What do you want us to do?" Bob asked.

"Get her out as quickly and as quietly as you can. I'll have admitting assign her a bed. For the moment," the doctor said, looking toward Jessie, "it's probably better that she doesn't know I'm here. We don't want her to cause a scene in intensive care."

"Thank you, Doctor," Sue Martin said. "That's wise. I'll help you," she added, looking at the Bakers. She, Tracy, and Bob walked toward Jessie.

Just before they arrived, Jessie felt a cold draft on the back of her neck and turned toward them sharply. She did it with such definiteness, it brought a look of surprise to the nurse's face and a gasp to Tracy's lips. It was as though Jessie had miraculously regained her sight. Even though her head was directed at them, however, her eyes remained dull, lifeless.

"Jessie," Tracy said, reaching her first and taking her hand into hers. "Why did you sneak away like that? You gave Bob and me some fright."

"Get away from me. Get away." Jessie pulled her hand from Tracy's. "Leave us alone. Leave us alone," she repeated, raising her voice sufficiently to set the head nurse moving.

"Mrs. Overstreet, you will have to leave now. This is intensive care. You're permitted only a short visit," Sue Martin said.

"No," Jessie said, shaking her head. "I must stay with him, protect him. Please."

"You can't do anything for him right now, Mrs. Overstreet, and as I told you before, we have many critically ill patients in here. Please. You can return later."

"I won't make a sound. I won't do anything. I'll just sit here and hold his hand. I swear it," Jessie pleaded.

"Mrs. Overstreet . . ."

"I must stay with him," Jessie said firmly. "If I don't, they will take him from me. Don't you understand?" she insisted, raising her voice again. Sue Martin signaled another nurse, who came across the room quickly.

"You're making things much more difficult for everyone, Mrs. Overstreet, including your husband," Sue Martin said.

"Really, Jessie, you are," Tracy added. "Bob and I are here to be with you and—"

"NOOOOO," Jessie cried. She stood up and held her hands out to ward them off.

"Oh Jesus," Sue Martin said. She and her assistant moved forward and seized Jessie firmly at the upper arms and waist. "If you don't walk out, Mrs. Overstreet, we will carry you out."

Jessie started to resist, but their grips tightened.

"You don't understand," she cried.

"We understand, Mrs. Overstreet. Really we do. We

know what you're going through." They started her forward.

"You have no idea." Jessie couldn't stop them from leading her away. "Dr. Beezly is going to take my husband's soul. He's going to put another soul in him, an evil soul. They're digging up the grave right now," she whispered. The two nurses looked at each other and then at Tracy and Bob, who shook their heads sadly.

"Just a little bit farther, Mrs. Overstreet," Sue Martin said. "You can wait with your friends downstairs. If there's any change whatsoever, we'll call you."

"I want another doctor. Will you call another doctor?" she pleaded through her tears.

"Of course," Sue Martin said. "I'll do that right away," she said, but Jessie heard her condescension.

"No, you won't. You don't believe me. Maybe you're one of them," she said weakly. It was all overwhelming her again. Her legs felt so soft, her body wilting like a flower without water or sunlight. A deep sadness filled her. It was as if the darkness in her eyes had spread like a rash over her body, making her other senses just as dull and ineffective. She could barely feel anything or hear anything. The world around her began to drift away, leaving her alone in some dark corner, washed in a shadow and becoming little more than a shadow herself.

Just before they reached the door, she lost consciousness.

She had no idea where she was when she awoke. She felt she was adrift in space, floating in some dark limbo. She heard the murmur of strange voices. There was the rattle of wheels, the click of footsteps. Someone's thin laugh threaded its way through the tapestry of confusion.

She lifted her hands and began to explore her immediate surroundings. She felt a starched, stiff bed sheet over her body. Gradually the scents of the hospital began to announce themselves clearly and she remembered.

She groaned and tried to turn, but found she had been strapped into the bed. One strap was over her thighs and one was over her ankles. She struggled to get her hands over the strap across her thighs to find where it was fastened, but she discovered no way to release herself.

How had she gotten here? Who put her here? She labored to recall the final moments before she lost consciousness and remembered she had been with Lee.

Lee!

"Help!" she cried. "Someone, please . . . help!"

She heard a rush of footsteps outside the door of the room and moments later a soft, female voice.

"It's all right, Mrs. Overstreet. It's all right," the nurse said, and took her hand. She felt her place her other hand over her forehead and wipe back some strands of hair.

"Where am I? What happened to me?"

"You're in the hospital. You fainted in the intensive-care unit, but there's nothing seriously wrong with you. Dr. Beezly checked you over."

"Oh no," Jessie said weakly. "Why am I strapped in?"

"It's just a precaution, Mrs. Overstreet. We don't want you trying to get up and falling. You can hurt yourself seriously doing that. You're too weak and unstable right now. But after a day or so . . ."

"It will be too late by then," Jessie said. "Please, let me get up."

"How about we get something in your stomach . . . some nice hot tea, some oatmeal—"

"I'm not hungry. I just have to get up and get back to my husband," Jessie replied, and struggled to sit up.

"That's all right. You just get something into your stomach anyway. That's the fastest way for you to regain your strength, and you want to regain your strength, don't you?" the nurse asked as if she were talking to an infant.

"Yes, yes," Jessie said. They weren't listening; no one would listen.

"Good." The nurse fluffed up her pillow and set it behind her so she could sit up comfortably.

"Please unfasten me," Jessie begged again.

"For the time being, let's just leave things this way. If you need to go to the bathroom, I'll bring you the bedpan."

"No, I need to get up."

"In due time."

"I'm strong enough. Really."

"Now, now, Mrs. Overstreet. Do you want Dr. Beezly to be angry with us? Let me get you something to eat and then you will feel better, okay?"

Jessie nodded and sighed. She lowered her head. It was no use, no use. What was it her father always said? "A branch that doesn't bend, breaks."

"Now there's a good girl," the nurse said. "Your friends wanted me to tell you that they would be back as soon as they could and they would keep you informed about your husband's condition," she added.

"They don't have to," Jessie said quietly, her voice soaked in defeat. "I know his condition. He's going to die, if he's not already dead."

"Oh, you must not think that way, Mrs. Overstreet. You must have faith. Are you a Catholic?" she asked.

"Not a practicing one," Jessie replied.

"Well, Father Rush is here visiting patients. Would you like me to send him in to see you?" the nurse asked. "He's a very nice man. I happen to be a Catholic, too," the nurse added.

Jessie didn't reply. She just fell back against the pillows.

"I'll send him by," the nurse said, and left.

Jessie felt herself drifting off again. The weight of the battle was too much. She thought about all that had happened, all the warnings they had had: the things she had heard, had sensed, and had felt. Lee should have listened. "He should have listened," she murmured.

"Who should have listened, Mrs. Overstreet?" a deep, strong voice asked. At first she thought she had imagined it, but then she felt the warm hand over hers.

"What?"

"I'm Father Rush," the man said. "How are you doing, Mrs. Overstreet?"

"Father Rush?" Jessie started to sit up again.

"Now, now, take it easy," he said softly. "I understand you're having a bad time of it. Your husband was in a car accident, I know." He continued to pat her hand softly.

"Oh Father," Jessie said. "You don't know. Satan is here. The devil is here to take him."

The priest's fingers stopped stroking hers, but his hand lingered over her palm. Jessie seized his hand quickly and squeezed.

"You must believe me, Father. You must."

"You're quite overwrought, Mrs. Overstreet. Just try to relax a bit."

"Father . . ."

"I'm here. I'm listening to you," the priest said calmly, but before Jessie could go on, the nurse returned.

"Oh, you've got her sitting up, Father. That's good," she said. "I've brought her some tea and hot oatmeal."

"Very good."

"I don't want to eat. Please, I—"

"You should get something hot in your stomach, Mrs. Overstreet," the priest said.

"All right, all right. I'll eat if you will stay and listen to me."

"I'm not going anywhere," he said. She could hear the amusement in his voice. Maybe he wasn't a priest; maybe he was one of them. . . .

She pressed her palm into his again and held it there as tightly as she could, concentrating, searching, listening for the voices, reaching deeply. There was nothing dark, nothing sinister.

The nurse set up the bed table.

"Do you want me to feed you, Mrs. Overstreet?" she asked.

"No, no. I can feed myself. I'm not a helpless child," she snapped. A thread of hope renewed her strength. She took a spoonful of oatmeal and then sipped some tea.

"That's a good girl," the nurse said. "I'll be right outside, Father, if you should need me."

"We've got things under control here, Suzanne," he said. "Mrs. Overstreet is fine."

Jessie listened for the nurse's departing footsteps. The moment she was gone, she dropped her spoon and turned to the priest.

"Father, my husband is in great danger if he is not already lost," she began. "You must believe me. You're my last hope."

"I'm here to help you, my dear," he said.

"You believe in the devil, in Satan's existence, don't you, Father?"

"Yes, I do."

"Can he be defeated? Is there anything we can do to overcome his hold on us?" she asked desperately.

"Lead a good life, keep our fortress strong, love the Lord, and do His bidding. The devil can't plant his seeds of evil in a garden of goodness."

"But we all sin, Father."

"Alas, we do, but we must be remorseful and repent, and then the devil is driven out of our hearts. I will pray with you, my dear," he said. "Together we will ask the Lord for forgiveness."

"Father, I will do that, but we must do something to keep the devil away from my husband now, and my husband can't pray for forgiveness. He's in a coma."

"The Lord understands that, my child. We will pray for him, and I assure you, God will listen."

"No, Father," Jessie insisted, "it's too late for only prayer. We must do more."

"Do more?"

"Father, I beg you. Don't think I'm crazy."

"You're not crazy. You're upset. I understand and—"

"No, you don't, Father. Let me tell you all of it," she said, and began with the first night they had arrived and the voices she had heard wailing in the cemetery.

"I'm not sure I quite understand what you mean when you say the devil is exchanging souls, Mrs. Overstreet," Father Rush said after Jessie had brought him up to date. She had been encouraged by the way he sat quietly and listened, never interrupting, never trying to tell her she was mistaken or hallucinating. He sounded thoughtful, concerned, and nowhere near as skeptical as she had feared.

He was especially attentive when she had described

the way Dr. Beezly had metamorphosed during his
examination of her, and how Satan had tried to rape
her. Her description of the way she envisioned Satan
had apparently struck a note with the priest. Furthermore
he didn't challenge or express incredulity when she told
him Dr. Beezly was evil.

"Somehow he is replacing the souls of these people
with souls from hell. Maybe . . . maybe it's the way
the devil rewards those who are most loyal to him in
hell. And that's why these people who have been close
to death or died are so different afterward. I certainly
sensed it in Marjorie Young and Tracy sensed it in her
husband. I'm sure her time is coming, too. I've been
doing a lot of thinking about it ever since I realized why
Mr. Carter was out there digging up the graves and why
I heard the wail of the dead."

She reached out and found the priest's hand. Seizing
it, she cried, "I don't know why, but God has given me
this power."

"Perhaps for this very thing," Father Rush said softly.

"Then you do believe me. You do."

"Let me say that I have been disturbed by many things
in our community over the past year or so."

"And Dr. Beezly?"

Father Rush was quiet for a long moment. Jessie was
afraid he wouldn't respond.

"Father?"

"I have had troubling feelings about him. Yes," he
confessed.

Jessie breathed with relief. She had finally found an
ally.

"Oh Father. It's not too late. I know it. What can we
do? How can we keep the devil away from my husband

and perhaps save those souls he has taken?"

"I am not an expert in demonology, but I have some knowledge of it. Perhaps holy water," he mused aloud.

"Holy water?"

"Yes. The devil is not supposed to be able to abide it."

"Then . . . if we put it around Lee's bed, we can keep the devil away from him?"

"Perhaps."

"Oh Father. Let's do it. Please," she begged. "If Dr. Beezly is unable to approach my husband, that will be proof, won't it?"

"To us certainly."

"Father, will you help me? Will you do it?"

"I will try," he said. He stood up. "I'll go to the church and get the holy water and return. Until then don't say anything to anyone. Finish your food and rest."

"Will you hurry, Father? Will you?"

"I'll be back as quickly as I can, but remember, we don't want to attract attention and warn the evil souls around us," he said. He patted her on the hand. "Pray, my child. Pray," he said, and left.

She ate a few more spoonfuls of oatmeal and drank some tea. Then she lay back against the pillows. The nurse returned.

"Oh, that's good. You've eaten some of it. Now you just rest, and before long you will feel much better. Isn't Father Rush a nice man?" she said, taking the tray.

"Yes. How old a man is he?"

"Oh . . . I'd say he's in his fifties."

"How long has he been in this community?"

"Almost twenty years, I think," she said, and then she laughed.

"What's funny?"

"Oh, it's just the way everyone in the parish puts it, those who have lived here for years and years, that is."

"Puts what?"

"Father Rush's arrival. They came about the same time, you know."

"They?"

"A doctor of the body and a doctor of the soul. That's the way the parish puts it."

"A doctor of the body and a doctor of the soul?"

"Dr. Beezly and Father Rush. One day one was here; the next day the other. Now you just lie back and rest. I'll be right outside if you need anything. Here's the buzzer," she said, putting the button in Jessie's hand.

But Jessie didn't feel it; she didn't feel anything.

— 15 —

Weak with disappointment and still strapped firmly in the hospital bed, Jessie lay there as still as a corpse. For all the good she was able to do Lee and herself, she might as well be dead, she thought. Why was the devil so powerful? Why could he reach almost anywhere he wanted in order to get his way? Where was God?

Father Rush had told her that God permitted the devil to exist so that man could make moral choices. In rejecting evil, man became good and was embraced by God. But after what the nurse had told her, Jessie thought the priest was simply justifying the existence of evil.

And yet she had to wonder why she had been given this power, this ability to see and hear beyond. Was it meant to be some exquisite torment? What were her great sins? Why was she being punished so? She knew that Lee believed he was being punished for his sins when they had had their accident and she had been hurt so seriously. It was part of the reason why she had accepted her fate so stoically: she knew how much he blamed himself and how the weight of that guilt could destroy him.

Now he was being destroyed by the Prince of Evil himself and there was nothing anyone could do. Maybe it was best she died with him, she thought. Leave this world, a world Satan was claiming. If she were to believe tradition, Satan had tried to claim the world after God had first created it and had created Paradise and Adam and Eve. The devil had been defeated, but not before he had corrupted Adam and Eve and had left enough of himself behind to set the stage for his second attempt. This was the beginning of that new attempt, and Lee, she, and the others were the first to fall victim.

She was too weak and frustrated to cry, almost too weak to care. Let sleep come. Let it all end, she thought.

She wasn't sure how much time had passed, but suddenly she felt someone unfastening the belts that strapped her into the bed. In moments her thighs and legs were free. She sat up quickly, about to scream. Father Rush put his hand over her mouth.

"Shh," he said. "We don't want anyone to hear or know what we are about to do."

Her heart pounded. The evil ones were going to make sure she presented no more danger to them. Surely that was their purpose now.

Father Rush took his hand from her mouth and pulled back her blanket so she would be able to get out of bed. Then he went to the closet and got her clothes.

"I'll watch at the door while you get dressed," he said, setting the clothing on the bed. "Hurry. The nurses are taking a break."

Jessie said nothing; she hadn't moved.

"You've known Dr. Beezly ever since he arrived here, haven't you?" she asked quickly.

"Yes."

"My nurse told me you both arrived around the same time," she said in an accusatory tone.

"Yes, we did, and for a long time—actually until up to a year or so ago—Dr. Beezly and I were very good friends. We often dined together, and he was a member of my church. He was a warm person, compassionate, and very intelligent. We had many philosophical and theological discussions."

"Then why are you doing this?" she demanded. "Dr. Beezly is highly respected in this community. Aren't you afraid you will get into trouble or look foolish?"

"Those who do the work of God can never look foolish," he replied. "I know there are many who don't believe the devil exists the way we believe he exists; there are even many in the Mother Church who don't, but I have reason to know it is so," he added softly.

"What reason? My story?"

"No." He returned to the side of the bed and took her hand into his. "I myself have been tempted by Satan," he confessed.

"How?" she asked. The priest was quiet for a long moment.

"All of us, being mortal, have our weaknesses, even priests."

"And even Dr. Beezly?"

"Oh yes. He was a man who had his own weaknesses and sins, some more serious than others, perhaps. Perhaps there were sins he didn't want to confess, sins he hadn't repented.

"Suddenly he stopped coming to church, and in fact, those whom he had treated for serious injuries or illnesses stopped coming as well. I found him a changed man, yet a man who still had a major influence on others, even me."

"How?" Jessie asked.

"Dr. Beezly developed an uncanny knack for knowing what our weaknesses were and finding ways to tempt us to damnation through those weaknesses. That's what I meant when I told you I've had troubling feelings about him, especially during the past year."

Jessie still didn't move.

"You don't trust me, I see. I can't blame you. Under the circumstances, if I were you, I would probably be the same way. Is there anything I can do to convince you that I have reason to believe your story?"

Jessie thought.

"What was your weakness, the weakness Dr. Beezly appealed to and almost caused you to damn your soul?"

Father Rush hesitated.

"I should confess only to another ordained priest," he said. And then, after a moment, in a low voice, he added, "There was . . . is . . . a married woman in town. I have always had strong romantic desires for her. Of course I told no one, least of all Dr. Beezly. But one night he invited me to his home for dinner. He hadn't been coming to church and we hadn't seen each other for so long that I readily accepted the invitation. She was there without her husband, and never did she look more beautiful, more enticing.

"I drank some wine . . . too much wine, and suddenly she became amorous and Beezly left us alone. Only my faith gave me the strength to resist."

"If you hadn't," Jessie said, "you would probably have become a candidate for a deadly resurrection yourself and been a victim of an accident or some serious illness."

"Yes," Father Rush said. "Now, because of you and the things you have told me, I believe that. Up to now my own failures, weaknesses, have prevented me from helping the people I should have helped. I was blinded by my own sinfulness. I have not been a good soldier of the Lord," he lamented. "And for that I am most dearly sorry."

Jessie reached out and found his face. She moved the tips of her fingers over his cheeks and felt his tears.

"We should hurry," he whispered. "I have brought the holy water."

"Yes." She turned herself out of the bed and he went to the doorway to stand guard until she got dressed.

When she was ready, he took her hand and brought her to the door.

"Wait," he cautioned. One of the nurses at the station began to come their way. Fortunately she turned into another room about halfway down and all looked clear. Father Rush stepped forward and led Jessie down the corridor toward the elevator. When the doors opened, they stepped in and he pressed the button for the floor on which the intensive-care unit was located.

"The head nurse will wonder what I'm doing back there," Jessie cautioned.

"There's been a shift change by now. It will be a new head nurse."

They got out and went to the doors of intensive care. As Father Rush had predicted, there was a new head nurse on duty, and she knew him well.

"Good evening, Laurie," Father Rush began. "You have a Mr. Overstreet here?"

"Yes, Father." From the way Laurie Smith looked at Jessie and then quizzically at him, the priest knew she had been told about her.

"Everything's fine now," he said quickly. "I've volunteered to escort Mrs. Overstreet here to see her husband.

We want to pray at his bedside. If that's all right with you," he added diplomatically.

"Oh. Of course, Father. Right this way."

"How is my husband?" Jessie asked. "Has there been any change?"

"I'm sorry, no. But his vital signs remain good," she added.

"We can be thankful for that," Father Rush said. "We'll be all right," he whispered when they arrived at Lee's bedside. Laurie Smith looked at Jessie again and then nodded. As soon as she walked off, the priest took out his bottle of holy water.

"I'm going to encircle your husband's bed," he told Jessie. She took Lee's hand in hers and waited while the priest went around, offering a prayer in Latin as he sprinkled the holy water. Then he sprinkled some over Lee. After that, he joined with Jessie and they both bowed their heads to pray. But before they were finished, Jessie heard those now-all-too-familiar footsteps.

"Michael, I should have known you would do something like this," Dr. Beezly said as he came up behind them. Jessie and Father Rush stood up and turned his way, Jessie clinging tightly to the priest. "You've been a naughty little clergyman, Michael." He waved his right forefinger as if he were talking to a bad little boy. "You have my nurses downstairs quite frantic. Really, Michael, stealing away a patient like this." He clicked his lips and shook his head.

"You're the one who's been stealing people away," Father Rush replied.

"Oh no. Don't tell me you're listening to anything this woman says, Michael." Dr. Beezly grimaced and shook his head. "She's in the midst of a serious nervous breakdown," he said as Laurie Smith came up beside him.

"Is anything wrong, Doctor?" she asked.

"I'm afraid Father Rush has gone beyond the call of duty, Laurie. He has taken Mrs. Overstreet out of her room where she had been restrained for her own good, and brought her up here without the nurses on the floor knowing."

"Oh dear," the nurse said. "I had no idea."

"Of course you didn't. Who would think our good Father Rush capable of anything evil?" Dr. Beezly smiled.

"You would certainly," Father Rush said sharply. Dr. Beezly's smile faded quickly. His eyes became cold, sharp, and his lips tightened into a pencil-thin line. Then his smile returned, only this time it was chilling, more like the grimace drawn on the face of a corpse by the hand of death itself.

"You will be so good as to take Mrs. Overstreet back to her room please, Father Rush," he commanded.

"Mrs. Overstreet doesn't want to go back to that room. She doesn't need any of your treatments, Doctor."

"I can't force her to listen," Dr. Beezly said. "But you're making a mistake and doing her a terrible disservice by encouraging her hallucinations. In any case I have to examine my patient."

"Of course," Father Rush replied, and pulled Jessie gently to the side. She tightened her grip on his hand. Her heart began to pound in anticipation.

"Father . . ."

"It's all right," he whispered.

Dr. Beezly watched them suspiciously for a moment and then started toward the bed. He stopped abruptly a foot away and brought his hands to his face as if he had gotten too close to a blazing fire. Then he moaned.

"Are you all right, Doctor?" Laurie Smith asked quickly.

"Yes, are you all right?" Father Rush chorused.

"What's happening?" Jessie demanded.

"Dr. Beezly isn't feeling well himself," Father Rush said.

Beezly lowered his hands from his face and backed away. His skin looked sunburned. His mouth twisted up into his cheek and his eyes blazed in rage.

"Doctor?" Laurie Smith said. She pressed her hand against her bosom and stepped away from him.

"You've made a tragic mistake interfering with me, Michael," the doctor said in a loud whisper.

"I think not, Dr. Beezly. In fact, I think it would have been a tragic mistake had I not," Father Rush replied.

Beezly glared at him a moment and then made a second attempt to approach Lee. This time he pulled his hand back as if he had touched an inferno. He groaned in fury.

"Doctor?" Laurie Smith said, coming to his side.

"It's all right," Beezly muttered, rubbing his hand. "I've forgotten something. I'll return," he added, and quickly turned to walk out of the intensive-care unit. They watched him pound his way down the floor and out the double doors.

"He's gone." Father Rush released the air he held in his lungs. "The Lord be praised."

"But he will return," Jessie warned. "We must get to the cemetery."

"The cemetery? Why?" Father Rush asked.

"To lock the door. Please, take me there and bring your holy water," Jessie pleaded.

"What's going on here?" Laurie Smith asked, her face twisted with confusion. "Cemetery? Holy water? What happened to Dr. Beezly? I don't understand."

"You don't have to understand. Just don't move my husband from this bed," Jessie commanded, "or you will bring about his death for sure. No matter what Dr. Beezly asks. Please. Anyway, he's not my doctor."

Laurie looked at Father Rush.

"Not her doctor?"

"That's correct. I'm asking on Mrs. Overstreet's behalf, too, Laurie. There is nothing wrong with this woman other than that she suffers from blindness. She doesn't want Dr. Beezly treating her husband. Is that clear?"

"Well . . . I . . . what should we do in case—"

"Call Dr. Ross. Tell him Mrs. Overstreet would like him to take over her husband's case. I'll vouch for everything that's been said here."

"Okay." Laurie Smith shrugged. "I certainly don't want to get involved in any doctor-patient spats."

"Thank you," Father Rush said.

"We should hurry," Jessie whispered. Father Rush started to lead her away. "Wait," she said, turning back toward Lee. She made her way to the bed and found his hand. She held it to her lips and then placed it gently at his side, stroking his hair as she did so. Father Rush came up beside her.

"He'll be all right," he said.

"Yes. Soon. As soon as we get to the cemetery and make sure Beezly can't have his way," Jessie replied, and they left the intensive-care unit as quickly as they could.

No one interfered with their leaving the hospital. Father Rush led Jessie to his car in the parking lot. Then they drove off into the night.

"About four months ago," Father Rush said as they drove toward the cemetery, "a man in town came to me to complain about how his son had changed. The boy had been in a motorcycle accident and had nearly died."

"Dr. Beezly had treated him?"

"Yes. The man wasn't a regular churchgoer. He was raising the boy on his own ever since his wife had died. Up to that time he hadn't had serious problems with his son. Oh, he was a bit of a Huckleberry Finn, just like the rest of the boys his age in this town, but he began to degenerate rapidly—stealing, drinking, smoking dope, staying out until all hours of the night. That sort of thing. He became a serious discipline problem in school, too, and the former basketball coach, Kurt Andersen, was going to boot him off his team."

"His name was Benson," Jessie said quickly.

"Yes. How did you know?"

She described the incident with the truck.

"I should have taken him and the things he had said more seriously," Father Rush said with regret. "He insisted his son was not his son, but Benson was drinking heavily and I attributed it to that. If I had listened . . ."

"Let's hope we're not too late," Jessie said.

They were both silent for a while, each saying his private prayer. When they arrived at the cemetery, Father Rush drove through the gate slowly. Jessie asked him to stop.

"I need to get out to listen," she said.

"Okay. I have a flashlight in the glove compartment."

"What are we looking for exactly?" he asked after they had both gotten out.

"An open grave," Jessie said. She held his hand and signaled him to be quiet for a moment as she focused her concentration on the dark and gloomy surroundings. Soon she heard the whispering. It grew louder, some of the voices warning her, some of them urging her forward.

"They know they have been violated," she suddenly said. "That's what I've heard them complaining about ever since I arrived."

"Who?"

"The dead. Let's go forward, to the right."

She and Father Rush began to walk down one of the paths. An overcast sky had shut out the moonlight and stars. To Father Rush the darkness around them seemed more like fog filled with soot—grimy, thick, all-encompassing. The thin ray of light emanating from his small flashlight barely penetrated the dense shroud of night. It sliced the darkness, but once they moved through it, the sheet of black fell behind and around them with the finality of a stage curtain at the end of a play.

Jessie hesitated and tilted her head. Someone, some decrepit soul of the damned was wailing and scratching at the inside of its decomposing coffin. The sound of its nails grinding along the walls of its death cell sent chills down her back, chills that turned into slithering snakes of ice. She squeezed Father Rush's hand tighter and stopped again.

"What is it?" he asked, his own heart now pounding so hard he could barely get up enough breath to be heard.

"Directly ahead," Jessie whispered.

He lifted the flashlight and aimed its beam. Twenty yards or so in front of them an old tombstone leaned precariously, its pale white surface now glimmering under his light like a giant old tooth. He lowered the beam slowly and saw the gaping hole before it.

"Yes," he said in a whisper, too. "The grave has been dug up."

"Take us there. Quickly," Jessie ordered.

The priest moved himself and her forward, stumbling over some rocks. When they reached the foot of the grave, he stopped and pointed his light down. The uncovered coffin was gray with decomposition. Through the holes that had formed like cancers in its surface, he could see the gleaming dust of bones.

"The coffin is uncovered," he said.

"Is the lid still down?" Jessie asked.

"Yes."

"Then we're not too late. The holy water," Jessie said. "Quickly. Cast it over the coffin and you will surely shut the door on this soul from hell and keep Beezly from resurrecting it."

"Yes, yes," Father Rush said, and shifted the flashlight to his other hand so he could dig into his pocket to produce the bottle of holy water; but as he raised his head to begin a prayer, they suddenly heard a gruff voice behind them.

They both turned and Father Rush directed the beam of light before them. It fell on old man Carter, who stood with his pickax in hand. It was as if he had been born of night itself, just instantly appearing.

To Father Rush the old man looked like a corpse that had crawled out of an open grave. His face seemed emaciated with its sunken cheeks and deep-set eyes now two yellowish orbs sucked back into the sockets of his skull. The bones of his jaw and his forehead looked like they would burst out of the thin layer of skin that covered them. His lips were dark purple and writhing like worms on a sidewalk.

Jessie inhaled the putrescent stench she had smelled in the hallway of the DeGroot house before.

"It's Mr. Carter, isn't it?" she asked in a whisper.

"Yes," Father Rush replied quickly.

"What are ya doin' here, Father?" old man Carter demanded in a voice that sounded like a death rattle.

"Did you dig up this grave, Mr. Carter?" Father Rush asked.

"It's no business of yours what's done in this cemetery. This ain't the church's cemetery no more," Carter said.

"You've been doing the bidding of the devil himself," Father Rush said. "We're here to put an end to it."

Old man Carter threw his head back so sharply it looked like it might roll off his neck. His Adam's apple thumped against the wall of skin as he released a bone-chilling, thin laugh that reverberated through the cemetery. Jessie pressed her hands to her ears quickly. All the voices around her cried in a chorus of pain.

"Put an end to it? You?" Carter laughed again. "A man who is a sinner himself, whose heart is rotten with lust?"

Father Rush held his ground. Sternly, his eyes fixed on the decrepit old man before him, he raised his bottle of holy water and declared, "You shall not open the portals of hell."

And then, in a loud voice, he cried, "SATAN, GET THEE BEHIND ME!"

He brought his arm back to cast the water over old man Carter, but the aged cemetery caretaker suddenly moved with the speed of a man a quarter of his age. He raised his pickax and stepped forward just as Father Rush began to sprinkle the water. Jessie sensed the confrontation and cried out as she retreated a few steps.

Some drops splashed on the old man's face. He yowled like a wolf whose leg had been clamped in the teeth of an iron trap, but his forward motion brought the pickax down sharply, striking the priest in his chest, just over his heart, the sharp end of the iron tool ripping into the organ. Father Rush turned in agony and fell against the retreating Jessie, his body knocking her back. His weight was too much and she fell, along with him, down into the open grave, both of them landing on the crumbling coffin, smashing through the rotted wood.

Above them, old man Carter writhed in agony as the drops of holy water singed and burned. The fire it created spread rapidly through his face and drew a line of flame down his chest, tearing it apart. He fell to his knees and quickly choked on his thickening, blackened tongue. Instantly his body fell prey to the degeneration held back by the evil soul that had been housed within. It turned to dust, smoking.

In moments the tiny cloud was swallowed by the darkness, and then an air of funeral quiet was restored to this small village of the dead.

— *16* —

Jessie moaned. She wasn't in pain so much as she was twisted awkwardly, her body half in and half out of the rotting coffin. Father Rush lay beside her on his back, his left arm draped over her waist. The stench of damp earth, rotting bones, and newly spilled blood enveloped her and caused her to choke and gag on her own breath. Her right shoulder had taken the full brunt of the fall, and a dull ache began to radiate down her arm and up her neck. She moaned again and tried to turn away from the priest, whose deadly stillness and silence filled her with renewed terror.

Slowly she was able to twist herself around and then began to disengage her body from his. She lifted his arm away and struggled into a sitting position.

"Father?"

There was no response. Gradually, with the caution of a munitions expert attempting to disarm a bomb, she inched her fingers forward over the clergyman's body. The handle of the pickax stopped her. She gasped and then followed it down to where the head of it joined with the priest's body. The tips of her fingers tapped around his opened chest like a giant spider dancing over a hot stove. Still lodged in his breast, the iron tool felt warm and wet. She realized she was gliding her fingers through Father Rush's trickling blood and screamed.

Trapped as she was in the open grave, her cry reverberated into the night. It echoed in her own mind, sounding like a second and then a third scream. Groping about, she felt the sides of the grave and pulled herself away from the priest's body. She pressed her cheek against the cool earth and cried, her body shaking. Finally getting hold of herself, she first got to her knees and then, bracing herself against the side of the grave, lifted herself into a standing position.

It was a deep grave, nearly six feet down. She would have to find some footing in order to pull herself out, she thought, and began to kick at the surrounding wall of earth. Her right arm and shoulder ached so, she feared she wouldn't have the strength, but once she realized she had some support, she stepped up and moved her hand over the ground, searching for something to grab.

Suddenly she felt a hand over hers. Thinking it was old man Carter's, she started to pull hers away, but the fingers tightened quickly. She gasped and then screamed, yet the fingers clung to her own.

"Easy," she heard a voice say. "I'll help you out."

Her mind reeled. She shook her head vigorously to refuse, but the hand moved down to her wrist and began to tug. Her body lifted and she was unable to resist being pulled out of the grave. When she was out and lying on the ground, the hand released her. Her arm recoiled like a frightened snake. She held her breath in anticipation.

"What a mess you've caused," Dr. Beezly said. "You

should just see what's left of my faithful cemetery caretaker. Oh yes, I keep forgetting you can't see. Well, here,
then. Feel what's left."

He dropped a handful of cremated dust over her face.
She cried out and covered herself. The dust continued to
fall over the back of her hands.

"Leave me alone," she pleaded. "Leave me alone."

"I'd like to leave you alone, but you won't leave me
alone," he replied. She heard him shuffle past and stand
gazing down into the grave.

"Thanks to you, Father Rush is dead. Actually I
always found him to be a grave man," he added, and
laughed hideously. "A fallen soldier of the Lord. And
he never had his last rites." He paused. "What will
become of his troubled soul, I wonder? You know,"
the doctor continued, turning toward her, "that's always
been one of the more interesting aspects of my existence
and power—not knowing the disposition of every soul.

"What I mean is some of the people I would never
have expected to turn up, do turn up at my door, and
some I expected and counted on never arrive. How do
you explain that?

"Could it be," he mused, "that there is no logic in the
spiritual world after all? That it resembles this world, a
world full of chance and accident, where good people
often suffer and bad people often prosper, where babies
die in infancy and cantankerous, mean old men live into
their nineties . . . like old man Carter there, now reduced
to a few ounces of gray dust?

"In your ruminating and pondering, did you ever con-
sider the possibility that this world is hell, and that's why
there is disease and war, crime and hate? Maybe you
are already a citizen of my kingdom, eh? Maybe this
decrepit priest lying below and all his fellow clergyman

of every denomination are clowns I've created for my own amusement?"

He laughed again, the sound of it stinging her ears. She pulled herself back and took a deep breath.

"What's the matter? Aren't you enjoying our little talk? Am I filling you with too many doubts?"

"No," she said in a voice barely above a whisper. "You can't fill me with any doubts."

"Ah, still defiant. Interesting, isn't it—the will to resist, the stamina you still possess.

"Here lies your savior, Father Rush, his heart crushed by a pickax. You are blind and your husband remains in a coma back in the hospital. Yet you fight on—futilely, I might add. Once you're gone, the nurses will listen to me again. I'll have him moved and then this loyal soul you and your priest nearly kept shut up will have a new home and become another of my faithful here on earth.

"Now, let's see," he continued, "your meddling cost me old man Carter, so I think I'll keep Lee living in the DeGroot house. He can become a part-time caretaker," he added, and laughed again.

"Just imagine the irony—he will be out here digging up the graves from now on."

"No," Jessie said. She backed away on her hands. "No," she cried. She turned and pulled herself to a standing position.

"Going somewhere?" Dr. Beezly asked. "Don't you want to rest with your priest? You will make such a nice dead couple. What do they say . . . 'the blind leading the blind'?"

His laughter propelled her forward. She charged ahead, but smacked right into a monument. Stunned, she spun and fell to the ground again. She moaned and struggled to her knees. She could hear his horrible footsteps, that step and slide, that step and slide.

"NO!" she cried, and stood up. Hands out, she walked quickly forward. The voices began to call to her, but all of them so loud and so mixed, they merely confused her. She stopped again when she felt another monument, only this one softened in her fingers and metamorphosed into the naked body of a man. She tried to pull back, but his skin was as sticky as flypaper. All the while she heard the hideous laughter behind her. Suddenly the body softened even more and her hands fell through, her fingers drowning in blood and becoming twisted in the organs. The revolting feelings brought her to her knees, and just as quickly as the monument had changed, it returned to being a monument.

She gasped; her mind reeled, yet she found the strength to stand again and start away once more. She moved slowly, her arms extended, sobbing, her chest aching, her body trembling so hard, she barely could keep her footing. She had no idea where she was heading; she even had the sense she was going in circles. Suddenly she heard a familiar voice calling from just ahead and stopped.

"Lee?"

"Jessie, what's happening? What are you doing here?"

"Lee? Is it you? Is it really you?" She listened keenly.

"Of course it's me," he said.

"But we left you in the hospital, in a coma . . . Lee?"

"I snapped out of it and came after you as soon as I found out what you were doing," he replied. "Now come away, quickly," he added. His voice became lower, thinner. He seemed to be fading, pulling back, away from her.

"Lee?"

".Jessie . . . come to me . . . Jessie."

"Why are you going away from me, Lee?" She surged to her left. "Lee, please, help me."

"This way, Jessie. I'm leading you out, away. Just follow. Quickly."

She walked faster. A great silence had come over the cemetery again. She could actually hear her own footsteps and that shuffling somewhere behind her. But Lee's voice had become so small and thin, it was lost in the wind.

"LEE!" she called, and walked as fast as she could without stumbling. Suddenly she heard him again, this time loud and distinct, only his voice was coming from below. She paused.

"Lee?"

"Just a few more feet, Jessie. Just a few more feet," he said.

"Where are you, Lee?"

"Right here, right ahead of you. Come to me, my Jessie, my love."

Slowly, hesitantly, she took a step forward and then another, holding her hands out.

"Lee, I'm afraid. Please."

"Right here, Jessie," he said, and she stepped out once more, only this time tumbling back into the grave that now housed Father Rush's dead body. Her scream followed her down. She just missed the handle of the pickax, struck his shoulder and arm, and rolled back to the position she had been in before. Miraculously she was unhurt. She groaned and started to sit up when suddenly Father Rush's hand seized her wrist.

At first she was too tired, too exhausted and shocked to scream again. Her body turned to ice; she didn't move.

"Hi, Jessie," he said, only he spoke in Lee's voice. "I'm glad you've decided to come back to me. We'll lie together here for ages and ages, and at night we'll scream with the rest of them, hoping someone else like you will come along and hear us. Won't that be nice?"

"NOOOO!" she cried, and with all the strength she possessed, she pried the dead fingers off her wrist.

"Not very courteous and grateful of you," Dr. Beezly said. He was at the foot of the grave again. "Do you know what cemetery space costs these days? Plenty, believe me. It's become a lucrative business for me; and here we are offering you one for free.

"Some people, it seems, don't know what's good for them," he added, "but don't worry, we'll be sure to tell them." He laughed again. "Well, I've wasted enough time and energy here. Yes, even I am occasionally concerned about such things. Eternity might not last forever, you know. I mean, I'm not one to take His word for anything."

Jessie shook her head and started to struggle to her feet again, but a shovelful of dirt hit her in the neck, some small stones in it stinging her and driving her back.

She screamed again and then another shovelful of dirt hit her. It began to come faster, one shovelful after another, some hitting her feet and legs, some hitting her head. She fell against Father Rush's body, clutching him as if she somehow hoped he would be resurrected in time to save her from being buried alive. She seized his coat and then slid her hands over his right shoulder and down his right arm, pulling at him and shaking him as if she thought that might awaken him.

"NO, NO," she cried.

And then her fingers found his right hand. Still clutched in it was the bottle of holy water. A surge of hope shot through her body and made her oblivious for the moment to the dirt that struck and pounded her back. She clutched at the silver container, but Father Rush's fingers had hardened like fingers of cement around it. She pried and tugged, now with both her hands.

"Oh God," she sobbed, "please help me."

Father Rush's fingers softened slowly. Gradually she inched the silver container out of his palm, and when she had it firmly in her own, she called on all her strength and spun around to stand.

Dr. Beezly paused in his shoveling and gazed down at her.

"Shall I bury you standing?" he asked impishly.

With a faith that filled her voice with power, she cried, "GO BACK TO THE HELL WHERE YOU BELONG!"

She whipped the holy water in his direction and heard it splat like drops of cold water on a blazing campfire. The sizzle instantly produced a putrid stench.

Dr. Beezly's scream seemed endless. It was so sharp and shrill she had to cover her ears. Along with it came a chorus of piercing shrieks, rising from beneath numerous tombstones. The symphony of hellish agony filled the night, resembling a thousand alley cats tearing away at each other's flesh. It ended with what sounded like a clap of thunder and then all became deathly quiet, so still and silent that the sound of her own heart beating against the walls of her chest now seemed thunderous.

She started to cry and the sobbing was a catharsis, freeing her of terror and pain. When she stopped, she felt renewed and strong enough to help herself. She found footing in the wall of the grave again and this time pulled herself out. She rested for a moment on the cool earth, still afraid she was not fully out of danger. But there was nothing around her, no sounds, no sense

of any being, nothing but the solitude and stillness of a
country graveyard.

Confident she was safe, she got to her feet and began
a careful walk back down the path she now could clearly
sense led to the stone-arched entrance of the cemetery.
She was nearly there when she heard a car come to a
stop and then heard some voices.

"Father Rush's car is here," she heard Bob Baker say.
She paused and then she heard Tracy cry out.

"There she is, Bob. There she is!"

Jessie waited, anticipating some sort of new attack on
her person or her soul. She raised her arms instinctively
to protect herself. In her hand she still held the container of holy water. But Tracy Baker quickly embraced
her and held her the way a mother would hold a lost
child.

"Oh, you poor dear," she cried, and brushed back
Jessie's disheveled hair. "Look at you. What happened?
Why did Father Rush take you out of the hospital and
bring you to the cemetery of all places?"

"What happened, Jessie?" Bob echoed. He was standing at Tracy's side. "Where is Father Rush?"

"Give me your hand, Bob," Jessie demanded instead
of responding.

"What?"

"Hold out your hand," she said, "so I can feel it."

"Hold out my hand? What's she talking about? Look
at what she looks like," he said to Tracy.

"You're afraid to hold out your hand because you
know, don't you?" Jessie said in a mad whisper. "You're
one of them. He is, Tracy, don't you see? That's why
he's been so different."

"Different? Who's been different?" Bob asked. He

looked down at Jessie's extended hand. "What does she want with my hand?"

"Just do it, Bob. Can't you see she's terrified and hysterical."

"Sure," he said, shrugging. "No problem. Here's my hand, Jessie."

Jessie closed her fingers around it. She brought the container of holy water to it and sprinkled some drops over Bob's knuckles, anticipating the sizzle and the stench, but nothing happened.

"What is she doing, washing my hand or something?"

"What is that, Jessie?" Tracy asked. "What are you putting on Bob's hand?"

"It's holy water," Jessie replied, confused for a moment. "Father Rush brought it."

"Well, thank you for the blessing," Bob said, taking his hand from hers.

"They've gone with him," Jessie realized. "When I drove him away, they had to go, too. Of course," she added, nodding. "Without him, they couldn't remain. He gave them life."

Bob shook his head at Tracy.

"What in hell is she talking about?" he whispered.

"Poor thing," Tracy repeated. She put her arm around Jessie's shoulders. "What happened to you, Jessie? What's been going on here?"

"I told you the devil had possessed the body of Dr. Beezly," she said. "Father Rush suspected it himself. He and I kept him from doing any more to Lee. Once we surrounded him with holy water, he was safe in the fortress of the Lord and Beezly was unable to touch him. Then we came out here to lock the evil soul in its grave and in hell," she added in a breath. She lowered her head.

"Its grave in hell? Jesus. Well, where is Father Rush?"

Bob asked. "Why is he letting you wander around here on your own?"

"He's back in the grave. Old man Carter killed him," Jessie muttered.

"What?"

"Killed Father Rush?" Bob said.

"Yes." She lifted her head and took a deep breath. "He's back in the opened grave, a pickax in his chest. Just follow this path back and go to your right."

"Oh my God, Bob. Go see if she imagined it," Tracy directed. Bob shot off down the cemetery path.

"Let me take you back to the house, Jessie. Your dress is torn; you're covered with mud and grime. . . . You do look like you're the one who has been through hell."

"Almost," Jessie replied. "Almost."

Tracy led her to their car. The headlights were still on; the engine still running. She opened the door on the passenger's side and began to guide Jessie in when Bob appeared in the stone arch.

"She's telling the truth," he announced, his face in a ghastly grimace. "Father Rush is lying at the bottom of a grave with a pickax in his chest."

"Oh Bob."

"I'll run ahead to the house and call the police," he said. "You okay?"

"Yes, go on. Go on," Tracy said. She continued to guide Jessie into the car.

"Jessie, why did Mr. Carter do such a thing?" she asked after she got in behind the steering wheel.

"Because we were about to cast holy water over the coffin and keep the evil soul within. I told you; I kept telling all of you, but no one would listen. No one . . ." she said, her voice trailing off. She laid her head back and let her body sink into the seat.

Tracy drove her to the house and helped her in, leading her directly back to her bedroom. Bob joined them in the corridor.

"The police are on their way," he said.

"All right. Put up some water for tea and I'll get her as cleaned up and as calm as I can," Tracy said.

"Right. Jesus, what a night."

"I'll draw a warm bath for you, Jessie. How would you like that?"

"I'm so tired . . . sooo tired," she said, falling back on the bed. "I don't have the strength for a bath. I'll just rest here awhile."

"Let me get you cleaned up. I'll sponge you down at least," Tracy said, and began undressing her. Jessie was too exhausted to respond or help. Vaguely she felt Tracy washing off her face, shoulders, and arms. She heard her muttering about the dirt under her fingernails. After Tracy had cleaned her as best as she could, she got her into a nightgown and under the covers. Jessie let her eyelids close and permitted herself to start to drift off, but she heard Bob come to the bedroom door to announce that the police had arrived.

"I'll take them to the grave," he said. "The tea's simmering. How's she doing?"

"She's very tired. Bob, what could have happened here?"

"I don't know. We'll get to the bottom of it soon. Be right back," he added, and left.

Jessie moaned.

"I'll bring you some tea," Tracy said. She returned with a cup and began to spoon-feed her.

"Thank you," Jessie smiled. "It's so quiet now, no more voices . . . very quiet."

"Voices?"

"I'll just get a little rest now," Jessie said, letting her head fall back to the pillow.

"Okay, I'll be right nearby if you need me," Tracy said, rising. She fixed Jessie's blanket and left her.

A little while later Jessie was awakened by the excited voices of Patrolmen Peters and Daniels in the hallway just outside her door. After Bob had taken them and shown them Father Rush's body, they had gone upstairs to speak to old man Carter.

"The door was open," Jessie heard Peters telling Tracy, "so we went in."

"You wouldn't believe the stench," Bob said.

"It's like he kept dead bodies up there or something," Daniels said.

"But the old man isn't there," Bob added.

"His car is here, so we'll start looking for him in the cemetery, but we'd like to talk to Jessie first," Peters said. "How is she?"

"She's very, very tired," Tracy replied. "I'm sure she's sleeping."

"I'll talk to them," Jessie cried. "Tell them to come in, please."

The policemen entered and stood just inside the doorway. She beckoned them closer.

"What happened here, ma'am?" Burt began. "Where's Mr. Carter? Do you know?"

"He's been turned to dust," she said. "Dust to dust . . ."

"Dust?"

"Father Rush hit him with the holy water before he was struck with the pickax. Now it's over; it's all over," she said softly.

"Over?" Peters asked. "What's over?"

The telephone rang.

"I'll get it," Tracy said, and lifted the receiver. "Hello." She listened for a moment. "No, this is a friend."

"What is it?" Jessie asked fearfully, and turned toward the phone and Tracy.

"Oh, thank God, thank God," Tracy said. "Yes, I'll tell her immediately. Thank you."

"What?" Jessie said before Tracy hung up the receiver.

"It's Lee. He's come out of his coma. He's going to be all right, Jessie."

Jessie pressed her small closed fist into her mouth and began to sob. Tracy sat on the bed to embrace her.

"There, there," she said. "It's all right now, Jessie. It's all right."

"I know," Jessie muttered, and smiled. "I know."

"Ma'am?" Greg Daniels said. "I'm afraid we still don't understand what happened here."

Jessie widened her smile. "I sent him back to hell."

EPILOGUE

Tracy Baker and Jessie, both wearing flannel shirts and jeans and both with bandannas tied around their hair, came out to the porch of the DeGroot house into the bright morning sunlight, their arms filled with clothes on hangers. It was a great day to move, everyone thought, blue skies, cool and dry.

"Watch your—" Tracy began, and then stopped her warning as Jessie accurately began to descend the small stairway. Bob and Lee paused in their loading of the U-Haul and looked back, smiling as Jessie sauntered up the walk toward them without hesitation.

"I can't keep up with her," Tracy cried, rushing down the steps.

"You don't have the same motivation to get out of here," Jessie said. She turned toward the cemetery.

"You're not hearing the voices again, are you?" Bob asked, and glanced at Lee.

"No," Jessie said.

For a long moment no one spoke.

"Let me take that," Lee said, scooping the clothing out of Jessie's hands. Bob took the clothing Tracy held.

"We're almost finished," Tracy said, and the two women started back into the house.

"I must say, Jessie looks radiantly happy these days," Bob commented. Lee nodded.

"She is. Funny thing was, I didn't think she could be as long as we remained in Gardner Town. I thought she would want us to move more than ever, but she believes in her story so much . . . she's so confident." Lee turned to Bob. "She's got me believing it." He had to confess to himself that part of the reason for that concerned his act of adultery and how Jessie's story of evil and possession helped justify it. It made sense. Hadn't Monica London resigned from her position at the school and left Gardner Town?

"And when Henry and Marjorie Young came by to visit and brought along their son," Lee continued, "Jessie didn't seem at all surprised. She said she knew they would all make up and Henry would accept what the boy was doing. He's a fine young man, with a true love for spiritual things. Henry's changed, too, hasn't he? He's firmer, more supportive, and as a result you can see and feel a difference in the school. There's an air of control, discipline. It's the sort of school I originally thought I was coming to," Lee said.

"I know," Bob said. He leaned back against the car.

"What's the matter?" Lee asked. "Aren't you happy about all that?"

"Oh sure."

"So?"

"Swear you won't say anything?" Bob replied.

"Of course. What is it?"

"Every once in a while I come across something I did after my heart attack . . ."

"Yeah?"

"And I have no memory of doing it. Tracy swears I did, of course, and there's evidence I did, but . . ."

"Like what?"

"Well, the most astounding thing is I just don't recall how I got involved in the cemetery corporation with Dr. Beezly. I mean, I know it's my signature on those documents, but it's like buying a stock and forgetting it, forgetting what you originally paid for it. That sort of thing."

"You're still getting your dividend checks, aren't you?"

"Well . . . there's a problem. I had to turn it all over to Willy Stevens. Something with the mortgages."

"Wasn't Henry Young involved in that, too?"

"Yeah and Willy's his attorney, too." He paused and then looked up. "We're going to have to sell the house."

"Oh no."

"It's too much house for us anyway. Which is another thing," he added.

"What?"

"I don't feel like it's my house . . . like it's my home. Sometimes I wake up at night and wonder where the hell I am. Really. It takes me a moment or two. Now, don't you go telling any of this to Jessie," Bob warned.

Lee smiled.

"I think she already knows."

"Yeah, yeah." Bob started to put a carton into the back of the U-Haul.

"What about Dr. Beezly?" Lee asked, coming up beside him.

"What do you mean?"

"I've heard the rumors and I'm sure you have, too, but none of us—not Henry, not you, not me—wants to talk about it."

"You mean the stuff about the burns over his body?"

"Yeah." Lee gazed back at the house quickly to be sure Jessie wasn't returning yet.

"All I know is they found him dead in bed and the coroner ruled it a heart attack. You missed quite a funeral while you were still in the hospital."

"Somehow that doesn't upset me," Lee said.

"I know, but you've got to give the devil his due."

"Don't say that, even in jest," Lee warned. The girls had reemerged and were carrying additional armfuls of clothing.

"A lot of people miss him. He was a throwback to a gentler age—house calls, real involvement with his patients. I miss him myself."

"Who do you miss?" Jessie asked, halfway down the walk.

"Sorry, I keep forgetting how keen her hearing is," Bob said. "Nobody."

"You don't have to lie, Bob," Jessie said, stepping up to hand Lee the clothing. "You were whispering about Dr. Beezly."

"Jess . . ." Lee warned.

"It's all right. The Dr. Beezly Bob, you and other people miss was the real Dr. Beezly. How the devil got possession of his soul is something between the doctor and God," she insisted.

"Okay, Jess," Lee said. "We agreed."

"Regardless of what everyone agrees and thinks and says," Tracy said, unloading her armful of clothing into Bob's arms, "the fact remains that this town now has only one physician."

"Maybe not for long," Bob said.

"What do you mean?" Lee asked.

Bob loaded in the garments and turned back.

"The real estate agent called this morning before we left to come over here. We've got someone biting on the house . . . and his name is Dr. Timons."

"Is that so?"

"You're selling the house?" Jessie asked, and then quickly said, "Of course."

"Jessie Overstreet," Tracy said, her hands on her hips, "you're getting to sound like a regular fortune-teller."

"Yeah, Jessie," Bob said. "If you're going to practice predicting the future, how's Lee's team going to do this Friday night?"

Jessie hesitated and then moved closer to Lee.

"His team's going to win, and fairly," she said.

"Spoken like a true coach's wife," Bob said.

"Well, why not? That's what she is." Lee threw his arm about her shoulders. They all laughed.

When the last of their personal possessions was loaded, they got into their cars to drive off. Jessie rolled her window down and turned toward the cemetery. Lee started the engine and began to drive off, but he saw the way she was listening.

"Hear something?" he asked softly as they drove past the stone arch.

Jessie turned and smiled at him.

"No," she said.

He hoped and prayed she was telling the truth.